S0-BYW-746

# The Geronimo Breach

## Russell Blake

Copyright 2011 by Russell Blake. All rights reserved. No part of this book may be used, reproduced or transmitted in any form or by any means, electronic or mechanical, including photocopying, recording, or by any information storage or retrieval system, without the written permission of the publisher, except where permitted by law, or in the case of brief quotations embodied in critical articles and reviews. For information, contact Books@RussellBlake.com.

ISBN: 978-1480277724

Published by

**Reprobatio Limited**

# CHAPTER 1

Bullets peppered the dirt around Al and his partner. They instinctively returned fire, the barrels of their automatic rifles pulsing hot from burst after burst of armor-piercing slugs. Thick smoke belched from a crippled station wagon lying on its side by the mouth of the rural alley where they'd taken cover. The glow of burning fuel intermingled with the unmistakable stench of seared flesh, creating a nauseating haze. A slug ricocheted off the peeling wall, gouging a chunk of brick from the dilapidated surface.

A flickering of illumination from ancient streetlights succumbed to the gloom of late evening, casting otherworldly shadows over the rustic thoroughfare – now transformed into a killing zone.

White noise and static shrieked from their radios – not that they could distinguish anything in the cacophony of the firefight. The concussion of gunfire had devastated their hearing, and the ringing from tinnitus obliterated all sounds besides the percussive chatter of their guns.

Squinting down their sights at the blurs of motion on the rooftops of the bombed-out buildings across the street, they paused, turning to give each other a knowing glance before returning their attention to their assailants and squeezing off their last rounds. They weren't going to make it. This was a deathtrap; they'd been boxed in with no hope of escape. Help was at least fifteen minutes out, assuming their base had received the solitary frantic distress call before the radio had been taken out. It didn't look good.

The incoming fire escalated to a hail of screaming death. Rifle ammo depleted, they un-holstered their army-issue Beretta pistols and fired intermittently in the direction of their attackers, to no obvious effect. They exchanged panicked looks – this wasn't supposed to happen; just a routine patrol in a secure area with no reason to expect hostiles, much less heavily-armed ones intent on slaughtering them. It was supposed to be a cakewalk.

Dave's gun jerked as he reflexively squeezed the trigger, again and again, even after his magazine was spent. Al glanced at him with alarm and then elbowed him back into the fight. Dazed, Dave stared at the useless weapon in his hand, before dropping the Beretta and frantically fumbling for the scarred knife handle protruding from his belt. He almost had the serrated edge free from its sheath when his head exploded in a blast of bloody emulsion.

Al spat out fragments of his mutilated partner and expended his last rounds in a defiant salvo, squinting at the shadows in an effort to make each shot count. Cursing silently when his ammo ran dry, he tossed the handgun aside and bared his trusty blade for the final reckoning.

Shouts in an unfamiliar tongue drifted from beyond the dense smoke at the alley's mouth. A bright flash momentarily blinded him as a flare bounced down the length of the cobblestone passage before coming to rest a few yards from his trembling body.

Four figures emerged from the gloom, cautiously approaching the soldier's hiding place through the fog of burning oil, their rifles trained on his blood-spattered profile. Pointing at the ludicrously inadequate combat knife clutched in Al's shaking hand, the tallest of the bearded, turbaned warriors barked a guttural cackle. He handed his firearm to the figure beside him and from beneath his filthy robe withdrew a gleaming, viciously curved blade as long as his arm. He sliced at the air with it, savoring Al's horrified gaze as it whistled its grim tune. The turbaned warrior grinned maliciously and moved forward.

The angel of death had arrived, and it was time for Al to die.

He shielded his head with his arms, all thoughts of attacking with the knife now gone.

The bearded executioner smirked.

Sobbing, the last thing Al registered as the scimitar descended to sever his head was a bloodcurdling scream from his executioner; a victory yell as old as the god-forsaken hills of the foul dustbowl that had claimed his mortality.

Al bolted awake, the image of the flashing blade still vivid, even as the specter dissolved into a muddy, waking awareness.

What the hell?

His chest heaved from the adrenaline rush triggered by the nightmare, his heart trip-hammering in his chest as he shook off the bitter remnants of the dream state. He sluggishly scanned his surroundings; dimly visible silhouettes of furniture offered a quiet reassurance he wasn't anywhere near a gunfight in some non-specific shithole, or being decapitated by a malevolent mullah straight out of central casting. *Damn, that had been realistic.* He cleared his throat, wiping the sweat from his face with a damp hand.

A battered air conditioner wheezed from its position on the wall, barely denting the heat and humidity in the squalid room. The bed sheets beneath him exuded an odor of sour perspiration and years of marginal laundering. A car's un-muffled exhaust roared down the street outside the window; the moth-eaten curtains providing slim insulation from the racket.

Still, it was better than being beheaded in a mud-hole.

Al tried to sit up but was sapped of energy. Pausing to muster his strength, he registered a tickling on the skin of his right leg, as though ghostly fingers were brushing at the hair just below his knee. He groped for the small bedside lamp on the table by his head and after several seconds found the power switch. A weak yellow light flickered on and he gingerly pulled the threadbare sheet off his naked lower body.

He froze.

Two claws gnashed at the air over the greenish black carapace of a highly agitated scorpion. The arched tail lashed at Al, its venomous stinger fully exposed. He went rigid, his skin instantly covered in a film of clammy sweat. The poisonous insect became more agitated by this physiological change and, enraged, it scurried up Al's thigh and plunged its deadly barb into the soft, exposed flesh of his groin.

Al thrashed to full wakefulness, clutching his calf in agony, expunging the scorpion dream as he dealt with this all-too-real distress. The pain was blinding as the large muscle of his lower leg cramped into a rigid ball, taking his breath away as he pawed at it, trying to persuade it to release. His back shuddered with spasms from the effort of bending nearly double – he wasn't exactly in prime shape for gymnastics, and the effort of stretching to loosen the knot had pinched his sciatica, compounding the excruciating discomfort from his traumatized lower leg.

Harsh experience had taught him to maintain a grip on his toes no matter what and exert steady pressure on the Achilles tendon, pulling and coaxing the contracted muscle until it relaxed. If he surrendered to his back's protestations the cramp would worsen and the ordeal would go on seemingly forever – either way there would be pain, garnished with even more pain.

He groaned with anguish. What kind of fresh hell was this anyway? Why him?

A blurry flash of the prior evening's debauchery intruded into his labored calisthenics. He vaguely recalled lurching up the stairs to his dingy apartment swigging the last of a cheap bottle of coconut rum after many hours of drunken gambling at the neighborhood watering hole, and a loud argument with the bartender about soccer, transvestites and how the Chinese were Satan's henchmen, but the rest was a blank, with the exception of copious quantities of alcohol. The memory of the rotgut triggered his gag reflex, filling his mouth with bitter saliva as he choked down vomit.

The spasm in his leg eventually loosened and he cautiously slid his legs off the bed and stood up. So far, so good. He kicked an empty bottle out of his path and leaned against the wall, stretching his hamstring while he massaged his back with his free hand. Hopeful the worst was over, Al limped to the coffee table in the studio apartment's sitting area and collapsed onto the sofa, dimly aware of something wet adhering to the side of his head. He reached up and peeled off the offending item; a slab of congealed lard and dough.

Pepperoni.

*Nice.*

*How did this get any worse?*

His head swam through the waves of dizziness that assaulted him and bile seeped out of his nose. What time had he gotten in? That he'd passed out was a given – meaning today had to be either Friday, Saturday or Sunday. He had a strict rule, or at least a semi-strict rule, against getting obliterated on weeknights so it had to be one of those. He was pretty sure it wasn't a Monday. He desperately hoped it was the weekend – there was no way he could make it in to work in this condition.

The luminescent wall clock above the TV read 5:30. Probably a.m. given the dearth of daylight. So maybe he'd gotten three hours of sleep. The nightmares were no doubt a result of plummeting blood sugar and dehydration.

He really had to stop overdoing it.

Soon.

After he got through the present, that is. Right now he was in no shape to make rash decisions.

He groped through the accumulated trash on the scarred table surface until he found what felt like a cigarette packet.

Empty. Of course. It would be, wouldn't it?

Rooting around in the accumulated refuse, his hand bumped a cold metal ashtray reeking of a rancid blend of carbon, alcohol and nicotine. He fished around among the butts, trying to find something only half smoked.

Great. They were all soaked.

The stink caused him to retch again. Now he could add vomiting on himself to his pre-dawn party tricks. Gagging, Al struggled upright and staggered toward the dim outline of the bathroom door, hands fumbling for support. He switched on the light and was transfixed by his reflection in the hazy mirror.

Even for him, this was a new low.

Red, bleary eyes had the bleak thousand-yard stare of a chain-gang prisoner. Tomato paste crusted around his right temple created the impression he'd been in a collision, as did the now hardened mozzarella flecking his cheek. What was left of his hair was matted into a greasy clump. He resembled nothing so much as a puffer fish that had been hit in the face with a brick. Several times.

At least he still had his health.

Al crumpled onto the floor in front of the toilet and grabbed the cracked rim for support before spewing the night's excesses into the grimy bowl. He was afraid to look too closely.

He smelled blood.

The cramp threatened to revisit his leg as he heaved and it was all he could do to keep from crying in frustration at the accumulated misery of a body that had completely betrayed him. The spell passed. His hand reached for toilet paper to blot his mouth and instead found the coarse cardboard of an empty roll.

Perfect.

He dried his face with the filthy bath mat, absently wondering whether it would wash clean, and depressed the toilet lever, anxious to flush the toxic soup from the prior night's episode down the pipe. He heard a snap rather than the satisfying flushing sound he'd hoped for. The rusty rod in the tank had broken again; his temporary fix with fishing line and super glue having obviously proved inadequate.

A glance at his watch confirmed it was Friday the 29th. Dammit. He had to make it into the office. There was no choice. He was already in deep weeds due to chronic absenteeism.

There'd better still be some emergency vodka stashed in the freezer, or he'd never make it.

He regarded his bloated, ravaged countenance in the mirror. A network of ruptured capillaries lent him the flushed glow of a seasoned vagrant, with yellowish skin that was disturbing, at best. To say he looked like shit was pejorative to excrement.

He was a complete mess.

Al flicked a speck of vomit from the corner of his mouth and splashed some lukewarm water on his face, knocking his toothbrush into the noxious toilet in the process.

*Superb. Thank you, universe.*

He considered his reflection once more. This had to stop. He'd never seen anything looking so bad that was still breathing. It couldn't continue. And then he grinned, a lopsided smirk devoid of humor.

Albert Ross, proud member of the U.S. Diplomatic Corps in shit-swamp Panama, Central America, at your service.

# CHAPTER 2

Ernesto gripped the metal handle for support, swaying with the rest of the passengers as the brightly painted bus bounced along the rutted street. Faded Spanish advertisements for breath-freshening gum and miracle kitchen cleaning products punctuated the ever-present graffiti scrawled over every interior area of the vehicle.

Most of the occupants were dark-skinned Panamanians wearing colorful shirts or dresses, as if the vibrancy of the colors could ward off the stifling temperature. A few intrepid tourists sat toward the front, their pale complexions and floppy hats proclaiming them as aliens in the tropical landscape. The rich aroma of coffee sloshing in Styrofoam cups mingled with less identifiable odors in the confined space, and for those unaccustomed to such constant humidity and heat it was almost unbearable. But for the locals, this was merely the start of another workday – a Friday exactly like thousands of others before it.

The creaky fifty-year old conveyance might have seemed primitive to outsiders but for the commuting laborers it was a blessed alternative to walking miles in each direction to and from work. Sure, air conditioning would have been welcome but compared to trekking two hours to get to a job that barely paid for food, water and shelter, the ancient converted school bus was welcome progress.

Ernesto tuned out his fellow travelers and watched the scenery go by. Every day it was the same cast and the same landscape. There was the graveyard followed by several *barrios* leading to a haphazardly laid out strip mall, and then increasingly condensed homes of progressively larger size. He knew how close he was to his exit point by the landmarks. When the old pink shack appeared with its rows of chickens roasting on the makeshift grill, Ernesto rang the bell to signal his stop, fifty yards past it.

For eight years now he'd taken the same bus to this very stop and it never once occurred to him to question whether his life had turned out the way he'd wanted, or if some alternative, better reality could be his with just a little more initiative or effort. No, Ernesto was comfortable in his role. He was a cook – not a chef or a showman – just a cook; like his father and mother before him had been in his native Colombia. He actually felt he had it pretty good – his current job was hardly demanding; creating three meals a day in a large colonial villa a quarter mile down a side road from the chicken shack. True, the cuisine requests had seemed odd at first, but he'd long since become accustomed to preparing the largely-vegetarian fare and it was second nature to whip up a lentil soufflé or zucchini curry.

Beyond those simple culinary exercises, work was invariably tedious. He was the only kitchen staff and, but for the small black and white TV he was allowed on the counter by the refrigerator, he would have died of sheer boredom. Still, many workers had it far worse; and the pay was good, as were the hours. Nine to seven, six days a week, with Sundays off – he always prepared Sunday's meals on Saturday so the staff only needed to warm them in the microwave.

Ernesto had mixed feelings about his existence in Panama. He lived in a small row house in an outlying *barrio*. It wasn't bad – had running water – and four years ago they'd finally installed electricity. To an outsider it would have been a frightening area; run down, poor, and dangerous, but to Ernesto it was simply where many people like him lived. Sure, it had its fair share of crime – mainly burglaries at night, and assaults on weekends when disagreements broke out after a long day's drinking – but he knew all his neighbors, and they watched each other's' backs.

He wished he'd met and married someone special and started a family but with his schedule and limited means there hadn't been a lot of prospects. Even in Panama, a chubby, thirty-seven year old cook who spent his free evenings and discretionary income at the bordellos in town wasn't at the top of the food chain for desirable mating material. Besides, the *barrio* women were usually dark and coarse and illiterate. Ernesto considered himself superior to them.

Originating from Colombia, with light brown skin and hazel eyes, Ernesto not only knew how to read and write but also had a vocational skill that earned him more than most in his circle. Getting trapped in a marriage with a flat-footed mestizo girl who'd swell to two hundred pounds within a few years of their nuptials wasn't for him. He preferred the company of the professional ladies of the city, and if he had to pay, well, that's why he worked and made money. It wasn't like he had an extravagant lifestyle; no car, a few hundred dollars a month rent between him and his roommate, thirty dollars for utilities, and the rest for entertainment, with a small portion set aside for savings with the local loan shark

Nobody used banks in his neighborhood – they asked too many questions, were suspicious of cash and paid laughably low interest. In virtually every *barrio* in Central America the neighborhood convenience store ran a profitable side business lending money; and they tended to be trustworthy custodians for savings. He methodically gave the local market owner $200 each month, as he had for three years, and earned fifteen percent annual interest. Sure, the owner lent the money out at sixty percent, but Ernesto was satisfied with a quarter of that as his cut because the owner took all the risk. And Ernesto was building a nest egg. Perhaps one day he could return to Bogota and meet a nice girl – someone with an education who worked in a shop or an office – his savings could easily provide the beginning of a life together. But for now, a little paid romance twice a week did the trick.

Such were Ernesto's thoughts as he strolled toward the familiar high-walled compound. He punched the red intercom button by the ornate iron gate and the overhead camera mounted at the top of the support beam swiveled to scrutinize him. Just as it did every day. The lock buzzed and he entered the grounds. It was a large piece of land, no doubt had belonged to a wealthy colonial landowner back in the day. There were a number of buildings scattered around the two story main house – several garages, servants' quarters, a kennel and stables, and a large corrugated steel storage shed he knew was used as an office. He believed the place was owned by a powerful Gringo because there was always an armed retinue of at least four Gringo guards patrolling the interior, day and night, often accompanied by several large German Shepherds.

Armed compounds weren't particularly unusual in Central America, given the often bloody manner in which the *narcotraficantes* settled their disputes, along with the ever-present danger of kidnapping for the wealthy and their families. Ernesto had grown so accustomed to the presence of the gunmen he barely registered them beyond giving them a salute or a wave, which they always reciprocated. The entire time he'd worked there he'd never heard of any altercation or problems, so the sentries and high walls topped with razor wire had obviously served their purpose. This was one the of the last places on the planet anyone would want to rob. There were far easier targets.

He'd never met the owner he'd been cooking for – not once in his eight years at the villa. Clearly the man or woman had reclusive tendencies. Fine by him. His weekly salary was always paid in American dollars, and never late, so as far as he was concerned things couldn't have been better. He simply had to follow the written menu that invariably awaited his morning arrival, but was largely left to his own devices beyond that. The shopping was done by parties unknown and the pantry and large double-width refrigerator were always brimming with fresh supplies. It was like working in a small hotel – he kept to himself, stayed out of the way, did his job, and everyone left him alone. His contact person was a bi-lingual Gringo named Stanley, who checked in with him several times a week in addition to handing him his pay envelope.

This morning was Friday. Payday. Ernesto knew that at 10 a.m. on the dot, Stanley would enter the expansive kitchen, chat for a few minutes and then give him his wages – always in twenties. The routine never changed.

But today the activity around the villa was unusual. Four new vehicles sat by the garages – big SUVs, late model, with their rear deck lids open. The sentries no longer carried their weapons and were ferrying crates and boxes from the house. There were at least fifteen unfamiliar people helping move the items, some of which were large trunks.

Ernesto was troubled. This was a first.

He entered the kitchen and placed his backpack onto the counter by the TV as he did every day before approaching the large island to see what the day's menu consisted of. But today there was no menu. Instead, there was a handwritten note in Spanish, signed by Stanley, along with a brown envelope. He picked up the note and read the terse missive.

"Ernesto, your services won't be required any longer. Sorry for the lack of notice but I just found out last evening. We're moving on Friday. The envelope has two week's pay in it. Good luck finding another position. You're a good cook."

Ernesto opened the flap and peered inside at the paltry wad of twenties.

Unbelievable.

He was now unemployed, even though he'd never missed a day's work – except when his mother had died – and all he got by way of thanks was one lousy extra week's pay? Ernesto sat heavily beside the island and read the note again. Stanley hadn't even bothered to show and personally deliver the news – Ernesto just got a short letter. Why not just text message him on the bus on the way in? What a thoughtless way to reward almost a decade of loyal service. Gringos were all the same. You couldn't trust them; they viewed anyone foreign as beneath contempt – just cheap little robots for their own convenience, unworthy of the most cursory consideration.

He deserved better than this. Whether Stanley wanted to talk or not, Ernesto intended to have a conversation with him. This wasn't over – not like this. For the first time after his eight years in the compound he shouldered his backpack and moved through the connecting double doors into the hall that led to the main house. It was buzzing with activity; men hastily carting boxes from the house to the vehicles. Ernesto was invisible to them; just another of the locals hired to move their belongings and clean up after them. He realized he had no idea where to find Stanley – even if he was still in the villa. His indignation rapidly fading, he stopped outside one of the open doorways halfway to the main wing. Glancing inside, he saw several monitors, some audio-visual gear and a case filled with about a dozen late model video cameras.

Ernesto looked up and down the hall. It was temporarily deserted. Overcome by an impulse he didn't completely understand, he leaned into the room and grabbed the nearest camera, hurriedly stuffing it into his bag before closing the lid on the camera container. He scanned the hall again. Nobody had seen anything.

He stood for a moment in the hall, internally debating his next move, when a man in one of the house 'uniform' windbreakers rounded the corner. The Gringo stopped when he saw Ernesto and spoke to him in rapid, clipped Spanish without any hint of an accent.

"What the hell are you doing here?" he demanded.

Ernesto's righteous indignation buckled, replaced by fear of being caught. "Er, nothing, sir…I was actually looking for Mister Stanley…"

"Stanley? He's gone. Who are you?"

"Ernesto. The cook. I really need to speak with Mister Stanley…"

"He's gone, and he's not coming back…just like you." He narrowed his eyes. "You shouldn't be here. You need to leave the area right now."

"But I–"

"I'm not going to repeat myself. Get out of here – now – or I'll have you removed by the guards."

Ernesto weighed his anger at his abrupt termination against the likelihood of being prosecuted for stealing an expensive piece of electronics.

Discretion won the day.

"All right," Ernesto protested. "But you tell Mister Stanley the way he treated me isn't right. It isn't right."

The man regarded him with a stony stare and pointed to the kitchen door.

Ernesto got the message. He turned and slunk back down the passageway, through the kitchen and out of the compound.

Eight years, and the bastards boot him out just like that.

*Chinga tu Madres, Putas.*

# CHAPTER 3

Sam Wakefield sighed contentedly as the climate control in his Range Rover dropped the interior temperature to a comfortable 69 degrees. Late Spring was hellish around the equator. It was all he could do to make it from his waterfront Panama City high rise condominium into his car without sweating through his hand-tailored dress shirt. True, his condo and elevator were also air conditioned but the underground garage wasn't. He dreaded the fifty yard walk from the elevator to his vehicle. It was bad enough being stationed in the tropics without having to suffer the heat and bugs like a local ditch digger.

When he saw Sam's daytime headlights approach, the uniformed security guard raised the access gate so Sam didn't have to slow before pulling onto the side street that ran alongside of his building. This was a daily ritual, as Sam was a creature of habit. Every morning at 9:45 he left home, making the drive to the embassy in exactly six minutes.

Sam hummed along with his stereo – he'd just had the latest satellite system installed to keep up on the latest tunes and news from the States. Panama wasn't bad, overall, but he despised what passed for the culture; you'd have had to hold a gun to his head to get him to listen to the salsa that permeated virtually every location in the country. Let the natives dance around the fire to whatever jungle stomp floated their boats – he'd take Aerosmith or Brooks and Dunn every time.

His official title was Commercial Attaché but the closest Sam had ever gotten to anything commercial was watching ads on TV. As the top man in Panama for the CIA, he was chartered with overseeing the local efforts in the war on drugs, and keeping his other eye on the various narcotics cartel factions, along with ensuring the local DEA guys didn't get too militant in their attempts to quash the inevitable cocaine traffic. He also spent a fair amount of time spying on the Chinese – who were everywhere since the new canal project had gotten underway.

He viewed his position as a springboard to greater things and secretly loathed anything to do with Panama, including his colleagues on the ground there. The country served as a backwater posting for losers and most of his peers with State Department credentials were has-beens and casualties rather than fast track achievers.

Sam arrived at the U.S. Embassy gates and honked. The marines on duty saluted and opened the gate. He roared into the walled parking area and skidded to a stop in his assigned spot by the side entry door. He'd connived for a full year to get that slot, in order to avoid having to walk across the lot. During the rainy season it was a pain in the ass, and he'd trashed several pairs of Johnson and Murphy loafers negotiating the puddles surrounding his old parking place on the far side. Thank God those days were over.

Once inside the building he strolled to his second floor wing of offices, enjoying as always the plush feel of the thick carpeting underfoot. As expected, his special blend espresso roast was brewed and ready when he entered his suite. His secretary, Melody, automatically brought him a cup, handling the tray with efficiency. Sam had drilled into his staff again and again that they were a bastion of American civilization; that it was important to get the small details right lest they slip down the slippery slope and become savages. In his mind, having coffee out of genuine china cups represented an important line in the sand, as was speaking English at all times, even to the locals, and even though his Spanish was fluent. Inside these walls lay American soil, and English was the official language of America. If you didn't like it, the door was that way.

Sam scanned the daily briefing that had been deposited into his inbox and reviewed his itinerary for the day. Meetings all morning before lunch at the Boxer Club in the penthouse of the shiny new HSBC building, followed by several hours of conference calls with DC. The usual grind, in other words, and he secretly counted the days until he was re-stationed in three months. He'd been pushing Langley for a position on the Beltway, where all the power players gravitated to, and hoped his exile in mosquito-land would shortly be over. Sam understood that a few foreign postings were mandatory for a well-rounded Agency resume but that didn't mean he had to like living in this cesspool. True, Panama City was cosmopolitan as they came and more akin to New York or Singapore than his preconceived image when he'd received the assignment – visions of Toucans and jungle huts abounded – but it was a far cry from Georgetown and he couldn't wait to get the hell out. His wife felt much the same way; she lived as a virtual shut-in at their condo, spending her days glued to their 50-inch television watching U.S. programming and gobbling Vicodin for her non-specific back pain.

Reclining in his padded leather swivel chair, feet on the desk, he savored his coffee and contemplated his misfortune. Only a few more months and then it was *hasta la vista, baby*, and Panama could continue rotting without his skilled supervision. He would miss his mistress, but that was about it – anyway, there were plenty of available hotties on the Beltway circuit so any discomfort would be short-lived. Even so, he had to admit some of the local talent was top shelf – about the only thing this hellhole had going for it.

Sam was the ultimate paradigm of a mid-level bureaucrat. More than just petty and vindictive, he also possessed a unique exclusionary mechanism for his own weaknesses and lapses in ethics. Though a harsh judge of others, he had an elastic sense of right and wrong when his comfort or convenience were at stake. He lacked self-awareness to an Olympic degree, making him a perfect candidate for government work; especially when involving clandestine activities, because he had no messy internal barometer which might cause him to question his orders. Whereas many of his peers struggled with the toll their professional choices had taken on their personal lives and integrity, Sam remained blissfully devoid of introspection. He was selfish to the exclusion of all else, lacking any ability to empathize with his fellow man. He perceived others as extensions of his own desires and needs – like characters in his personal movie – worth no intrinsic value other than as objects within his cozy microcosm.

If asked about his philosophy, Sam would have launched into a long-winded description of an Ayn Rand-ian 'heroic' objective individual whose sole duty was to his own happiness. This amounted to nothing more than a rationalization mantra to justify his lack of concern for anyone but himself, though he'd learned to cloak his selfishness in a high moral tone.

In his youth, he could have gone either way – his temperament and psychological makeup were eerily similar to that of many serial killers. One of his greatest regrets in life was having never been in combat while in the service – not because of a desire to hurt others – but because he'd been deprived of an experience that would have made him a more attractive candidate for his chosen career. While still in high school, Sam had decided that he really, really wanted to be a spy. The primary attraction had been a lifestyle that rewarded deception, together with his internal perception of the job – molded by a voracious diet of Le Carre and Ludlum novels. Other humans were boring, useless creatures – and here was a job that required one to be a consummate user of others, while affording the luxury of living in exotic locales.

Unfortunately, for all his ambition, Sam had gotten shortchanged in the intelligence department. Not that he was a stupid man – he just wasn't a particularly smart one; beyond a certain ruthless cunning, bred from infancy, of habitually lying to everyone around him. Still, the CIA had embraced him with enthusiasm, just as he had selflessly committed to the Agency as though he'd finally discovered his real family.

But as he'd aged, Sam had discovered that not only was he unsuited for field work, having been exclusively stationed in desk job roles from the onset, but his natural limitations were compromising his ambition of ascending to the upper tiers of the Agency. That was intolerable. Finally, after a string of postings to obscure locations in second and third world countries, he'd gotten the plum position of Station Chief in Panama, which signaled an opportunity to move up the food chain and take his rightful place back in the real world – once he was finished here. The end of his Panamanian tour was approaching and he'd soon be off to DC for an enviable life in the fast lane.

He was so close he could taste it.

"Melody? Can you get the maintenance guys to adjust my chair so it doesn't squeak? I can't hear myself think," Sam called to the outer office.

"Yes, sir," she replied. "I'll get someone on it while you're at lunch. I asked yesterday as well, but they never showed up."

Good Lord. How hard was it to get the locals to do their job? Their laziness was incredible – he was almost compelled to oil the thing himself, but he'd be damned if he would let them get away with shirking.

It was the principle, after all.

# CHAPTER 4

The commandos rehearsed the attack scenario for the seventh time that day. They functioned like an organism; a single entity with a single purpose, controlled by a single mind.

The elite group of two dozen hand-selected combat veterans, SEAL Team Six, was augmented for this operation by several veterans of a different sort – older men, hardened, who kept to themselves and didn't waste words. While most of the team members were in their early thirties, the eight men who had been added – and who would be playing point – were a decade more seasoned.

They too checked and rechecked their weapons before the next rehearsal, though there was a different tone to their routine, and it wasn't lost on the rest. These were serious bad-asses of a special caliber, unusual even among this most exalted of select operatives; who were used to being dropped alone behind enemy lines and left to fight their way out with only a handgun and a stiletto.

The obvious leader of the older men had worn the insignia of a colonel when he'd arrived at the rehearsal site – a rarity in itself; this rank would never usually enter the field on an active op. But this clearly wasn't your typical mission, so nobody questioned that someone had called in the heavy artillery. They were all proud to have been chosen, even if the eight old dogs were going to do most of the heavy lifting.

All had specially designed earpieces through which communications would be handled. It was understood that once on the ground they'd be limited to hand signals but any detailed mission instructions would come via the com channel. It was highly irregular to have a strike force modified with new personnel for only one operation, however, the service always had its reasons, and part of being one of the elite commandos in this group was not questioning those reasons when you didn't understand them.

They'd been joined by the veterans ten weeks earlier; when preparations for the mission had suddenly stepped up several gears. Nothing was left to chance and the operation notes and instructions ran to a length normally associated with novellas. But, unlike many SEAL Team Six operations, this one was being overseen by the CIA – it was tacitly understood that the new additions were CIA operatives. Maybe that would have raised eyebrows among most combat teams, but this was no ordinary team.

The rehearsals had taken on a deadly earnest quality as word had come down that they were going to load up and go active that evening. This was the culmination of hundreds of hours of training and there wasn't a man among them that didn't feel a certain quickening at the prospect of going live.

This is what they lived for. What they did. They ran the drill again, for the umpteenth time. Their com channel crackled into life. They were instructed to stand down and prepare to ship out.

It was show time.

They were ready.

# CHAPTER 5

Al sat in his ancient wooden chair, the nearly non-existent ventilation from the creaking overhead fan delivering scant relief from the oppressive stifle. Beads of sweat ran down his pallid forehead, collecting in his unruly eyebrows before continuing their descent down his face. He mopped his brow periodically with a cloth napkin he'd pilfered from the corner seafood restaurant, and for the tenth time that day, cursed his fate.

His hands trembled like a crack fiend's trying to light a midnight rock – the three shots of eighty-proof *Seco* in his morning OJ had barely dented his hangover, and the two *Cuba Libres* at lunch had been like pouring a glass of water on a bonfire. Fortunately, he was able to hide from any public encounters, claiming to be inordinately busy on this muggy Friday afternoon – should anyone have been interested in meeting with him.

Nobody was.

What he really needed was a solid *siesta* for a few hours. That wasn't going to happen today. He'd exhausted his funds the prior night betting first on a cockfight, when he'd backed the losing-est rooster in history and then had made matters worse by having a few too many cocktails and doubling down on a soccer game where his team had done nothing but welcome the ball into their net like a long lost relative. By the time he'd paid his tab he was broke – he'd had to borrow a ten spot from the long-suffering bartender to cover some cigarettes and today's lunch. His bi-weekly pay got deposited into his account by five that evening but much of it was already spoken for. So any chance he had of slipping off to grab a room at the fleabag motel, a few blocks from his shabby satellite consulate station in Colon, had gone down the drain when his soccer call had screwed the pooch.

Al considered lying naked on the floor of his dingy office for maximum cooling, but dismissed the idea. With his luck his chronically absent secretary would take that moment to stop in and claim some sort of sexual harassment, so the nude nap was out of the question. He'd just have to wait. He reached into the top drawer of his scarred desk and extracted a pint bottle of *Seco* with a merenge-ing coconut on the label – he presumed it was dancing because it was shaking maracas in its stick-figure hands.

Strictly for medicinal purposes, he reasoned. He had a delicate system and it couldn't take the shock of the DTs hitting full force without a chemical buffer. He took a long pull, grimacing as the cloudy fluid seared his throat. Al absently wondered what dirty sock the manufacturer filtered it through and considered it nothing short of a miracle he hadn't gone blind drinking it.

He lit his seventeenth cigarette of the day from the ember of the sixteenth, nearly burning his hand when the rotary-dial desk phone rang. Good God almighty. How did they get them to ring so loud? It was worse than an air-raid siren.

Al lifted the handset, primarily to stop the clamoring, and gave a lackluster greeting.

"Al Ross."

Sam's voice boomed on the line. "Albert, me boy, how hangs it? Any breaking news in exciting Colon today?"

"Sure, Sam," Al replied. "I've got three teenage nymphomaniacs seeking asylum here. Kinda got my hands full. What's up?"

"Oh, nothing. Just cutting out early today. Got to get the Range Rover serviced. Fuckers gave me a three-series Benz as a loaner. What am I supposed to do in a shitbox like that for the whole weekend?"

Al scowled at the handset, his dislike of Sam palpable. He was convinced the man only called to torment him. He glanced through his dingy window at the 1990 Ford Probe he'd been tooling around in. Listening to Sam whine about the Mercedes caused his annoyance level to spike – just over the course of the few sentences they'd exchanged. "Hey, Sam, I'm sort of swamped here right now. Is there anything urgent?"

"No. Just wanted to touch base, make sure tha wild man is still in the mix." In other words, he'd called because he was bored and wanted to torture Al with stories of his Benz.

"I'm in da house, big dog," Al countered. "Maybe tomorrow we can hook up and pound some suds…" There was no chance in hell Sam would go anywhere near the places Al frequented.

"Yeah, uh, maybe I'll call and we can work it out. Gotta run – the frigging AC in the Benz is stuck at the coldest position and it's uncomfortable. Take it easy, wild man."

Al hung up.

Sam called a few times a week, generally to report on some item like attending yet another lavish soiree for diplomats or to complain about his wife spending thousands on some absurd piece of furniture. Al had no doubt that the only reason Sam stayed in touch was so he could feel superior and lord his station in life over him. Al thought Sam was a tool, but a largely harmless one; an annoyance from his past who'd established an orbit around him for unknown purposes other than to piss him off. Sam feigned friendship but the true dynamic of the relationship was one of a spectator being horrified and titillated by the observed. In this case, Al was clearly the observed and his meteoric fall from grace provided endless fodder for Sam's underdeveloped self-esteem to do victory laps.

They'd been in the service together during Desert Storm and Sam had never been able to get over Al receiving a Purple Heart and a Bronze Star. Sam's resentment over them always bubbled below the surface of any conversation they had, which secretly delighted Al as much as Al's misery seemed to titillate Sam. Al's greatest pleasure during their discussions was knowing that the medals ate at Sam's soul like a cancer. If only Sam knew the truth – his head would explode.

The one redeeming moment in Al's life, when he'd received honors for bravery and merit, had occurred somewhat differently than the official versions documented. When he'd been stationed in Kuwait, in addition to occasionally acting as a quasi-public defender in court-martials, he'd been in charge of the mail – an administrative function that kept him far away from any combat action or danger of anything worse than a paper cut. But his assignment placed him in a unique position over letters and packages to and from home, affording him the opportunity to devise a nice little side business with high income possibilities – namely, helping two of his buddies set up a smuggling operation to get religious icons out of the country and onto the black market in the U.S. – without any annoying paperwork or intrusive inspections.

One fine spring day, they'd set up a meet with a new group of locals whom Al believed were going to become a conduit for the icons – unbeknownst to Al, his buddies were thinking bigger money and had forgotten to tell him they were actually doing a heroin buy for one of the buddy's cousins, who was active on the West Coast in the pharmaceutical distribution business. Long story short, someone tried to rip off someone else at the meet, guns came out and nervous trigger fingers got the better of the situation. Both his buddies got killed, along with the four natives.

Al took a slug in the upper chest, but survived – barely. The Army concluded that the three brave marines were ambushed by bloodthirsty terrorist insurgents intent on murder, and Al, the survivor of the altercation, was decorated for his bravery. That marked the high point of his career – instead of being a paper-pushing cog in the army postal machine, he became a decorated combat veteran. Sam had never known the details and Al obviously preferred the army version to the actual one, and so the story stuck, there being nobody alive to contradict it. Al certainly had no interest in confessing, so 'don't ask, don't tell' took on a whole new meaning. But Sam, who had endured a completely unremarkable stint in the service with zero opportunities for bravery, had developed a fixation on Al – remaining convinced he was a lowlife shirker.

Which wasn't far from the truth. Only he was the lowlife with the two medals. And Sam had nothing.

Al idly wondered if he could pawn them and get enough cash to bet on the dog races tonight. Likely more trouble than it was worth – plus, he wasn't sure where he'd stashed them; one of the last times he'd been indisposed, he'd hidden them to keep himself from doing exactly that. In the end that was probably for the best. He slapped his neck, then studied his hand, where the bloody crushed carcass of a mosquito adhered to his palm. Great. He probably now had malaria or dengue to add to the day's horrors. Al couldn't wait for the hemorrhagic fever to start him leaking blood out of every orifice like a giant exsanguinating yogurt machine.

Fidgeting from hangover anxiety, he flipped open his cell phone and placed a call to Carmen; the owner of one of the more upscale brothels in town. Besides being a regular client of her establishment, Al periodically made extra money by running 'errands' that she brokered.

It was well over a month since he'd run one and he could really use the cash — he didn't mind leveraging the wave-through border security checkpoints his diplomatic passport entitled in exchange for some token remuneration. Sure, it might be technically against the rules, and some would label it with pejorative terms like 'smuggling' or 'human trafficking' or 'money laundering', but Al had a broader, more cosmopolitan view. Plus, when he was really in the shit with his bets and drinking, a little trip escorting someone to a rendezvous point could make everything better — at least for a while.

His only rule was no drugs — no way did he want to get involved in the cocaine traffic that claimed so many lives in the region. The groups involved in that were bugfuck crazy and would just as soon kill you as scowl at you. Al had enough excitement in his life without having to worry about some real-life Scarface with an Uzi waiting for him outside his apartment. Even Al had limits and standards — most of which were predicated on survival rather than ethical niceties — but they were still standards. He wasn't an animal, after all.

Carmen answered, and Al greeted her with enthusiastic affection. His voice cracked several times during the niceties, making him sound somewhat worked and desperate, even to himself.

"Oh, *Amor*, are you coming in tonight?" Carmen cooed, always promoting. "I have a couple of new girls who would love to meet a real gentleman."

"Not tonight. I'm afraid I can't afford even a few minutes in paradise right now." This was his way of indicating he needed a gig.

"Ahhh, your Lady Luck has been unkind to you lately? She can be a bitch, no?" Carmen commiserated.

"Si. She no like my Gringo ass anymore. Anything shaking on your end?"

"No, my love," Carmen said. "But I'll keep you in mind. It's been slow around here without you keeping us company."

This went on for a few minutes, until his headache forced him to terminate the call, his message delivered — Al was available and anxious to help anyone in need. Carmen was always good for something when he was down. And the last week had been a killer. He really could use a little tax-free kiss on the lips, hopefully over the next few days. Al owed a bookie $500 from a disastrous wager on Tuesday and really didn't want to have to spend the weekend dodging him. The guy was good natured enough about a little loan, but at 50 percent weekly interest it could get silly quickly, and he'd rather not dig himself any deeper in that particular hole. Allah willing, Carmen would find someone who wanted a package transported to Colombia or back and wanted to avoid customs formalities, or need an escort to or from that fine misunderstood nation but didn't want to have to wait in line at immigration. Whatever it was, Al was ready for it.

Assuming he could make it through his hangover without passing an organ or stroking out.

He sat, sweating and paranoid, counting the minutes until he could leave his oppressive little office and make his steady way home for a *Mojito* or five and some badly needed sleep. Al's Friday night was going to be a calm one.

And this time he meant it.

Really.

# CHAPTER 6

Ernesto spent the day as a tourist would. He rarely had free time, so suddenly finding himself with an oversupply of it he decided to take the bus to the waterfront and meander there; have a lunch of seafood washed down with some local Panamanian beer. One led to three and it soon became dusk, so there he was, walking the streets of the big city with some money in his pocket and a bad attitude.

Resolved to make the best of an otherwise negative event, he calculated the cost of a few hours at one of his favorite whorehouses. It would cut into his two week's pay, which would have to last him a while, but sometimes a long term sacrifice was worth it if there was short term pleasure to be had. He rationalized that this was the first holiday he'd really had, in eight long years, where he didn't have to be at work any particular day or time. Why not let his hair down and live a little?

He took the bus back toward his *colonia* and stopped about thirty minutes short of his house. There, by the roadside, lurked a number of rough-looking saloons advertising billiards, 'Showgirls' and 'Ladees Bar'. Paintings of cowgirls in chaps, or ponies running wild, adorned the stark hoardings. All had roughly the same layout – a one or two story main building joined to a motel-like structure where rooms could be rented by the hour or the night. Ernesto normally frequented a club closer to home but he'd heard good things about this cluster of bars and had been meaning to stop in to see whether the scenery was any better than at his local place.

He entered a dark watering hole, improbably named *Tres Palomitas* – the three doves – and allowed his eyes to adjust. It was all locals, with groups of two and three men sitting at the small tables nursing buckets of beer as women in nighties and negligees circulated between the tables, sitting on laps and joking with the customers.

He took a seat. A tall, gangly waiter with a pencil-thin moustache materialized at his side and took his order. A bucket of four beers was $2 for locals – a more than fair deal given the air conditioning and the two big screen televisions broadcasting soccer and ultimate fighting. Latin pop music blared from a sixties-era jukebox on one side of the room – Juanes' *La Camisa Negra* filling the room. Twenty seconds after the waiter appeared with his beer a short girl of no more than twenty came dancing up in impossibly high platform shoes, wearing little more than a couple of cocktail napkins held together with dental floss. It was a compelling look, coupled with obviously artificial breasts and long, curly brown hair with highlights framing her pretty face.

She came from Peru, and had been in Panama for two months. Angel claimed to be nineteen but Ernesto expected that was a lie. It didn't really matter – after half an hour of ritual flirting he had a good buzz going with this attractive and affectionate girl. Just what the doctor ordered. The place was hardly jumping, so after a starting price of $100 for an hour of pleasure he negotiated a full night with Angel for $60, with an additional $15 for the room until morning.

Ernesto was on vacation, he reasoned, so why not throw a little money around? By his reckoning he had something like $6,000 saved with the market owner so he could afford a night of harmless slap and tickle. Maybe even two nights, if he liked his trip to Peru…

Negotiations and the bucket of beer concluded, the unlikely couple made their tipsy way to the rear of the club. Ernesto bought a bottle of rum and a couple of Cokes on the way out the back door to the waiting room. He wasn't planning to vacate till morning, so that would suffice for a combination late dinner and social lubricant. Angel wobbled to the third door from the end on the shabby courtyard, high heels sculpting her legs in an appealing manner. Ernesto followed. Angel was taking him to heaven. What more could any reasonable man want on a Friday night in the tropics?

ॐঙ

"We have a problem." The voice on the phone was almost a whisper, and had a sibilant, reptilian quality that oozed latent menace.

"Yes, sir. What is it?" Sam asked, eager to solve whatever crisis had summoned the man on the other end of the line. Late night calls at home from Langley were almost unknown, and this operative wasn't just anyone – so Sam viewed it as an opportunity to prove his worth.

"We've had a complication on a little off-grid op in your backyard. We were sanitizing a safe house and had an item go missing. We believe it was pilfered."

"Can you send me the details, sir? Do you have any suspects?" If they had an idea of who might have taken whatever it was, this would be easy enough to fix.

"You'll have a full report waiting for you in your office. I can't underscore enough how sensitive this item is, or how important it is we recover it immediately," the voice continued.

"I'll get right on it in first thing in the morning," Sam promised. "You can count on me, sir."

"Perhaps you should go in now," the voice suggested. "Time is of the essence."

Sam glanced at his watch – it was three in the morning.

On a Saturday.

"Can you tell me anything about what I'm looking for?" Sam was curious about what could be so pressing.

"It's all in the report," the voice continued. "We're not sure who took it – there were a number of locals helping clear things at the site – so you'll need to mobilize several teams."

That didn't sound promising. Needles in haystacks came to mind. "Any G2 as to what the op was, sir?" It would help to at least understand what had been compromised.

"That's need to know. You don't need to know. We just need the item recovered," the voice cautioned.

"I…I think I understand," Sam said, who didn't understand at all, but didn't want to appear provincial.

"Focus on locating the item. I'll make arrangements to get someone down there within 24 hours to deal with any logistical issues."

Sam didn't want anyone from headquarters banging around in his turf if he could help it. "I, err, there's no need…I can handle whatever needs to be done from here," he ventured.

"Just find the item. I'll handle everything from that point. You should probably head into the office now – time's wasting."

Sam very nearly protested, but something inside advised against it. The caller wasn't the sort to be trifled with. If he wanted to fly someone in to handle a messy situation maybe Sam really didn't want to know anything more about it. The most prudent course at this point was to do as he was told, and go read the report before responding appropriately. "Yes, sir. Of course. I'm on my way," Sam declared. "Whatever it is, I'm on it, sir."

"Good." The line went dead.

Sam regarded his wife, snoring rhythmically on her side of the bed, visions of opiate-friendly pixies no doubt dancing in her head. She hadn't even registered the unusual conversation. Probably a blessing.

He stifled a groan, stepped into his slippers and trudged to the bathroom. Whatever was going on that had caused the caller to be so concerned about some 'missing item' of indeterminate origin and purpose didn't auger well. Something very serious must have happened. It was only an hour later in Washington, which meant the caller was awake at 4 a.m. on a weekend dealing with some mystery item gone walkies. That was definitely not standard operating procedure. Especially not for the man on the other end of the phone. This was as unusual as anything Sam had ever been involved in.

It promised to be a very long morning.

☞☜

The sound of Shakira's 'Loca' filled the small room, rousing Ernesto from his boozy slumber. Angel had already flown a few hours earlier; duties performed and with a cozy bed at home calling to her. He looked around the room until he spotted his shirt crumpled in a ball under a chair and stumbled over to it, retrieving his ringing cell phone in the process.

"*Hola*," Ernesto greeted.

"*Hola*. Ernesto? It's Miguel, from across the street," a male voice said in Spanish.

*Who?* He racked his brain for a few moments, trying to place the name. Oh, his neighbor Miguel. Of course. "*Si*, Miguel. How are you? What's up?" Ernesto asked.

"I don't know, *amigo*," Miguel said hurriedly. "But there are people in your house. They arrived a few minutes ago."

What? In his house? There had to be some sort of mistake. "What do you mean? What people?" Ernesto demanded.

"It's none of my business, man. But there are two Gringos, and a couple of police."

Ernesto stiffened. "Police?"

"*Si*. The cops are sitting out by their truck and the Gringos are inside," Miguel explained.

"What are they doing?" Ernesto asked. "Can you see anything? Where's Andres?" Andres was his roommate.

"Let me get closer. Hey, it looks like they're going through your stuff. Oh, and there's Andres. One of the Gringos just took him out to the police truck."

What the hell? That wasn't right. Why would the cops be standing around while a couple of Gringos ransacked his place? And what were they doing with Andres? He was completely harmless.

"Miguel, go back inside your house. Try not to look suspicious. I don't know what's going on, but whatever it is, you don't want to be involved."

"Yeah, okay, man. I don't need no trouble. I just wanted to warn you...you know, in case...in case you needed to know," Miguel hesitated. "Ernesto, you into anything dangerous? Is there anything you want me to do? They're cuffing Andres..."

Dangerous? Not good. Now his neighbor thought he was in the dope game. "No, Miguel. I don't know what they want," Ernesto said. Which was true.

"Awright, I hope you figure it out. Good luck," Miguel said, then hung up.

A pair of Gringos in that neighborhood, escorted by the *Policia*? What would Gringos be looking for in his house? He didn't have anything...

Shit. The camera. They must have figured out he'd taken it. But how?

Ernesto remained a little fuzzy from the night's *fiesta* but the scenario wasn't that hard to figure out. He'd been seen by the guy in the hall. And there were few other locals to choose from who worked at the villa and had the same access he did. Maybe there were security cameras in the room where the equipment had been stored? He hadn't troubled to look very closely, just acted instinctively.

God, that had been stupid. Why on earth had he done it? It was just a spur of the moment, childish move. What had he been thinking?

❧❧

The two men went over every inch of the little cinderblock dwelling, methodically checking for hiding places. There weren't a lot of options, given that the walls and floor were concrete. The air inside the house was stifling – there were only a few small windows for ventilation with bent rebar over them – acting as security bars – and no air conditioning. The tiny, two bedroom house couldn't have been over 300 square feet, with a pair of microscopic bedrooms, a primitive bathroom and a combination living room/dining room with a strip kitchen. After half an hour, they were done, and the brains of the operation pulled out his cell phone and placed a call.

"The place is clean," he said. "Or at least, there's no camera."

"What do you mean, at least?"

"Well, it seems like our boy had sticky fingers. Probably a kleptomaniac, by the looks of it. We found a windbreaker, a bunch of utensils, some office supplies, about eighty pens and pencils, some small kitchen appliances, even a flashlight from the villa – but no camera," he explained. "There's a roommate here; doesn't speak a word, but he seems terrified. Claims he hasn't seen the cook since he left for work yesterday. I think I believe him."

"And there's no sign of him? Just the roommate?"

"Yup. Just him. Maybe we should park someone here to watch the place? There's a good chance he'll come back – seems like everything these guys own is in the house, and that isn't much. They're about as dirt poor as you can imagine."

"Good idea. And have the cops bring the roommate in to grill him – no, better yet, tell them it's a U.S. federal investigation involving the DEA and we'd be very obliged if they'd allow someone from our offices to question him."

"Okay. I'll call you if there's a problem. Doesn't seem like there should be. Worst case, maybe we have to donate a few hundred bucks to the police retirement fund. I get the feeling they'll play ball."

Sam hung up. It looked like they'd identified their perp. Now it was just a question of finding the guy. He'd just collected two weeks pay in cash, so it was likely he was off on a bender somewhere and would return once the money ran out. That was how they played. Almost like children. Couldn't be trusted not to steal everything that wasn't bolted down; they were even worse with their own money. Probably one of the reasons they stayed destitute instead of making something of themselves.

Sam twitched his computer mouse to wake up his monitor and typed in a brief status report for Langley.

☙❧

Ernesto took a quick shower and hurriedly dressed, slicking back his hair with water. He had invited trouble; that much was obvious. He'd clearly stepped on the wrong toes by stealing the camcorder and they were taking it personally. Ernesto opened his backpack and fished around inside, retrieving the camera. It looked expensive; a Sony, like new. The dreadful realization hit him that, since they'd gone through the house they would know he'd been stealing things for years, so any chance of mercy was gone. Maybe if he'd been able to explain it away as poorly-advised angry impulse and returned the camera, they would have let him go. But now the police were involved to a point where they were willing to escort Gringos out to search his place. This was serious.

Ernesto fought back a rising sense of panic. He couldn't really resist pocketing items that weren't his whenever the opportunity afforded – overtaken by a compulsion inherent since childhood – but he'd never imagined it would get him into any real trouble. But now it had, and in a big way. He cursed under his breath. Why did he do this shit? He never even sold any of the stuff he snagged. It was just automatic.

To make matters worse, his passport had expired several weeks ago; so not only was he a serial thief, but also living illegally in the country. He didn't know that much about how the law worked in Panama, but if it was anything like Colombia he could expect a long time in jail until he got to trial, followed by an even longer term once he was sentenced, especially since he'd also demonstrated complete disregard for Panama's immigration rules.

So what was he going to do?

He couldn't stay in Panama; it was simply a matter of time until they caught and imprisoned him. He'd never been in jail but the thought petrified him – jails were stark, miserable places back home and he had no reason to believe they were any better here. If only he knew how to sneak across the border into Colombia. Easier said than done, especially since he didn't have a valid passport. Colombian officials would certainly not just take his word for it and let him back into the country. No, they'd turn him away at the border and force him to get a new passport at the consulate in Panama City, which would result in him going straight to jail, because the Panama side of the border would do a police check, and bam – on would go the cuffs.

No matter how he sliced it, he was screwed.

On the plus side, the crimes of theft and being an illegal alien were nowhere nearly as serious as rape or murder, so it was doubtful there would be a manhunt. After all, how much crap got stolen every day without anybody ever getting caught? Then again, how many times had he heard of Gringos ransacking a house while the cops stood watch? The only safe assumption was to expect the worst. He'd have to be very careful.

Ernesto would never get another job in Panama without legal papers, so his future in the country was over. Plus, he wasn't getting any younger. If there wasn't a chance of better paying work for him in Panama he might as well return home and find employment there. The economy in Colombia had picked up since he'd left, and he did have some savings – so maybe all of this was a blessing…

Shit. Savings. His money.

Ernesto needed to visit the convenience store owner and get his cash before the day got much later. With a fat wad of hundreds, he had options. As things stood now, he was a sitting duck. As he considered his next move, a plan started to take shape in his head. It might cost him a bunch but he suspected he knew a way to get across to Colombia without any problems, leaving the stolen camera drama in Panama City.

Maybe everything happened for a reason.


Ernesto opened the door and stepped out into the muggy sunshine, backpack in tow. He made his way to the main road and waited for the bus. On weekends they only ran half as often so he figured he might be there for a while. His head ached from too little sleep and a too much alcohol, but it had been worth it. Traffic was sparse with not a single bus in sight. He continued down the road until he reached a small market, where he bought cookies and a soda. Breakfast of champions.

Ernesto walked back to the opposite side of the thoroughfare and stood under a tree, sheltering himself from the unforgiving rays of the mid-day sun. Half an hour later, a bus groaned to a stop and he boarded. It was almost deserted, a far cry from the weekday throng. Settling into the worn bench seat, he realized this would be one of the last times he ever watched the scenery along this stretch of road go by. For eight years he'd been taking the ride automatically and now that was over for good. He didn't have any regrets, especially as he sat roasting in the poorly ventilated old relic.

After ten minutes he saw the familiar pink chicken shack on the opposite side of the road. He'd be at the villa road in a few more seconds. A siren screamed behind the bus, forcing it to lurch onto the shoulder, chilling Ernesto's blood. How was it possible they'd caught him? How had they known he was on the bus?

Two fire trucks roared by, horns blaring and lights flashing, and turned the corner onto the villa road. A police car screeched by and followed them. Ernesto let out his breath and peered through the dirty window as the bus rolled slowly by the turnoff. Clouds of black smoke wafted into the partially overcast sky.

From the exact place where the villa sat.

There weren't a lot of homes there – it was rural, and he knew its geography by heart. The closest house to the villa was a quarter mile away, right by the intersection. What the hell was going on? Curiosity clawed at him, and he almost yelled 'stop' to the driver so he could jump off the bus. Then his survival instinct kicked in. How smart would it be to rubberneck at the scene of his crime, surrounded by emergency vehicles – including police – with the stolen property still in his backpack?

Maybe not so smart.

Besides, whatever had happened at the villa wasn't his problem anymore. Ernesto's only concern was now Ernesto. He remained seated, biding his time until he got to the outskirts of his *colonia*, where he descended from the bus and entered the neighborhood convenience store.

# CHAPTER 7

Al sat on his couch in his underwear, munching on leftover Chinese food and watching a DVD he'd downloaded from a pirate site. He favored simple-minded action plots but this one was lowbrow even by his liberal standards. How did garbage like that make it into production? He daydreamed about having written a hit screenplay based on his experiences in Desert Storm, savoring the seven figure bonus he'd been paid as an advance, and imagined the hot, young starlet who'd been cast as one of the leads. The poor thing had fallen head over heels for the enigmatic but brilliant author – no, make that author/producer. Their biggest annoyance were the paparazzi, who would follow them around to the five star restaurants they regularly frequented, and the award ceremonies where he was routinely honored, and even on their private jet vacations to the islands…

The cardboard food carton leaked a viscous brown sauce onto his undershirt, startling him out of his fantasy and burning his stomach. He jumped to his feet. God, that hurt. He inspected the shirt. Ruined.

Al carried the container to the kitchen before padding to the bathroom to turn on the shower. He'd managed to jury-rig the toilet into operation last night, and so far, so good. He caught a glimpse of himself in the mirror – paunchy, out of shape, a good thirty pounds overweight.

Okay, forty.

Maybe it was the stained shirt that made him look fatter. Whatever. He knew he wasn't in exhibition shape, by any means. Al peeled off his underwear and twisted a tepid stream of water on before stepping into the shower and scrubbing at the sauce on his shirt with the remaining sliver of soap. His home phone interrupted his interlude. Dripping wet, he slipped and almost went down as he hurried out of the shower toward the telephone, tweaking his sacroiliac, which had only recently stopped throbbing from the twisting it had received during the calf cramp episode.

The ringing stopped a second before he was able to pick up. Al stood, dripping onto the floor of the living room, naked from the waist down, glaring at the evil handset in his hand. He flopped onto the bed, and hit redial. Music boomed in the background as the caller picked up.

"*Amor*!" Carmen exclaimed. "I'm so glad I got you."

"It's been a long time since a woman said anything like that to me."

"Oh, you. Listen, I have something I think you can help with. Are you busy tonight?"

Al paused a moment, considering his soaked, semi-naked, Chinese food-stained state. "I think I can break away. What's the deal?"

"Eighteen hundred dollars if you can be here by seven p.m."

"Who do I have to kill?" Al deadpanned.

"See, that's why I love you, *Amor*," Carmen squealed. "You're so funny!"

"Yeah. I missed my calling."

"So you can make it?"

Al looked at the clock over the TV. He had two hours. No problem. "I'll be there. You want to fill me in now, or later?"

"When you arrive," Carmen said. "I need to make some calls to see if I can set everything up for tonight. I'll see you when you get here…"

"All right. Thanks, Carmen. *Ciao*."

"*Ciao* to you too, *Amor*…" Carmen hung up.

*Well, what do you know?* Maybe his luck was turning around. Eighteen jings, just when he needed it most! Ask and ye shall receive. He flipped open his Zippo and lit a Marlboro red, exhaling a satisfying cloud of smoke as he absently fondled his belly; which seemed to grow bigger by the day. At one time, he'd been somewhat of a lady-killer – piercing blue eyes, high cheekbones, a smirking self confidence that knocked the *chiquitas* dead. The years hadn't been as kind to him as he might have hoped – actually, the years and a steady diet of alcohol and tobacco. But he still had some game, and he could always lose the weight.

Maybe after this weekend he'd start working out.

Anything was possible.

❧

Esperanza was a brothel with a difference. Situated in a colonial mansion on the outskirts of old town in Panama City, it aspired to a higher tone, a more select clientele, than the typical whorehouse. Red velvet draped the foyer and incense permeated the air, and instead of the typical squalid ambiance, an aura of seedy refinement was the ethos within its walls.

Carmen Ortega presided over the establishment with an iron fist in her proverbial velvet glove. Her girls were among the most attractive, and her prices the highest because she believed you got what you paid for. And the popularity of the venue vindicated her choices. There prevailed an appetite for a higher-end experience in the burgeoning city. As the money steadily gravitated to Panama, so too did the requirement for a platinum-level den of iniquity. Her customers came from all walks of life and no one was ever overtly excluded, though she unabashedly courted and catered to the well heeled, whether that meant new fast money from the drug trade, the established business-elite, or as in Al's case, the embassy crowd. If any rowdy college kids wandered in, the prices shut down their party faster than any burly bouncer could.

Carmen's vision had been of a classy club with a veneer of sophistication, and when she'd happened across the dilapidated building in need of major refurbishment she'd known instantly that this was the place for her. Six months of round-the-clock construction had resulted in a kind of baroque Disneyland for horny men, where they weren't just paying for a one hour roll in the hay, but rather an entree to a wonderland of possibilities.

She was making a killing and she knew it was all in the packaging.

A natural entrepreneur, Carmen had also become a discreet go-to source for solutions to mundane problems such as border crossings, smuggling, money laundering and the like. Her intricate network could get anyone anything – for a price. And because she avoided narcotics trafficking and murder-for-hire, she didn't step on the more established operators' trades, thus providing a complementary service rather than outright competition. This enabled her to leverage relationships and stay on good terms with the whole twisted web of conflicting networks in the region. Everyone needed a little help from friends sometimes and Carmen had a menu of necessary, but obscure, services that were lucrative, but not to a degree that anyone would want to muscle in and cut her out.

Take her current project: a simple cook who had slipped on his paperwork and found himself experiencing a minor misunderstanding with local law enforcement. He'd been an occasional client of her place – maybe three times a year, likely birthdays or other special events – but was a decent sort in need of help, and with cash in hand. So what to do?

Rather than charging him an exorbitant fee for a relatively straightforward service, Carmen had offered a solution to him for forty-five hundred dollars. That was a bargain for what she was offering: guaranteed safe passage to Colombia, escorted much of the way by a highly-regarded member of the diplomatic corps. Obviously, the cost would have been triple if he'd wanted to come the other direction – most questionable traffic tended to move north through Panama, not south – however, she avoided that trade; preferring to leave it to those who were more comfortable with the increased risk. So Carmen pocketed a grand, paid the border patrols near the rendezvous point a few hundred each to get busy for a few hours, and arranged for a guide to meet her client and get him into Colombia. No questions asked. And of course, the eighteen hundred for her friend Al to shepherd the client south ensured his trip would be uneventful and uninterrupted. Money well spent.

It was a win-win deal for everyone. A nice little sideline to her prostitution business. She was owed many obligations by grateful clients on both sides of the border, and this provided a means to monetize her favor bank. And all for just a few phone calls. It was perfect.

Ernesto sat in the downstairs bar, fortifying himself with Seven and Sevens as he waited for word he'd be departing that night. The bartender's black slacks and tuxedo shirt, fitted with an ebony vest and bowtie, reinforced the formality of the room. There were worse places to kill time – the scenery was first rate; a steady stream of exceptionally beautiful young women in various stages of undress moving through the lounge, trolling for clients among the exclusively male patrons seated at the circular white marble tables. The gold brocade and velour trappings created an aura of quiet sophistication for the drinking gentlemen.

At first he'd balked at the cost of getting across the border, but upon consideration he'd realized it was unlikely he'd find a more reasonable or dependable avenue. Carmen was top notch – he'd get his money's worth – and at the end of the deal he'd still have almost $1500 left when he landed in Colombia; more than enough to support himself while he got a job in Bogota or Medellin.

The price was steep, but it beat the hell out of rotting in prison for a year or two.

That choice was no choice at all.

Carmen presided over the scene like royalty, greeting new entrants and thanking departing customers. A striking brunette with an eerie resemblance to Salma Hayek, she wore a long, red silk sheath with a slit up the side that almost reached her hip – a suitably provocative yet elegant ensemble that somehow resonated with the decor. Carmen fancied herself the consummate hostess – her charms weren't for sale; rather, she was the mistress of ceremonies.

As Al entered the foyer, she waved and blew him a kiss, disengaging from the two men she'd been entertaining.

"Alberto, *Amor*, welcome again. You look thirsty," she said, smiling warmly.

"It's hotter than usual out. Easy to get parched with this weather," he conceded. "And you look ravishing, as always."

"Let's get you something cool to drink and slip upstairs to talk business."

"I like the way you think, Carmen," he flirted, eying the bartender. He crossed the room in a few strides and ordered a double vodka tonic; easy on the ice and tonic.

Carmen waited until he returned, tumbler in hand, and they climbed the curved stairway to a room at the far end of the third floor – all the other rooms had been converted to bedrooms but Carmen had reserved this suite as her office.

"I have a friend who needs to get to Colombia in a hurry," Carmen explained. "I've arranged everything – a guide will be waiting in the jungle to walk him over. The usual spot near Meriti. He'll be there at 6 a.m.."

"Brutal hours," Al observed. "But should give us plenty of time. When do we leave, and what's the traveler's story?"

"His name's Ernesto – a cook who's been unfairly accused of theft and has also lost his passport," Carmen said. "A simple man with a problem. A Colombian who just wants to get home."

Put that way, Al almost felt guilty accepting the $1800 Carmen was going to pay him. Almost. He downed his drink and rose to his feet, feeling better than he had all day. "Okay, so it's an escort job. Fair enough." Al paused. "I'll be back at ten to meet him and give him the rundown. We should plan on leaving at eleven. Thanks for setting this up, Carmen. Couldn't come at a better time."

"Are you sure you don't want to spend an hour here? I have some remarkable new arrivals…"

"Thanks, but no. I need to grab my passport, gin up Ernesto's paperwork and change into something more comfortable. I'll take a rain check though," Al promised.

"Okay, *mi Amor*, it's your loss. Don't say I never offered," she said, feigning offense.

"If it were you, Carmen," Al said softly, "I'd change my mind."

"Ah, *Amor*," Carmen flirted. "If only it was a different time and place – you wouldn't even have to ask."

This was a common theme in their interactions; a harmless diversion. Both enjoyed the banter, and neither took it seriously. Their relationship was far too lucrative to ruin business with anything personal.

"What's your friend's full name?" Al asked. He'd need it for the document he had in mind.

"Ernesto Cortez Sanchez, spelled like it sounds," Carmen replied. "Sanchez might not be his real name, though," she cautioned. "Here's a photograph for the document you'll need to create…" She placed a passport sized color headshot on the table – her digital camera and photo printing setup in the corner of the office came in handy for such assignments.

"It'll take me a few hours," Al said. "I'll see you at ten. Thanks again."

"*De nada*, Al, *de nada*." Carmen waved her fingers at him. "Now come back downstairs with me – I'll accompany you out. It's a busy night so I have to be available to help the clients make smart choices. Otherwise I'd stay and chat with you forever, *Amor*."

Al understood. It was time to hit the road and get his stuff together. Carmen had money to make and the evening wasn't getting any younger.

Neither was he.

They walked down the stairs, arms linked, Al playing the gallant courtier to Carmen's regal descent.

❧

Al sat at his ancient computer and typed in *Senor* Sanchez' name, then printed the document. It was pure bullshit but would suffice when the police decided to stop and check cars going toward the border, which they routinely did. Purporting to be a photocopy of the photo and signature pages of an American passport – the story being that he'd lost his original, which accounted for Ernesto being escorted by State Department personnel – it was pure invention; one of Al's many sleights of hand he'd come up with for his little side business.

Al knew from past experience he could bluster through by waving it around and leaning on his diplomatic passport. Truth was, very few folks were trying to slip from Panama to Colombia at night with a U.S. diplomat escorting them, which made his job all the easier; the scrutiny traveling south was typically lackadaisical. Other than a few routine traffic stops by bored, tired, disinterested policemen, they'd be golden.

Getting near the border wasn't that tough, but making it out of Panama and into Colombia was harder than it sounded, at least if you didn't have the right paperwork and couldn't travel in a legitimate manner. If you'd had a misunderstanding with law enforcement and couldn't hop on a commercial airliner, there were only three options: boat, private plane, or foot.

Cars and buses were out because there were no roads between the two countries, nor any rail service – just some of the densest jungle in the world. That created a natural, virtually impassable barrier to movement between South and Central America, which was where he and Carmen came in.

Al ran the timeline in his head. Pick up Ernesto at ten, fill out the blanks in the bogus document, like birth date and physical characteristics, and then drive to Meteti – which would take almost all night. Ernesto then faced the hard and dangerous part – forty-four miles of jungle skirting the northern section of the infamous Darien Gap. Fortunately for Al, he didn't do that part of the trip – his brief was to get the customer to the rendezvous point outside of Meteti, and his part of the transaction was done.

There was no frigging way he'd have taken the job otherwise.

Rightly considered one of the most dangerous areas on the planet, due to the drug smugglers' rebel forces or armed militia – often one and the same – that controlled the area, you'd need to have a death wish to stray anywhere near the Gap. Normally, Al wouldn't have ventured within fifty miles of it, however, Carmen's contacts with the border shadow organizations ensured safe passage, at least to the rendezvous point. After that, Ernesto would be on his own with the guide Carmen had arranged and Al would return to his car, eighteen hundred dollars richer. He'd done the trip a dozen times and by now had full confidence in the arrangement – after all, he was still around to tell the story, so the system obviously worked.

He didn't envy this Ernesto character the next part of the trip. If you somehow managed to evade being shot to pieces by homicidal drug smugglers or bloodthirsty armed insurgents, you'd likely succumb to any number of toxic plants, insects or animals. It was the perfect place to disappear if you wanted to drop off the face of the earth, but in the absence of someone like Carmen's guarantee of safe passage, trying to make it through was an imminent death sentence. Every year an occasional hiker would ignore the plentiful warnings and try his luck crossing the tangled, verdant expanse and inevitably disappear, never to be heard from again. Even the police were terrified of that frontier, and wouldn't approach even the perimeter.

Not that Al cared – he was only playing glorified chauffeur, and after going for an early morning hike, would be out of the deal. He understood his role; the police had checkpoints all along the southern part of the Transamerica highway, as the two lane strip of asphalt was self-importantly labeled, and unless one had, say, a diplomat for company, it could be difficult to make the last fifty miles. That was his value. Al had zero issues with ferrying a fugitive to the middle of nowhere as long as he got paid. Who was he to judge his fellow man? Carmen wouldn't have helped a murderer or rapist, and anything less was just a question of local laws being bent. He'd been around long enough to understand that everyone made mistakes – his philosophy was to do the job and let God sort it out in the end.

He sat back in the creaky wooden chair and inspected the bogus paperwork with satisfaction. This was the easiest money he'd ever make. Beat the hell out of roasting in his oven of an office, that was for sure.

# CHAPTER 8

The rutted dirt runway glistened with dark mud following the constant afternoon showers. The private twin-prop plane struggled to maintain control as it came in to land, bouncing on descent from updrafts caused by the heat of the jungle rising into the cooler air. The pilot wrestled with the flaps, eventually straightening the craft and gliding to a slithering halt by a waiting late model Toyota Land Cruiser. A weary customs agent emerged from the small shack near the end of the landing strip and waved at the pilot. Inside the plane, *Don* Tomas reflected on how relaxed crossing international borders could be when the local officials had gambling debts they needed to pay off. The pilot killed the engines, restoring the hushed quiet of the thick jungle on all sides of the clearing.

The door of the Cessna opened and a small folding ladder descended gracefully from the fuselage, coming to rest on the waterlogged gravel. Two black-haired males in their late twenties followed the white-suited *Don* Tomas as he made his way toward the Toyota. The younger men, one tall, one stocky, scanned the surroundings and slipped into step on either side of the Don in a protective formation. The driver, who waited by the vehicle, stepped forward as they approached and hugged *Don* Tomas, enthusiastically shaking his hand in greeting. "*Don* Tomas. Always good to see you."

"Thank you, Cesar," the *Don* replied, an easy smile complimenting his cherubic, yet forty year old face. "It's good to be seen."

The stocky young man waved at the pilot. After a few moments the props slowly turned as the starter fought to engage. After a splutter or two the engines roared to life, leaving a puff of black smoke hanging in the air as the plane taxied to the far end of the runway. The motors howled as the RPMs went into the redline. It leapt forward and within a matter of seconds was airborne, its wheels narrowly clearing the surrounding tree line.

The tall man attended the passenger door for *Don* Tomas before getting in the back with his partner. Cesar took the wheel and started the engine.

He opened the center console and extracted a small black nylon sack. He handed it to *Don* Tomas, who unzipped the bag and extracted three Glock 17 pistols, one of which he slipped into his jacket pocket, passing the remaining pair to his two younger bodyguards.

"*Gracias*, Cesar. You did well," *Don* Tomas said.

"*De nada, Don* Tomas. Any time I can be of assistance, you know you only have to call," Cesar replied. "And how long will you be with us *this* trip?"

"Just for the weekend," *Don* Tomas said. "We'll be leaving tomorrow, about the same time. The pilot knows to arrive at seven."

Cesar frowned. "A very short trip indeed."

"*Si*. And how are things?" *Don* Tomas asked Cesar.

"Ah, you know. Always the same. The police want more money every month. The politicians want more money every month. Everyone wants to do less for it," Cesar complained as they navigated the road north.

"It's the same everywhere, Cesar." *Don* Tomas raised an eyebrow. "And have you had any trouble with our associates here?"

"No, it's been business as usual. Seems like things have settled down since the last disagreements," Cesar said cheerfully. "But I still don't trust them."

"The only ones you can trust are family, and even then you have to sleep with one eye open."

The three men laughed at the *Don*'s dry observation, and when the mirth subsided Cesar said, "When the police stop us at the checkpoint ahead, let me handle it. There won't be any trouble."

"I trust there won't be," *Don* Tomas said.

The bumpy dirt track steadily wound its muddy way to the intersection with the Transamerican highway.

"Do you have any special requests for your only night in town?" Cesar asked. "Do you want entertainment brought in, or are you in the mood to go out?"

"I think I'd like to go out. Surprise me. Somewhere *tranquilo*, but where the ladies are friendly," suggested *Don* Tomas.

"I know the perfect place," Cesar assured them, as he turned onto the main road. A rusting green sign, almost hidden by encroaching vegetation, advised *Panama City, 32 KM.*.

~⚬~

They'd had no luck locating the cook. He hadn't returned to the house and his roommate had come up empty, so now it was time to move to plan B. Sam's only problem was that he wasn't sure what plan B should be. There was a limit to how much he could get the local police involved. Pulling a few strings to have them accompany his team while they searched a house was one thing, but doing a nationwide manhunt for a camera thief wasn't practical. And if he stretched the truth and accused the cook of something appropriately serious to get the cops mobilized it would invite undesired attention. Sam tried to think like a petty crook. What would he do?

Probably sell the camera.

Which would introduce yet another layer of complexity. It was clear that Langley wanted exposure limited to as tight a circle as possible. And of course, it would mean yet more people to track down. It wasn't as though Sam had an unlimited team to follow up every lead. Panama wasn't exactly a hot zone, and he only had four men for field work under his command. He'd requested additional manpower and been assured it would be forthcoming within a day, but that didn't do much for him right now. And as he'd learned in the classroom, as well as from *CSI Miami*, the more time that passed after the commission of a crime, the longer the odds of catching the perp.

Hardly consistent with his desire for a meteoric rise within the service.

Sam understood he had a problem, all right. But the part where he came up with a brilliant complementary strategy for closing the box and catching his man was proving more difficult than he'd hoped. If he were in the U.S. he could have commandeered traffic camera footage from the time the cook had left the villa – assuming the NSA played ball. But in Panama there was no technology to work with, unless you considered mud huts high tech. So he was out of luck – and ideas.

Except for the phone.

He'd put in a demand for the cook's cell phone, and was still waiting for the info. The data they'd had on file was out of date; the number he'd given them long disconnected and moved to a new owner. But Sam had headquarters working through channels with the phone company to see if they had a new cell on record. If so, once they got the data, they could use

NSA – even in Panama – to track the clipper chip in the device and locate the cook to within a few meters.

That would be a game changer – leading to a simple snatch operation. Find him, grab him, and pray he hadn't sold the camera. His men were standing by but, unfortunately, nothing moved quickly in the boonies.

Frustration mounting, he opened a bottle of Maalox and chugged it. The acid from tension was eating away at his ulcer, increasing his discomfort. Why the hell had this, whatever this was, happened on his watch? He only had three lousy months left, and now a stolen camera conspired to make the agency look inept in his backyard?

The worst part of it all was that he didn't know why the damned thing was worth so much effort and concern. Nobody was telling him anything other than 'find the camera', which didn't speak too highly of Langley's faith in his abilities. And soon he'd have some stuffed shirt looking over his shoulder from headquarters, no doubt taking all the credit for any success and blaming any failures on Sam. He knew the way things worked and could see that this was going down the bad road.

Sam rubbed his face, tired from being there since 3:30 that morning. He paced around his office, trying to get the blood flowing so he would stay alert. His computer beeped, and he moved the mouse, activating the screen.

They'd gotten a match on the cook's number.

Maybe things were looking up after all.

# CHAPTER 9

Ernesto fiddled with his drink coaster, glancing around the room every few minutes. The waiting had made him edgy, and the parade of scantily-clad young Latinas had grown stale after a few hours. Adrenaline from the day's events had faded, replaced by a crash, and it was all he could do to keep his eyes open.

The stream of clients in the brothel had increased to full flow – unsurprising given that it was Saturday night. The diverse crowd comprised a mix of locals and visitors. One group in particular drew his attention – three obviously Colombian men hanging out in the lounge area with *narcotraficantes* written all over them. That also wasn't surprising because the drug traffickers packed the kind of money that made a night at Carmen's about as financially significant as a trip to a fast food restaurant for a Happy Meal.

At nine forty-five, Carmen came downstairs and escorted Ernesto up to her third floor office. She explained that the trip across the border that night was a go, and that it was time to settle the tab before they went any further. Ernesto fished out a wad of cash from his backpack and carefully counted out forty-five hundred dollars. Carmen, satisfied after confirming the count, excused herself for a few moments and slipped into the attached sitting room.

Ernesto stuffed the remainder of the money into the hygiene kit at the bottom of his backpack, scuffing his knuckles on the video camera in the process. He extracted the cursed device, having largely forgotten about it other than as the source of his current misery. Although he'd never used one before, he figured it couldn't be too difficult to operate. He punched at the buttons and fiddled with the controls until the unit beeped. A small screen popped out of the right side and flickered to life. Ernesto vaguely hoped it would be a sex tape, but with the way his luck was running it was more likely footage of the villa owner's colonoscopy.

Carmen closed the concrete-encased floor safe, securing the handle and spinning the dial. She sealed Al's payment in a plain white envelope, and kissed it, leaving a scarlet lipstick print on the white paper.

She inspected herself in the full-length mirror attached to the door that connected her office, and nodded, satisfied with her choice of outfits. She leaned a few inches from the glass surface and patted at her carefully applied makeup with a tissue, then brushed a lock of hair from her forehead. There were many more hours to go this evening and she prided herself on being a consummate mistress of ceremonies. It wouldn't do to appear fatigued – her clientele expected a departure from dull reality when they passed through her doors and she was one of the top representatives of the dream. Even though she wasn't on the menu, she still needed to look like a tempting dessert. After all, this was show biz, and you always wanted to look your best for the audience.

Carmen heard a muffled knock on the door of the other room, and glanced at her diamond-encrusted Piaget. Ten p.m. on the dot. At least Al was on his game tonight – regardless of her constant doubts about him he'd always been reliable. At least so far. He had his problems, but then again so did everyone. She had a soft spot for the poor sot, so as long as he could keep it together she'd throw him a bone now and then. It was convenient to have one's own State Department official to run errands, and he was cheap, so the relationship worked for them both.

"Coming, *Amor*. Let yourself in. Don't be shy, I won't bite," she teased as she entered her office.

Al closed the office door behind him and gave Carmen a courtesy hug and peck on the cheek. He plopped down in the chair next to Ernesto and put his satchel on Carmen's desk, then swiveled and extended his hand to the cook.

"*Hola, amigo*. I'm Alberto, and I'll be your pilot on this short flight," he proclaimed in Gringo-accented, but understandable, Spanish. A lingering odor of alcohol hung in the air; the residue of Al's fortification at home before the long night ahead.

*"Con mucho gusto,"* Ernesto replied, barely acknowledging him – he was white as a sheet and sweating in spite of the powerful air conditioning. Fumbling to zip his tightly-clutched bag, he grabbed Al's outstretched hand.

Al gave Carmen a worried look. What was the cook on? Was he a nutcase? Dangerous? Carmen threw them both a thousand kilowatt smile and acted like everything was normal. Maybe Ernesto had the jitters now that it was time to actually go? She'd seen that before – the client got cold feet once he'd had enough time to imagine all the ways things could go horribly wrong in his escape. It was her job to calm nerves and break things down in a comprehensible, organized manner, so the client not only understood they'd done this many times before, but that he was in safe and competent hands.

"Boys, here's how this'll work. Al will drive down to southern Panama tonight. That will take around six hours, assuming numerous police checkpoints and occasional washouts from rain damage. Once you're at your destination, he'll escort you to the meeting spot on the outskirts of the jungle, where my guide will be waiting. Ernesto, you'll go with the guide, who'll take you across the mountains to the other side of the border. From there, he'll explain how to get to Medellin, from which point you're on your own." Carmen paused. "You're not to give the guide any money – that's already taken care of. And you must do everything he says, exactly as he instructs. Your safety and survival depend on it. He's the only thing between you and death, so pay attention, and don't question."

Al had heard all this a dozen times before, with some minor variations. Sometimes it was a trip to a deserted port town for a boat trip down the coast, sometimes to an airstrip near the border for a tree-top flight into Colombia, and sometimes a hike, like tonight. It depended on the budget. Al intuited this was the bargain-basement tour, not the high-rollers' trip.

Ernesto nodded.

Carmen fleshed out the details and answered his questions before handing Al the cash-stuffed envelope, which he pocketed. Glancing at Ernesto, Al opened his bag and withdrew the paperwork he'd created earlier. It was time to fill in the blanks. Carmen excused herself, moving to her other room and leaving the two of them to complete the document in peace while she used the facilities.

# CHAPTER 10

A black Chevy Suburban pulled to the curb thirty feet from Esperanza, and four men exited the vehicle. All were Gringos with telltale military haircuts and athletic postures. They looked as though they were in uniform, in spite of their dark, nondescript civilian clothing. The lead man checked the screen of his iPhone and motioned in the direction of the brothel to the others – that was the place. The last man out of the truck took a bottle from his windbreaker and swigged from it, spitting out the fluid and placing the bottle in the gutter, well behind the vehicle.

The group moved silently up the dark, empty sidewalk, compact submachine-guns at the ready. Nobody spoke. The street was empty but for them, and the surrounding buildings were starkly uninhabited. Parts of the neighborhood had been undergoing renovation by entrepreneurial investors intent on retransforming the old colonial buildings into their bygone glory or converting them into stylish condos. But this far out on the fringe the homes remained deserted, other than occasional construction crews during the day. That would inevitably change, but tonight, Carmen's place projected the only sign of life on the street – now slick from a late-Spring cloudburst a few minutes earlier.

Checking the illuminated screen one last time, the leader made an abrupt gesture with his hand and two of the men positioned themselves out of sight on either side of Esperanza's entrance. One of the men lifted the battered iron ring attached to the center of the ancient wooden door and rapped. After a few moments a small wooden hatch opened at eye level and a man's face filled the space. Music drifted from behind him, along with occasional laughter and celebratory shouts.

"*Que Ondas?*" asked the doorman.

"Dude, I told you this was the place," the leader blurted to his companion in English, before switching to broken Spanish and addressing the face in the door. "Uh, a friend at our hotel said this was a good place to have some adult fun?" he slurred. The sour stink of hard liquor fumed on his breath.

"What hotel?" the doorman asked, switching to English.

"Hey, he speaks English!" the leader said. "The Intercontinental Hotel, *amigo*."

Ever suspicious, the doorman scrutinized them, then the little hatch closed and the scarred wooden slab swung open.

The leader stepped into the doorway and rabbit punched the doorman in the throat. He hit the ground like a wet sack of cement, emitting a low groan from his crushed larynx. Brandishing their guns, the group moved stealthily through the empty foyer and around the corner into the bar. *Don* Tomas' two security men, who were dutifully on guard in the lounge, registered the motion at the entryway, and seeing the Gringos' weapons, immediately pulled their Glocks and rapid-fired at the gunmen. The hail of rounds caught the intruders off-guard. One of the Gringos died instantly as a slug obliterated his jaw. A second collapsed screaming as several bullets shattered his legs. The Colombians tipped over their marble tables for cover and continued shooting into the foyer.

The pandemonium of women's panicked shrieks mingled with the concussive detonations of close-quarter gunfire as the remaining occupants scrambled for safety while hell was breaking loose. Machine-gun rounds peppered the wall behind the Colombians as they continued to blast away at the figures in the entryway.

On the second floor, *Don* Tomas pulled his pants on and drew his Glock from his jacket, ignoring the cringing girl on the bed clutching the covers to her chest. He pressed his ear to the door, and after confirming the hall was empty, padded silently on bare feet to the stairway. He peered downstairs. *Don* Tomas had survived many ambushes primarily due to his belief that when bullets started flying, the safe tactic was to shoot anything that moved and figure out who was who later. He had no idea why his Panamanian partners would want to eliminate him, but ruthless cunning had kept him alive when most of his peers were history, and this was just the latest betrayal in his brutal life.

Given the number of times rivals had tried to kill him, he always anticipated the worst – rule number one was to never allow yourself to be surprised. Whoever was coming for him had just made the worst mistake of their lives. *Don* Tomas didn't back away from fights. On the contrary, if you decided to take him on, you were buying a one way ticket to hell.

He chambered a round and cautiously descended the stairs, a bead of sweat trickling down his bare chest, gun held with both hands in a military grip.

❧

Carmen froze as she heard the unmistakable sound of gunshots from the ground floor. There had never been any trouble in her place but now it sounded like World War Three had kicked off downstairs. She ran to her monitor and flicked the mouse. A menu popped up with thumbnails numbered 1 through 25. She clicked on 2 and watched in numb horror as the close circuit cameras captured her lovingly restored cocktail lounge transformed into a battle zone.

"They're shooting the place apart!" she gasped. "It's those fucking dope dealers..."

Al stared at the screen in disbelief. Carnage reigned. Bodies littered what he could see of the area.

"Jesus, Carmen..." was all he could manage.

She clicked on number 25. The alley behind the building appeared on the screen. Devoid of activity.

"Al, quick, take Ernesto and go down the back way. End of the hall, then down the fire escape," she ordered. Without waiting for a response, Carmen ran into the attached room and rooted around in a closet. She emerged clutching a 12-gauge pump shotgun with a pistol grip. "Get going. Now, Al! The deal hasn't changed any. I can handle this."

"Are you sure, Carmen? It looks pretty messed up..." Al grabbed his bag and hastily retrieved the papers from the desk.

More shots exploded from below. Don Tomas had joined the fray with his associates.

"Just go, Al. I'll be fine." Carmen threw open her office door, peeked around the door jamb in both directions to verify no intruders were on their floor, and ran toward the stairs.

Al watched her head disappear down the main stairway before calling to Ernesto, "*Vamanos*. Now." He hurried to the window at the rear of the corridor and turned, looking for the cook. Ernesto popped out of the doorway a few seconds later and quickly joined Al, who was struggling to get the window open. Years of accumulated paint had sealed it shut. Together, they heaved on the window, forcing from it a creaking protestation until it opened with a sharp snap. Al climbed out onto the rickety metal platform and lumbered down the ladder to the second floor, where he kicked the ladder leading to the ground free. It slid downwards with a raucous screech. He jumped onto the pavement below and looked up. Ernesto was right behind him. The building was unusually quiet now, the shooting apparently over.

They circled around to the main street near Esperanza's front entrance, stopping close to the parked Suburban. Ernesto spotted the driver staring at them and nudged Al, who was squinting through the black of night at the intersection sign in the distance in order to get his bearings.

Al couldn't make out the sign but recognized the blue-green building that stood at the mouth of the alley where he'd parked his car. He whispered to Ernesto while he furtively scanned the street to ensure no homicidal drug dealers were about start shooting it out again. When he was sure it was safe, he beckoned Ernesto to follow him to his waiting vehicle.

The driver of the Suburban watched as they rounded the corner, and was preparing to go after them when the passenger window exploded in a spray of glass. The door flew open and the team leader threw himself in headfirst, holding his bleeding abdomen to stem the flow of blood.

"Go, go, go! Get out of here. Now," he screamed.

Panicked, the driver slammed the truck into gear and floored it, fishtailing as the rear window shattered from a burst of gunfire. More slugs thumped against the rear of the vehicle as they sped down the street.

"What the…" the driver yelled.

"Just keep moving. Get us back to base," the leader moaned. He slumped into the seat, which was already soaked through with blood.

The driver veered around the same corner the pair of men had run down and saw nothing other than deserted buildings and a pair of street dogs nosing through a pile of trash.

He saw tail lights turn onto another street several blocks up, and then disappear.

The driver flipped open his cell phone and hit a speed dial number.

# CHAPTER 11

"Jesus God. What the fuck? I mean, *what the fuck!*" Al babbled as he swerved down the small streets, racing away from the disaster back at Carmen's. Ernesto sat silently staring straight ahead, gripping the dashboard with one trembling hand and clutching his backpack with the other, his face ashen with shock.

Al was the polar opposite, animated and hyper from the excitement of the conflict. He hadn't stopped talking since he'd started the engine. "I mean, did you see that? It was a full scale war in there," he declared for perhaps the tenth time. "Unbelievable. Un-fucking-believable!"

He reached across Ernesto, popped his glove compartment open and withdrew a miniature single-serving size bottle of vodka. He spun the top with his teeth, bottle clenched with his right hand, and then blew the metal cap through his open window. He swallowed the contents in a single gulp. Al winced at the burn, and then burped loudly. The bottle followed the cap into the street.

Ernesto turned, woodenly examining Al's profile.

"Just my luck," Al prattled on. "I'm minding my business, just picking you up, and the entire Cali cartel decides to shoot it out a few feet from me. We're lucky we weren't killed. Really. It's a miracle we're alive to tell about it…"

Maybe that was overstating it, given they'd been two floors above the shooting and the floors and walls were constructed of foot-thick concrete. But still. He hadn't been near a discharging firearm since his service days, twenty something years ago. He knew the drug gangs routinely butchered each other, scrabbling over territory or routes, but those were usually lurid headlines in the local papers. It was different being proximate to a bloodbath.

Panama suddenly seemed far more ominous than it had a few hours ago.

Ernesto finally spoke, his voice a hoarse whisper. "But we're sticking to the arrangement, *sí?*"

Al thought about it. Other than the nightmare back at Esperanza, nothing had changed. They'd made it out without a scratch, and he'd already gotten paid, so in the end there was no reason not to go through with it. He toyed with the idea of fanning the entire adventure, dropping the cook off at the nearest bus stop and finding an air-conditioned bar to hide in for the next few days. He quickly dismissed the notion. His bookie needed to get paid and there would be plenty of time for fortification tomorrow, after he'd discharged his obligation.

"Yeah. Of course. Just fill in the last of the blanks on the form I stuffed in my bag and we're good to go. You'll need that when the cops do their routine stops on our way south." Al cranked the AC and rolled up his window – he was soaked through with sweat.

Al patted the breast pocket of his clammy shirt and felt the reassuring bump of his diplomatic passport and the folded envelope of cash. *Yeah, he'd go through with the deal.* He just hoped Carmen was okay. A massacre would certainly be bad for business, but if anyone could bluster through a difficult situation, Carmen could. She was a survivor, with enough friends and clients in high places to weather any storm.

He recalled her shotgun toting silhouette as she descended the stairs.

Al almost pitied the gunfighters. She'd looked pissed, and an angry Latina brandishing a twelve gauge was nothing to sneer at.

ॐ

"You're kidding me, right? Is this some kind of fucking joke…?" Sam was irate, yelling into the phone. He'd finally gotten the tracking info on the cook's cell number and placed it at a known whorehouse.

Then his four hard-case professionals moved in to do a snatch…and wound up butchered?

Sam slammed down the handset in frustration. How could grabbing a stupid cook and a pilfered camera turn into *Shootout at the O.K. Corral?* It was a whorehouse, for Christ's sake. The most dangerous part of this exercise should have been avoiding catching the clap. Now he had three dead men, a fourth in intensive care at the offices of the Agency's pet doctor, a driver with a head laceration, but no cook, no camera, and no explanation of how it all got botched. That, and a whole lot of 'splaining to do to the local cops – who were understandably curious as to how three Gringos with no IDs but identical military-grade weapons had come to wind up deceased in a gunfight with Colombian narcotics smugglers – all of whom were also dead.

And the Colombians hadn't gone easy – one of them had actually chased Sam's surviving man out of the brothel and single-handedly destroyed the vehicle with small arms fire. The only thing that had stopped him from tearing the truck apart with his teeth had been the Madame, who'd fired a shotgun blast through him as he emptied his clip into the departing Suburban.

This shit wasn't supposed to happen. This wasn't Beirut – it was frigging Panama. Nothing happened in Panama. It was a stinking swamp.

Sam's fury was modified by some particularly disquieting thoughts. Had the drug dealers been part of something he was unaware of involving the cook? Were they protecting him? Was this about to get much worse?

There were far too many unanswered questions. This had quickly degraded from a search for a mystery camera to an international incident with a bunch of body bags. And he still had no idea why the camera was so critically important to recover. Nothing made any sense. He paced his office, calculating how to frame his report to HQ.

A sharp knock interrupted his reverie.

"What? This better be good…" he yelled at the door.

A tall grey-haired man in his late fifties wearing a dark blue Tommy Bahama shirt and ivory slacks entered. He placed his briefcase on Sam's desk, and faced him. "Oh, it is good, Mr. Wakefield. It is," he declared.

"And just who the hell are you, and how did you get into this classified area?" Sam snarled, instantly regretting his harsh words.

The man smiled at him, but in a way that made Sam want to crawl under the covers and beg for Mommy. "Why, Mr. Wakefield – or shall I call you Sam?" The man paused. "Sam, I have a feeling I'm your worst nightmare," the man stated reasonably.

"Uh…err…" was all Sam could muster. He knew this was bad.

"I'm eagerly awaiting your next monosyllabic utterance, Sam. Given how you've attended to your duties so far today, I'm sure it will be a doozy." The man smiled again, enjoying his little funny.

Sam swallowed audibly. He tried again. "Look…I don't know what…" he croaked.

"No, you really don't, do you? Let me offer you a clue. I'm from Langley, my name's Richard Salero, and you're completely fucked," Richard said, deadpan. He smiled again.

"I...I see, sir."

"Yes, I believe you finally do." Richard nodded. "On the way in from the airport, I got an update on the situation. I understand you managed to get most of your working assets slaughtered this evening, in addition to failing to secure the missing item or the thief who took it? What do you do for an encore? Set fire to the flag and pass nuclear secrets to the Chinese?"

Sam wanted to punch the prick in his bony face but he choked down his rage, waiting to hear what came next. He'd never been spoken to like this in all his years with the Agency but something told him that now wasn't the time to defend his insulted pride.

"Cat got your tongue?" Richard asked. "Hmmm. Well, fortunately, Langley decided to send in adult supervision before this could get screwed up any worse – and I'm the new hall monitor. Effective immediately, you'll be reporting to me, Sam. And maybe if you're extremely lucky – and so far I see no evidence of that being the case – maybe, just maybe, by the time this is over, you'll still have a job." Richard gave Sam a searching look. "Now why don't you tell me in your own words how this turned into a complete clusterfuck during the few hours I was in the air, and then maybe we can be friends, okay?"

Sam stammered out his summary of what they knew so far, and waited for a response.

Richard stared at him as the office clock audibly marked the passage of time; seconds turned into minutes until Richard finally broke the silence. "So the driver got a good look at the cook and the man who helped him escape?" Richard asked.

"Yes, sir. He confirmed it was our target. But he didn't recognize the other man."

"What kind of shape is he in?" Richard inquired, almost as if he cared.

"The driver? He's got a minor head wound where he got nicked by some glass. Nothing serious. He lost a lot of blood, though. Head wounds bleed like a bitch. He's still in shock – he's just a local Panamanian asset, a reliable and discreet driver we've used before. Not a black ops guy or anything like that. He's pretty shaken up."

"Uh huh." Richard considered his options. "What about the cook's cell phone?"

"It's being tracked," Sam said. "Right now he's moving down the highway, headed south. I was just about to notify the local police to stop and hold him until we can get there…"

"That would be an extremely poor call. We can't have the locals involved from here on out. We'll handle everything internally." Richard saw the look of confusion in Sam's eyes. His tone softened slightly. "Look, Sam, headquarters flew me in on an Agency jet specifically to deal with this, and I brought some field specialists with me. We'll need to monitor the location of the phone real-time, and I'll handle the mission from here. I don't want the police involved any more than they already are."

Sam cleared his throat. "May I ask what's so important about a cook and a stolen camera that warrants your commandeering a jet and flying in a wet team at a few hours' notice?" He had to ask – couldn't help himself. What had been going on in his backyard, unbeknownst to him? What or who had been running an op without the local station chief being alerted? That was completely against all protocols.

"No, you can't ask," Richard answered.

"But…"

Richard's demeanor hardened again. "Here's what I want you to do, Sam. Don't think, and don't second guess me. I want you to find a sketch artist and get him to the clinic. Have him sit down with your driver and draw the mystery man. He's an unknown variable and I want him identified so we understand what we're dealing with. Do you think you can do that?"

"Uh, sure. But it's midnight. It'll take some time to find someone and get them out of bed on a Saturday night to do a sketch…" Sam thought aloud.

"Sunday. It's Sunday morning now, Sam. Saturday ended a few minutes ago. And yes, it will take some time. Which is why you should get on this instead of complaining about how difficult it will be," Richard said. "And I want you to run interference with the police and get the brothel Madame sequestered for us to question. I have a feeling we're not seeing all the pieces here. We need more intel. Do you think you can handle all that?"

"Of course. I'll get right on it, sir. But I still think we should notify the cops…"

Richard glared at him, what little patience he had swiftly dissipating. "Sam. I'll say this one more time, really slowly, so there's no mistake. I want to limit exposure on the recovery effort to just my group. Which means I need to figure out where the target's going and take effective countermeasures. I don't want local cops in the loop. I don't want to have to explain *anything* to them, and I certainly don't want to have to listen to your ideas about how I should or shouldn't proceed from here. Is that clear enough? As in, crystal clear?"

Sam's blood boiled again at the dismissive insult, but he said nothing – merely nodded assent. Which was hard, as he'd now been up almost 24 straight hours dealing with this mess, with no chance for rest in sight. But his instinct for self-preservation told him to bite his tongue and follow instructions without hesitation. He didn't know what he was involved in, but this Richard A-hole was obviously a senior field director, and they didn't fly those halfway across the world for amusement value. Sam completely believed him when he said his career was hanging by a thread.

That was one data point Sam knew he'd gotten completely right.

# CHAPTER 12

Inspector Jacinto Peralta of the Panamanian National Police was far from happy. Then again, he was rarely happy on weekends – when the lion's share of violent crimes occurred in Panama City and the surrounding *colonias*. Every Friday and Saturday night there would invariably be stabbings, shootings, robberies gone horribly wrong, grotesque crimes of passion, and every imaginable sort of retribution or vengeance killing. Following up on those was the workload and he was accustomed to his evenings being a parade of death.

Still, even by his standards the bloodbath at the Esperanza was gruesome. Nine people killed and six injured in one of the most savage episodes of his career; and of course, nobody knew anything. It was all shrouded in mystery. The few conscious witnesses had described an almost surrealistic sequence of events – armed men forcing their way inside, and within moments several of the customers who'd been quietly sipping their drinks blasting away at them. There was neither rhyme nor reason to any of it; unless it was one of the most indiscriminate drug-related execution attempts in Panamanian history.

That hypothesis seemed reasonable at first, given that three of the dead gunfighters had been known Colombian cocaine traffickers, in the country illegally. It would be easy to write a report that concluded their rivals had learned of their presence at the whorehouse and seized the opportunity to eliminate them. Though the niggling problem remained that their assailants were Gringos; none of whom had any identification on them, and all of whom were obviously athletic, in their late twenties and early thirties, with matching weapons. Standard characteristics for a team of professionals who knew what the hell they were doing.

Inspector Jacinto, known to the press and his subordinates as 'The Bulldog' knew from harsh experience that the drug trade attracted an international smorgasbord of criminal elements, but this was a first for him.

His lieutenant had opined the Gringos could have been Slavic – the Russian mob had been attempting to gain a foothold in Panama for some time – however a cursory inspection of their teeth, combined with a conspicuous absence of the ubiquitous gang tattoos, quickly sank that theory. The few Russians they'd arrested or found dead invariably had distinctively horrible dental work and were covered with dubious body art.

No, these men looked like NorteAmericanos. And that introduced a whole new set of complications for Jacinto.

The scene at Esperanza was chaotic. Police and emergency vehicles lined the block, which had been sealed off at both ends of the street. Floodlights illuminated the curb in front of Carmen's building and crime unit crews were photographing the area around the corpse lying on the sidewalk, as well as the glass trail from the vehicle that had been hit.

Carmen's customers had all prudently exited the area once the gun battle had obviously ended, as had many of the working girls. Nobody wanted to spend the night explaining their presence to the police. Many of the patrons were involved in questionable activities of one sort or another so they were naturally reluctant to being questioned by the cops for any reason, much less about being at a brothel during a shootout.

The foyer reeked with the distinct metallic odor of blood combined with the sulfur stink of cordite. Mosquitoes and other flying insects swarmed the area. The corpses of the Gringos were blanketed with flies, to the point that their buzzing was audible even out on the sidewalk. The crime scene technicians had their work cut out for them, in terms of securing any evidence that would amount to anything, due to the amount of traffic that had moved through the foyer after the shootout. Dozens of departing people had fouled the floor, tracking rust colored footprints everywhere. The entrance looked like a Jackson Pollack painting, the walls pocked with bullet holes and spattered with congealed blood.

While the devastation of the crime scene annoyed Jacinto, a large part of him didn't particularly care, as there was no question as to how the victims had died. Gunshot wounds were a pretty obvious cause of death, especially in the lounge area, where it looked like at least fifty rounds had hacked people apart indiscriminately. Good old machine-guns…

He didn't need a roadmap to guess how the Gringos had bought it, given the profusion of slugs in the walls behind their bodies.

The whole episode had lasted just a minute or two – at most – per the statements of the few witnesses. As the Gringos entered, two had been cut down almost instantly, with the remaining pair spraying the lounge with lead until the upstairs Colombian had opened up on them. One had been killed by him and another wounded, but had escaped, judging by the blood trailing out of the building and down the street.

That left the obvious questions of where the survivor had fled to, given that he would need serious medical attention, and the whereabouts of the vehicle or vehicles that had been hit by the Colombian. Jacinto knew the wounded man had made it to a vehicle because the blood trail continued far past where the dealer on the sidewalk had fallen, not to mention the glass littering the street. The police also knew for certain that the sidewalk shooter had been firing at vehicle or vehicles unknown – due to the eight shell casings surrounding his corpse; obviously ejected as he shot at a getaway car.

Must have been one tough son of a bitch, Jacinto mused. He'd shot and killed one of the two surviving assailants, taken a bullet in the thigh, wounded the second remaining gunman, and still was determined enough to make it out of the building to empty his gun at the departing vehicles before being blasted nearly in two by the Madame's shotgun.

One of the uniformed cops approached him. "We got a match on the prints from the sidewalk corpse. Tomas Cardinez Salazar, AKA *Don* Tomas. Bogota, linked to the National Liberation Army – the ELN. Suspected of being their number two man on the ground for narcotics trafficking."

"I've heard of him. So that's *Don* Tomas, eh?" Jacinto said.

"It certainly seems like he went down shooting," the officer observed.

"What about the Gringos? We need to run their prints through Interpol. They look professional."

"We already dusted them and sent them off," the officer said. "But you know how that goes. Maybe we hear something in a few days, maybe a few weeks."

"What about the woman with the shotgun?" Jacinto asked.

"Apparently the proprietor, Inspector."

"I sort of worked that out myself," Jacinto said. "Where is she? I want to talk to her."

"She's already been taken in for questioning."

"Taken? On whose orders? And taken where?" Jacinto demanded.

It was highly irregular for a participant in a shooting who'd actually killed someone, whether in self-defense or otherwise, to be removed from the crime scene before Jacinto had the opportunity to get some preliminary questions answered.

"I don't know, Inspector. I'll check. The order came from Headquarters. I assumed you had authorized it…"

This stank to high heavens. Jacinto had been in charge of Panama City homicide investigations for twelve years; first with the Judicial Technical Police, and later with the National Police. There were only two men above him, neither of whom worked nights or weekends, and they certainly wouldn't get their hands dirty in anything operational.

"Do so. Now," Jacinto ordered. "I want to interview this woman within the hour. There's no excuse for protocol to have been breached like this – find out what happened, and where she is."

Jacinto assumed that the Madame had pulled some strings to get herself extricated from an unpleasant situation. It wasn't unknown for the operator of a high-end escort business to have powerful clients, more than eager to help a valued friend out of a bind. He was realistic, but then again, this wasn't a burglar shot in some slum. This case was far too big for the woman to just disappear into the night without explanation. He didn't care what kind of clout she had. No way would she get to leave the area, even in supposed police custody, without answering to Jacinto. He guessed her story would be that she'd been trying to protect her place when she'd fired at the Colombian. But facts were facts – she'd blown a man in half on the sidewalk, pistol or no pistol, and if you did that you had to chitty chat with Inspector Jacinto.

Considering this new wrinkle, he drew a cigarette from a small metal case and lit it with a gold Cartier lighter – a gift from the last president. Very little impressed or frightened Jacinto. But this was one for the record books. He would get to the bottom of it, one way or another.

He was, after all, The Bulldog.

# CHAPTER 13

Ernesto regarded Al with skepticism and suppressed alarm. Even by Panama's lax standards, his driving was marginal to dangerous. More troubling to Ernesto, though, was the bank of warning lamps illuminated on Al's dashboard.

As the lights of Panama City receded in the rearview mirror another cloudburst hit, blinding them with a virtually impenetrable sheet of dense rain. The car hydroplaned, sliding this way and that before Al regained control with a series of parries. He twisted the wiper knob but only a small portion of the windshield cleared in the top quartile of the driver's side. The remainder of the wipers were either ragged, or metal.

Even more disturbing, whenever Al slowed and then gave the car gas, a howling issued from below the hood. Al seemed not to notice, but Ernesto, who had spent his childhood helping his father keep his ancient Fiat running, instantly recognized the sound of a loose belt.

"Alberto," Ernesto ventured. "I think you have a loose fan belt. That's what's making the horrible noise."

"What? What noise? Oh, you mean that? Don't worry, it's been doing that for months. Runs fine," Al assured him.

Ernesto wasn't convinced. "It's really not good. You should tighten it up. Do you have any tools?"

"Tools? No, don't need 'em. Never have," Al declared. "Don't worry. Everything's under control."

The howling resumed for several seconds as they slowed to avoid a large pothole. The man was an idiot, Ernesto concluded. Other than drink like a fish, he didn't seem to possess any other skills. Just where had Carmen found him? He hoped the guide he was meeting in the morning proved to be better at guiding than anything this Alberto had done so far.

Al scoffed inwardly at the cook's concern. Sure, the old Ford had a few dings and wrinkles, but it ran practically like new. He'd taken the same approach to his car that he had with his body – put fuel in it and hope for the best. After all, the car was only twenty years old; good for at least another decade before anything major needed to be done to it. At least, that's what he hoped.

As they pulled past San Miguelito the traffic thinned considerably and soon they were alone on the road. Lights from sparse residential developments had dotted the hills until they left the Panama City area; after that, signs of life were few and far between.

The Transamerican highway they were now traversing ran from Alaska all the way to the tip of South America, uninterrupted except for one section between southern Panama and Colombia. Every so often, a project would be proposed wherein the jungle would be cut back, and the highway would be continued through to Colombia. These proposals were ultimately shot down because the cost to construct a road through some of the most dense tropical growth in the world would be astronomical, and would also introduce a host of environmental issues. And the jungle was a toxic no-man's land of guerrilla fighters, rebels, drug and criminal gangs, and every sort of armed murderous miscreant imaginable. The notion that these predators would simply step out of the way once the bulldozers came in was ludicrous; it was a safe bet that if a road ever did get cut and paved, driving between the two countries would be like running a gauntlet of machine-gun fire for ninety miles.

To say that the prospect lacked practicality was an understatement.

Even just south of Panama City the road quickly became a two lane strip of asphalt with sporadic illumination and varying levels of maintenance. In the dry season the going was slow at night, and now, as the wet season began, some areas ground to a crawl due to flooding and pavements washing away – as well as occasional mudslides.

Al avoided driving anywhere besides Panama City and his office in Colon, which was all of fifteen miles away, so his understanding of current road conditions were about the same as Ernesto's, who took the bus everywhere and rarely ventured beyond a five mile radius of his *colonia*.

Ernesto inspected the bank of warning lights reflecting off Al's face. "Your gas gauge says empty," he observed.

"Yeah. Been like that for a while. It's broken," Al explained. "I put some gas in before I picked you up. We're golden."

Ernesto tried again. "Aren't you worried about all the hazard lights being on? Like the *check engine* light?"

"Nah. Those are just to let you know the manufacturer wants you to pay the dealer a bunch of money to verify everything's working. I know everything's working – if it wasn't, we wouldn't be moving right now…" Al's brand of logic was unassailable.

Ernesto changed his opinion of Al. He modified his internal evaluation of Al from idiot to sub-custodial mouth-breather. He just prayed they would make it to the rendezvous point so he'd never have to see the cretin again.

Unfortunately for Ernesto, tonight wasn't the night for prayers to be answered. At least, not his. A loud clunk and a series of shuddering slamming sounds came from the engine compartment, followed by silence, other than the motor running and the tires on the pavement.

"What the hell was that?" Ernesto asked.

"Dunno. Never done that before," Al observed. "But hey, she's running like a Cadillac, so no worries."

Which was true, until after a few minutes they both began to notice that the road was getting darker. The dimming headlights were soon barely illuminating the pavement. Al uttered an oath and pulled to the side of the road – in this case, the muddy shoulder.

Al popped the hood and Ernesto propped it open.

Ernesto pointed under the hood. "There's your problem. The belt for the alternator broke."

"Shit. Okay, so how do we fix it?" Al asked, his mechanical abilities limited to opening soup cans.

"Well, we can take the spare belt you no doubt have in your trunk, and using your tool kit, we can put a new belt on," Ernesto replied cynically.

"I told you. I don't have any tools. And no belts, either."

"*Si*, I figured that. I can tell you this car isn't going anywhere now, not until it's repaired."

"You're kidding, right? Al protested. "We're in the middle of the jungle, and it's close to midnight."

"I wish I was," Ernesto lamented. "I think our only choice is to walk. If you look south, down the road, you can just make out some lights maybe a mile and a half away. Perhaps we can find someone who does have a tool kit…"

"Are you crazy? Walk all the way there? Why not just drive without the lights on?"

Ernesto shook his head and closed his eyes. "Within minutes your motor is going to die, because anything requiring electricity isn't getting any from the alternator, and when the battery dies, the engine does."

"Jump in. Maybe we can make it most of the way there," Al said, smearing mud on the door as he reinstalled himself behind the steering wheel. Ernesto sighed wearily, and squelched his way round to the passenger side.

The car advanced for another twenty yards, and then all became silent.

Ernesto regarded Al's profile with disgust. He collected his backpack and his water bottle, and exiting the car, began slowly walking south. Al called after him, but Ernesto didn't turn. Head down, he just kept trudging. Al grabbed his bag and locked the doors before jogging clumsily after him.

"Don't worry," Al said. "I know a lot of people in Panama. I'll have us out of here in no time."

A strange smile spread across Ernesto's face. "I don't suppose," he said innocently, "you're on close terms with your mechanic, though?"

Al fell silent after that. They marched along the side of the road, the jungle sounds ever louder since the death of his beloved car. The rustlings of the bushes and the chatter of nocturnal bugs, punctuated by the odd indeterminate howl or shriek in the darkness, did little to calm the nerves of either man.


After half an hour they arrived at a little hamlet made up from a sorry collection of squalid houses stretching into the shadows of the ever-surrounding jungle. Incandescent lights glowed over a small market, still open, where a number of local residents were seated at white plastic tables near a portable food-service cart mounted to the back end of a bicycle. A small black and white TV sat on a shelf by the cart, providing free entertainment for the diners.

A tired looking sign a few yards from an ancient pay phone informed them they were in La Loma. Ernesto approached the man standing at the food cart and began an animated discussion in Spanish. After several minutes of hand waving, pointing, and gesturing at the sky with exclamations of wonder or amusement, Ernesto disengaged with his warmest handshake and returned to Al's side.

Ernesto reported his findings. "He says there's a mechanic who lives in this town, but he's gone to Panama City for the weekend, no doubt to party and wade in sin, leaving his poor mother to worry about whether she'll ever see him again. Apparently, he has a drug problem, and a number of loose women he sees in the city, while he ignores his live-in girlfriend here and their three year old daughter." Ernesto smiled. "Sorry I asked him…"

"So, no go on a repair tonight…" Al summarized.

"No."

Well that was just peachy. They were stuck in a backwater slum with no car, a tight deadline, and nobody around to help them. Al debated calling Carmen, but quickly reconsidered when he realized what she must be going through with the police after the shooting. And she'd never use him again if she discovered he didn't keep his car in reasonable operating shape.

Al fished through his wallet for a card, finally plucking out the one he wanted. "Ernesto. You have a phone I can borrow for a second? I need to call someone to come get us."

Ernesto pouted. "What's wrong with yours? Mine's almost out of minutes…"

"I…uh…forgot mine – it's at home," Al explained sheepishly. "Look, I'll only be a minute, okay? And this is to help you, not just get me out of here," Al reminded him.

Ernesto reached into his pants pocket and pulled out a micro-cell phone. He reluctantly handed it to Al, who glared at him before moving away to distance himself from the television noise. He entered a series of numbers and pushed send.

A bombastic voice answered. *"Hola. Quien Hablas?"*

"Sergio, it's Al. Al Ross."

"Al! What's up?" Sergio asked. "Why are you calling at midnight on a Saturday? Did you get arrested? In an accident? Start a fight?"

Al laughed. "No, no. It's nothing like that. Are you working right now?"

"I just got off my shift, and was about to head out for some entertainment, you know?"

"Hmm, nice," Al said. "But how would you like to make a little money for a very minor favor, my friend?"

Sergio's tone took on a suspicious air. "A minor favor at midnight on Saturday? Sounds like it might be expensive...*my friend*."

"It's really nothing, Sergio. My car broke down, and I just need a little lift."

"So all you need is a ride?" Sergio still wasn't convinced. He'd known Al a long time. "Where are you, and where do you need to go?"

Al paused. "Well, that's kind of the touchy part, Sergio. I'm about an hour outside of the city, in a beautifully quaint spot called La Loma. It's just a little south of Chepo...and I need to get to Metiti by morning."

"Metiti? As in, Metiti by Darien? Have you lost your mind? What did you do, kill someone?" Sergio fired back at Al.

"No, Sergio," Al explained softly. "My car broke down, and I was giving a friend a ride to see his sick grandmother in Metiti...she could go at any time. It's heartbreaking really, and you know what a soft touch I am..."

Sergio's good nature surfaced. "A friend, to Metiti, huh? That doesn't seem too suspicious at all."

"It is what it is, Sergio. I was thinking two hundred dollars for just a few hours of your time..." Al ventured.

"Two hundred? To blow off my Saturday night and haul you and god knows who else into the middle of the jungle? Al. Please. You're so way off. I think I'm hearing an $800 favor," Sergio replied.

"$800? Are you nuts?" Al exclaimed. "You think I have that kind of money lying around? If I did, don't you think I'd have fixed my car?"

"I'm just saying, it's not a $200 favor by any means," Sergio explained. "But hey, you called me, not the other way around. Do you want to take some time and think about it? I can't guarantee I'll be answering my cell much longer – I have a date for the evening I'd have to cancel. And she's very beautiful."

"Okay. $400. But that's all I have," Al countered.

"Did I mention she's young, too?" Sergio continued. "Young and beautiful. A rare and breathtaking combination..."

"Sergio, I really need your help. Fine. You're killing me. $500, if you can be here in an hour," Al conceded.

"It's a deal," Sergio said brightly. "Now, where in that shithole are you hiding?"

Al gave him directions and disconnected. He was pissed, but there wasn't much he could do. So now he was down to $1300 for the 'errand'

and by the time he was done with his bookie and fixing his car, he'd be lucky if he had a few hundred bucks left for himself. He returned the cell to Ernesto, who pocketed it and immediately resumed viewing the TV. Al told him a friend would be coming to give them a lift within the hour, so everything was fine. Ernesto shot Al a skeptical look but said nothing.

Frustrated, Al turned and ventured into the little market. He emerged in a few minutes with a quart of local beer. He chugged half of it before taking a breath.

"Hey, are you hungry? This is really good," Ernesto called to him. He was clutching a Styrofoam plate from the food cart with some steaming concoction on it, which he was eagerly consuming with a plastic spoon.

"No thanks. I don't eat anything but hot dogs and beer. American food. I don't like boiled cat or whatever that crap is." Al took another long pull on his beer.

Ernesto waved his spoon. "It's really good – *Sancocho* – a Panamanian specialty. I'm a cook, and I can tell you that this is not just good, it's great."

Al eyed the plate dubiously. "What's in it? Rat tails? Dog sphincter? Goat semen?" He had to admit it did smell pretty good. And the locals were munching it like it was opium.

"Chicken, meat, vegetables. It's practically the national dish. Come on, Alberto," Ernesto chided. "How long have you been living here, and you haven't sampled one of the best things Panama makes?"

"It's probably pig intestines and horse scrotum, isn't it?" Al said. But he was wavering.

"Just try some," Ernesto said, motioning to the man serving the food. He spooned a heaped portion onto a plate and handed it to Al. "It's on me," Ernesto offered. "My treat, Alberto."

Al took a tentative bite, making a face like he was chewing on live worms. "It's not bad," he conceded.

Five minutes later, both their plates were empty and Al had gone back to the market for a refresher of beer.

A guy had to keep up his strength, after all.

# CHAPTER 14

Sam burst into his office, which had been commandeered by Richard, who was busy murmuring into the telephone, feet up on the desk as he reclined in Sam's chair. Richard glanced at Sam and turned his head away so Sam couldn't hear the discussion. Sam paced around until Richard hung up.

"What?" Richard demanded.

"The GPS signal from the cell shows them stopped in a small town on the Transamerican highway," Sam said. "It's about 40 miles south of here. La Loma. If we scramble your team you can intercept them and this will all be over."

"Sam. Do I look particularly stupid to you?" Richard asked, conversationally.

That wasn't the response Sam had been hoping for. He tried again. "The point is, sir, that we could be there in an hour, tops, and…"

Richard held up a dismissive hand. "Da, ah, ah, ah. I asked you if I look like a moron. Do I? I must," Richard said, "because only a moron would consider sending a team into a situation they know nothing about, with no planning or information, at a moment's notice. That's the kind of whim that gets people killed," he continued. "Just like your men were slaughtered when they went into the whorehouse with no intel or plan."

"I…I just thought…" Sam stammered.

"No, Sam, you didn't think. That's the point. You didn't think at all. You just wanted to act. But we don't have the luxury of acting first and thinking later now, do we? You've seen how well that worked so far. I don't think we want a repeat of the last disaster, do we?" Richard asked.

"Well then," Sam blurted, "what are we supposed to be doing? What's your plan?"

Richard regarded Sam as though he were a paltry specimen under a microscope – a distasteful speck of something foul. "Sam, I can see you're confused again. You apparently think I need to report to you, or include you in my thinking. Let me clear this up – nothing could be further from the truth. I will move to neutralize this threat and recover the item when, and only when, I'm satisfied I can do it with a hundred percent certainty of success, and not before. And I won't be consulting you for your opinions when I do decide to move. If you're lucky, you'll be allowed to watch so you learn how a real operation is run. But your role will be limited to watching, hopefully in complete silence, and maybe bringing me coffee from that fancy gizmo you have in the outer office," Richard dictated. "Do we understand each other?"

"I…yes, sir. I was just trying to help," Sam explained. "I thought this might be the opportunity we were waiting for."

Richard turned and reached for the phone. He dialed a string of numbers and resumed studying the flat screen monitor.

The discussion was obviously over.

# CHAPTER 15

Carmen sat handcuffed to a chair at a metal table in a holding cell at National Police headquarters, wondering how long it would take for her to be charged – if she was going to be – or released. So far, nobody had questioned her or tried to take a statement. She was just placed in the cell, cuffed to the metal armrest and left to her own devices.

That struck her as odd, given that she was one of the few witnesses to the confrontation at Esperanza, not to mention she'd also shot one of the gunmen. All they had to do was ask and she would turn over the digital recording of the firefight. It was all there on her hard disk. Of course, they'd probably never figure that out if she didn't volunteer it because the cameras she'd installed were the size of pencil erasers – skillfully incorporated into the decorative moldings of the ornate ceilings. Patrons obviously wouldn't be thrilled at the idea of being recorded, so discretion was in order. But Carmen also needed to be able to watch over her flock, as well as monitor security, so she needed eyes everywhere. It was her little secret, and also her insurance policy – she had virtually every government official in the current administration on tape, so she was confident she'd be able to resolve any issues and get back to business soon enough.

By the time she'd made it downstairs the gun battle had been over, except for outside the front door. When she'd poked her head out to see who was shooting, the man with the pistol had turned his weapon on her. She'd had no choice but to shoot him – a simple case of self-defense. Carmen didn't think she'd have any problem convincing whoever was running the investigation of that.

She heard the echo of footsteps approaching down the concrete hall. The heavy steel door swung open and a man in a lightweight suit entered, a manila folder clasped under his arm. The uniformed officer who had opened the door for him remained outside the room until man in the suit nodded. He closed the door. Carmen heard the bolt slide back into place.

The man studied her face for a few moments before speaking. "Miss Ortega – Carmen. My name is Jenkins. I have a few questions for you, and it would be best if you cooperated with me and told me everything you know."

"Mr. Jenkins, I would like my attorney present before I say anything," Carmen responded, smiling sweetly at him.

"That won't be necessary," Jenkins stated. "This is an informal discussion we're having, and nothing you say will be used against you."

"That's all very nice, but I'd still prefer to have my attorney here," Carmen insisted.

"Why don't you listen to what I have to say, and then you can decide if that will be necessary, hmm?" Jenkins suggested, and before Carmen could respond, he continued. "Tonight was a regrettable and horrible slaughter. My concern, however, isn't with the shooting, nor with your role in the killing of the Colombian gentleman on the street. No, I'm here to seek your cooperation in a different matter," Jenkins explained.

"I don't understand. But I still want my lawyer," Carmen said. "This interview is over until he arrives."

"Yes, I see your point. And I understand. So now maybe you'll take a moment while I tell you a story, and then perhaps we'll both be on the same wavelength," Jenkins said, his fluent Spanish tinged with just the slightest Gringo accent.

"Do whatever you want," Carmen declared. "I'm not talking."

"The Colombian man you shot was a powerful cocaine trafficker. He was in Panama illegally. His name was Tomas Salazar – 'Don' Tomas – and he's reputed to operate one of the most brutal syndicates in Colombia. He's also believed to have a rather extensive operation in Panama, as well as in Costa Rica. If that wasn't enough, he's also rumored to have partners here who are Chinese Triad, and also considerable reach within the Mexican Cartels in the Yucatan and in the U.S. border states." Jenkins paused, watching her reaction.

Carmen was emphatic. "I have nothing to do with any of this."

"Oh, we know that," Jenkins said. "We also know you're one of the 'go to' people in Panama City for undocumented trips to Colombia and Costa Rica. Which brings me to the reason I'm here. You had a patron in your establishment tonight at the time of the shooting who I need to find, in the very worst sort of way. In fact, I'm so anxious to locate this man that I will do almost anything."

"I'm sorry I can't help you. Now I want my lawyer," Carmen demanded.

"That's a shame, Carmen. Because if you won't help me find him, I can see ugly rumors circulating around town that you not only cooperated with a rival faction and set up *Don* Tomas and his boys for execution, but you finished the job yourself. That would make for an extremely short life expectancy for you, not to mention destroy your source of income – Esperanza would be a ghost town within an hour of the story hitting the streets."

"But…that's not true!" Carmen protested.

"Maybe. Maybe not. I wouldn't want to be in your shoes, regardless. The Triads tend to be extremely sadistic in their retribution – even more so than the Colombians, if you can imagine that."

"Who…who are you?"

"Ah, Carmen, I'm your savior." He lightly touched her forearm. "I'm prepared to single-handedly prevent that story from leaking out. And all I need is for you to look at a photo and tell me what I need to know." Jenkins flipped open the folder and slid a black and white photo of the cook across the table to Carmen.

Carmen regarded the picture. It was Ernesto. Her expression didn't falter in any way. Jenkins watched closely for any tell-tale giveaways – ticks, rapid blinking, sidelong glances. There were none.

He waited for her to say something. She refused, and merely studied the photo.

"This man is a cook. We know he was in your establishment when the gunfight started," Jenkins probed.

"Mr. Jenkins, with all due respect, there were a lot of people there. It's Saturday night. How can you expect me to know every man who passed through the door looking for a little relaxation?"

"Carmen, this isn't a game. We know you're helping him out of the country. We don't even care that you're doing so – everyone's entitled to make money however they can. Same for Esperanza. Judge not, and ye shall not be judged. But this man is extremely sensitive for me, and I absolutely will find him, whether you tell me or not. Your cooperation will simply accelerate the inevitable, which is why I'm here," Jenkins explained. "Oh...and, of course...ensure your survival in the process."

"I'm afraid I can't help you," Carmen said. "You've made a mistake."

"Carmen, this is your last chance to save yourself. We're tracking him, and it's only a matter of time until we have him. We know he's moving south, down the Transamerican. My only questions relate to where he's headed." Jenkins watched her reaction. Nothing. She was very good. Figured, given her line of work. "We know he's headed for the border, so the only question is whether he's going all the way to Yaviza, or is he stopping in Santa Fe or Meteti and cutting over the mountains."

Carmen had blinked when he'd said Yaviza. Subtle, but it was there. And it was enough.

"I have no idea what you're talking about, Mr. Jenkins – or whatever your real name is. Maybe this man *was* at my place, enjoying the charms of one of my girls, but as to the rest of your story, it's way off base. I don't know what this man has done, but I have nothing to do with helping him get to Colombia. So you're barking up the wrong tree." Carmen's eyes narrowed.

Jenkins clapped, slowly, appreciatively. Carmen glared disgust at him, not bothering to disguise it. "I never said he was trying to get to Colombia, Carmen. I just said you were helping him get to the border. That could mean Costa Rica, too, couldn't it? But you said Colombia." Jenkins grinned, confident now.

Carmen frowned. "You said they were going south, and mentioned three villages near the Darien Gap. It doesn't take a genius to figure out they're going to Colombia."

"And I never said anything about 'they'. I only asked about the man in the photo." Jenkins reached over and slid the photo back into his folder, then pushed back from the table and stood up.

"It probably won't be safe for you to stay in Panama, Carmen, given the nasty rumors which will soon be circulating. A shame, really. I hope you make it out before someone gets you. You're a beautiful woman – I've seen what these characters do to beautiful women before they kill them." Jenkins held her gaze.

Carmen seemed deflated and her eyes filled with tears. She looked up at Jenkins, and said, "Meteti. Ten miles south of Meteti."

Jenkins smiled again, and turned to leave. He'd seen her blink when he'd mentioned Yaviza. He was almost certain she was lying now. He didn't blame her. He'd lie too, in her position. It merely confirmed his understanding of human nature.

"Good luck, Carmen. I think you're lying. I think you know 'they' are going to Yaviza and you're trying to throw me off the scent." He walked to the door, and knocked twice.

"You're wrong," Carmen insisted tearfully. "Absolutely wrong."

"Sure I am. Goodbye, Carmen."

# CHAPTER 16

Al wasn't feeling particularly good. He had heartburn from the goddamned sphincter soup or whatever the hell it was, and he had to pee away the three liters of beer he'd knocked back while they were waiting. Ernesto seemed content to stare at the jabbering on the TV, and he'd declined Al's generous offer of a frosty beverage to mitigate the heat.

Al stood, sweating from the humid night air, and told Ernesto he was going to take a leak. He wandered down the road about fifty yards and turned down a dirt track, moving toward the concrete wall of an industrial building – some sort of abandoned warehouse or storage facility.

Unzipping his cargo pants, he almost moaned aloud at the glowing sensation of relief. He urinated for over a full minute, focusing the flow on a crumpled beer can and hiccupping occasionally – the flavor of his nocturnal meal rose in his gorge each time, triggering a gag reflex.

Fucking monkey brain stew.

Finished, he retraced his steps down the dirt trail toward the main road, pausing by the corner of the building to light a cigarette.

A police cruiser screeched to a stop next to him and an officer leapt out, gun drawn. Startled, Al dropped the cigarette on his shirt, burning a small hole in it. He yelped. The policeman wrenched his arms behind him, and cuffed him expertly, then slammed him against the car, knocking the wind from Al's lungs. He threw the door open, and wordlessly stuffed Al into the back seat, then moved to the driver's door and climbed behind the wheel. The cop looked at his captive in the rearview mirror.

"Do you have to be such a dickhead? That was one of my last cigarettes, for Christ's sake," Al said conversationally, in English.

The cop chuckled. "You smell like a brewery, and smoking's bad for you. You really should quit. It's a filthy habit," he responded, also in English.

"Bite me, you prick," Al suggested helpfully.

"Not in this lifetime. Where's your friend?" Sergio asked, starting the engine and opening the door again.

"Over by the market. You gonna take the cuffs off, or are you going to rape me, you Latino homo?" Al inquired.

"Still have those prison rape fantasies, huh, Al?" Sergio responded. "It's a shame you're still fighting it – at your age, I'd just give in and live my dream." He opened the back door and playfully hauled Al out of the car before unlocking the cuffs. "Sorry. I just get all worked up whenever I see 'COPS' on satellite…and you caught me at a bad time when you called," Sergio explained with a grin.

"*No problema.* Thanks for coming. I owe you one," Al said; his tone serious.

"You damn right you owe me. Eight hundred bucks, I believe," Sergio said, returning to the driver's position.

Al moved around the car to the passenger side.

"Five hundred," Al insisted. "That's all I have."

"Yeah, but you smell like a goat soaked in beer piss," Sergio observed. "That costs extra."

They continued bickering as Sergio drove to the main road and pulled up to the market.

Ernesto was visibly alarmed at the police car, and almost made a break for it until he saw Al get out and head inside, muttering to himself.

"Ernesto, your chariot awaits. Meet Sergio. Don't let him try to kiss you," Al called as he walked through the door.

Ernesto looked dubiously at Al's back, and then swung around to meet Sergio.

They shook hands and exchanged greetings. Sergio was the exact opposite of Al. Short, muscular, obviously athletic, mid-thirties, dark skin, thick black hair cut in a military style, white teeth. His arms had almost the girth of Ernesto's thighs. He obviously spent a lot of time around barbells and looked like he could strip a car apart with his bare hands. Not a guy to cross, that was clear. Al, on the other hand, was a tall, doughy bag of goo on legs. Soft, pink-skinned, balding, puffy and overweight. Ernesto was willing to bet Al could do little more than walk into the market and back. Not exactly a confidence builder to have him as your escort into hell's backyard.

Ernesto started to feel a little better about his odds. All Al seemed interested in was pounding booze and chain smoking. At least Sergio didn't smell like someone had emptied a vodka bottle on his uniform – so their chances of actually making it to the rendezvous without crashing into a cow or a tree seemed to have picked up considerably. And he was a cop. A brilliant cover, Ernesto had to admit. He knew they'd be stopped at least a half dozen times on the way south, but they'd be waved through with little scrutiny in a police cruiser with a uniformed officer driving. Maybe Al wasn't a complete idiot after all.

Al stumbled out of the market and tripped on the small rainwater curb, dropping his beer in the process, which shattered on the hard packed dirt with a percussive crash. He did the classic drunk's double take, as if staring at the offending flooring would somehow warn it to be more careful who it trips next time. Al cursed, spinning around to procure another one for the road.

Ernesto took it all back. Al was definitely a cretin.

God help them getting to the rendezvous point without further incident. Maybe they could just leave Al there and proceed without him? Ernesto gave it serious thought, for more than a moment. But no, Carmen had a method to her madness. If Al was her chosen instrument to get him safely to the meeting with the guide, surely there had to be a reason. Maybe he just didn't show well late at night.

Anything was possible.

Sergio buckled in behind the wheel as Ernesto tossed his bag in the back and slid in after it, closing the door. Al weaved to the passenger side and wedged himself into the front seat, slamming his knee against the butt of the upright-mounted shotgun. He cursed again, and coughed alarmingly – his lungs wheezing like he had pneumonia.

Sergio gave him a sidelong glance, put the car into gear and smoothly rolled onto the Transamerica for the long drive south.

❧◈❧

Lilliana approached the bed. The man reclining against a stack of pillows had a bandage swathed around his head and an IV running into his arm. He looked pale and seemed uncomfortable in his hospital-gown, but beyond that, appeared unharmed.

Hearing her enter the room, or perhaps smelling her perfume, he opened his eyes, taking her in. Nice looking late-twenties Panamanian woman holding an oversized paper tablet. He closed his eyes, then opened them again, wondering if this was an hallucination. No, she was still there, and was pulling a chair up alongside his bed.

"Manuel, my name's Lilliana Cruz. The embassy sent me over to help create a likeness of the man you saw with the fellow everyone is referring to as 'the cook'. I'm a sketch artist and I sometimes work with the police. How are you feeling?" Lilliana asked. "Are you up to this?"

"I…well…sure – I suppose I am. It's not like I have anything else to do tonight." Manuel looked around for a wall clock. "What time is it, anyway? They took all my clothes stuff…"

Lilliana checked her watch. "It's two in the morning. I'm sorry to intrude so late, but this is apparently very important. They got me out of bed to come here." Lilliana shifted uncomfortably from one leg to the other.

"No, don't worry. After everything that's happened tonight, this is the one pleasant thing I'll remember," Manuel said, smiling at her. He gestured at the bedside chair. "You may as well sit down…"

"I hope it will be pleasant, Manuel. Let's start with a few questions. Are you married?" she asked before easing into the seat.

"No. It's just me. I'm single."

"Any kids?"

"No," Manuel answered.

"How old are you?" she inquired.

"Thirty-one."

"And you live in Panama City, or one of the surrounding *colonias*?"

"The city."

"Alone, or with someone?"

"By myself," Manuel said testily. He wasn't expecting the third-degree.

"Any brothers or sisters?" Lilliana probed.

"One brother. Older. What does this have to do with describing the man I saw?" Manuel asked, defensive about the strange line of questioning.

Lilliana removed her glasses and buffed the lenses on her skirt. She met Manuel's eyes. "Honestly? Nothing," she admitted. "I just wanted to know something about you before we start."

"Oh...Is that some sort of relaxation technique they teach you so I'll remember things more accurately?" Manuel was puzzled now, rather than rankled.

"Yes...well, truthfully, no. I just think you're a good-looking man and I wanted to know more about you," Lilliana said softly. She flipped open her sketch pad.

Manuel was caught completely off guard. He studied her carefully. Lilliana looked like she worked out and watched her weight. She had a nice body and a pretty face, especially when she lost the glasses. This suddenly got interesting for him.

Lilliana bent forward. He could feel her sweet, warm breath on his face. "Alright, Manuel, let's start with some basics on the man. What was he wearing?"

# CHAPTER 17

The huge transport plane lifted into the night sky, its massive turbines propelling it quickly to 40,000 feet. The lights of the East Coast receded behind it as the SEAL Team Six commandos settled in for the last rest they'd have for several days.

Their staging destination was Ghazi Air Force base. Many missions were launched from there into nearby Afghanistan, and the U.S. had a large presence in the region. All of the necessary large equipment had been shipped out a few days earlier, so when the team hit the ground they'd be ready to go.

The plan called for them to be at the base by late morning, and after a briefing and equipment check, to be ready to load up onto the helicopters at nightfall. This was a relatively small scale operation, but there were a lot of moving parts involved, all of which had to function together seamlessly to create a successful outcome.

The weather at Ghazi was iffy as of an hour ago, and they'd continue to monitor it throughout the flight. In the end, they could plan everything to the most minute detail, but if Mother Nature threw them a curve, there wasn't a lot anyone could do but wait and be patient.

ॐॐ

The police cruiser's headlights seemed inadequate as it rolled down the Transamerican highway. Road lights were all but absent, and the surrounding jungle was inky black. The incessant rain showers had left the pavement in rough shape in spite of the efforts of the nighttime maintenance crews they passed. A road in the middle of a jungle was very much like a bridge – you were never done with it; rather, you had to begin repairs at the start of the road all over again once you'd reached the far end.

There was long-term job security in maintaining the Panamanian stretch of the Transamerican Highway, that was for sure.

Sergio's cruiser crawled by the working men, most of whom leaned on their shovels and chatted as they watched a bulldozer-like contrivance distribute tarry asphalt on a section of highway. Some things were perennial regardless of what country you lived in – and road workers doing as little as humanly possible for long periods of time was a constant.

At the end of the section that was under construction, near a tiny hamlet, a uniformed policeman waved them down. Seeing Sergio, he didn't bother asking for papers. The two exchanged pleasantries, agreed that it was going to be a wet one this year, and commiserated at the cruel luck that had them working the midnight to dawn shift. The policeman only glanced at Al, who was dozing after all the beer had hit bottom, and then signaled to Sergio to proceed on his way.

Al woke up as they pulled back onto the road.

"Are we there yet?" he asked, only half joking.

"About ninety more miles to go, *amigo*. It will take around four hours, at least, not counting any more stops," Sergio replied, checking his watch. "If we're lucky, we'll hit Meteti at five. If this slows any further, maybe six."

"You drive like a grandmother," Al protested.

"Do you want to get there, or plow into a horse or run off the road? We almost broke an axle about five miles back, where part of the road had collapsed," Sergio reminded.

"Yeah, yeah. You're probably just too cheap to open this jalopy up and give it gas," Al said.

"No, the truth is I've never driven this stretch of road late at night, but I've heard horror stories about the general condition, as well as about animals and drunks, so if it's all the same to you I'll drive at my own pace and get us there in one piece," Sergio advised.

They watched the rolling hills go by in silence. Soon, they were winding their way up an incline, and then found themselves on a bridge, suspended high above a river. Just on the other side of the bridge there was another roadblock. This time, there were two police cruisers. One of the officers shined his flashlight across their windshield, motioning for Sergio to pull over. They did, and the officer demanded to see both Al and Ernesto's paperwork.

The cop regarded Al's passport, and then scrutinized Ernesto's papers.

"What's this supposed to be?" he demanded.

"That's a photocopy of his passport, officer. He had his original stolen. It's one of the reasons I'm with him," Al explained.

The cop studied the paper again, and then handed it back to Al, who gave it to Ernesto.

"Where are you headed?" he asked.

"Yaviza, down in Darien," Sergio said.

"That's an extremely dangerous part of the highway. What's the purpose of the trip?" the cop asked.

"They have reservations with an eco-tour in one of the private reserves there," Sergio explained.

"So why are you, a policeman, driving them in the middle of the night?" the cop queried.

Fair question.

Al interrupted the discussion, pulling out his passport again.

"Officer, my car broke down, and this man was kind enough to volunteer to get us to our destination. As you see, I'm a diplomat stationed in Panama City with the U.S. Embassy, and my guest is a VIP. I explained to your colleague here about the importance of us getting to the resort for the morning's meetings, and he was kind enough to volunteer to drive us – a selfless act that will not go unnoticed when I get back to the Embassy," Al blustered. "The retreat we're heading to is hosting a number of diplomats for meetings and lectures, so our arrival there is of paramount importance," Al concluded.

The officer took another hard look at Al's passport, then stared at his face, before finally handing it back to him and telling Sergio to proceed with caution.

"Keep your eyes peeled. There's been an increase of armed robberies and shootings on the road as you get further south into Darien. If it was me

I'd wait until daylight before driving much farther, but hey, it's your funeral," the officer advised, and then waved them through.

Al regarded Sergio with a deadpan expression. "You know, if I didn't know better, I'd say we were headed someplace pretty dangerous," he quipped.

"Yeah, who knew that the jungle between Panama and Colombia would be crawling with armed miscreants and homicidal killers. That's so, well, unexpected, you know?" Sergio opined. "Nice joy ride you have us on, Al. I think the price is climbing again, the more I hear…"

"I told you, five hundred's all I have," protested Al.

Ernesto was growing tired of the near-constant bickering, good natured as it was.

"Hey, I have a joke for you," he announced.

Sergio turned his neck to look at Ernesto.

"Yeah? Let's hear it," Sergio said.

Ernesto cleared his throat. "There's this man, walking down the street in Panama City, when he sees a sign in the window of a pet store. It says, *Talking Dog - Five Dollars.* The man, intrigued, decides to see what the story is, so he goes into the shop, where he sees a man behind the counter." Ernesto paused. "'Are you the owner?' he asks. 'I sure am,' answers the clerk. 'What's the story on the talking dog?' The clerk points to a doorway that leads into another room, in the back of the store. 'He's back there.'" Ernesto waited a beat before continuing, presumably for dramatic effect.

"The man enters the back room, and there in a large kennel cage is a handsome German Shepherd mix-breed. The dog's eyes glow with intelligence, and he has an almost human countenance.

'Are you the talking dog?' the man asks, dubiously.

'Yup. That's me,' the dog replies.

The man is stunned. The dog really can talk!

'How did this happen? This is amazing. How did you come to be here, and why can you talk?' the man asks.

'Well, I originally was the companion to U.S. President Bush. When he left office President Obama took me on, and I lived in the White House for several more years. After that, I wound up with Tom Cruise out in Hollywood, and then after seeing me on the set of one of his movies, I was recruited by the FBI, where I did undercover work infiltrating the mob.

You'd be surprised what people will say when there's only a dumb dog in the room…' the dog explains.

'That's…that's amazing!' the man declares.

He exits the room and approaches the counter, where the owner is stacking cans of dog food into a display.

'I'm astounded. That's unbelievable. Really. How much for the talking dog?'

'Like the sign says, five dollars and he's yours,' replies the owner.

The man opens his wallet and pulls out a five dollar bill, and puts it on the counter.

'But why so cheap? I mean, the dog can actually speak! It's a miracle. Why not more expensive?' asks the man.

'Because he's a fucking liar,' the owner exclaims."

The three men sat silently for a few seconds, and then Sergio started laughing uncontrollably. "Because he's a liar!" he repeated, tears of merriment rolling down his face. Ernesto laughed along. Al just stared glumly at the road.

"Come on, *amigo*, that's funny. What's wrong? It's really funny," Sergio insisted.

"Yeah, it's a real rib tickler. I don't know what's going on, but my stomach feels weird. I don't think I'm doing so good," Al complained. "It's probably that burro-dong gruel I ate back at the market. Probably teeming with parasites," Al said.

Sergio and Ernesto exchanged a sidelong glance.

"You didn't actually eat anything off that cart, did you? Those things are death traps! Yellow fever, e-coli, hookworms, burrowing liver flukes…" Sergio recited.

"Liver flukes?" Al stammered.

"Oh, *si*, they're the worst. They drill through your intestines and lay eggs in your liver and heart, and the larvae eat your organs as they mature…" Sergio offered helpfully.

"Jesus God. Pull over. Now. I'm gonna be sick," Al warned.

"We're on a schedule, remember?" Sergio reminded.

"Pull over now, or you're going to be swimming in liver flukes…" Al gagged.

They slowed and stopped on the shoulder, and Al leapt out of the car and waded a few feet into the brush. Ernesto and Sergio listened to him retching.

"Do you want to tell him the truth and put his mind at ease?" Ernesto said.

"No, let's see if this keeps him from smoking every five minutes and bitching about everything."

"Fair enough." Ernesto glanced at Sergio. "Because he's a fucking liar!" Ernesto exclaimed again, and both men broke into giggles.

❧

Sam and Richard were sitting at Sam's desk, studying a map of Panama. Real time, on the computer, was an overlay of the actual landscape taken from satellite, with a blinking red dot moving slowly down the Transamerican Highway.

"You can see they're headed south, staying on the road," Richard said. "There's no doubt the Colombian border's the destination. The only real question is where they plan to turn off the road and try to make it across."

"What about if they have a plane waiting for them, sir?" Sam pointed out. "There are plenty of dirt strips as they get closer to the Darien."

"That's doubtful. The man's a cook, who was living in a shithole," Richard snapped. "There's no way he has the kind of money it would take to get a private plane to run the border. We're talking tens of thousands of dollars. Not a chance..."

"Well then, sir, shouldn't we just grab him while he's on the road?" Sam reasoned.

"Again, I don't send men into harm's way without a strategy inked out. Jenkins interviewed the Madame and came away with a strong impression that they'll be continuing as far south as the pavement goes. That puts them in Yaviza shortly after dawn."

"Then what? What's the plan?" Sam asked.

Richard glared at Sam, annoyed at the constant interruptions. "The plan? Here's the plan: go brew some fresh coffee," Richard ordered. "This stuff's stale."

Sam bristled, but decided not to fight it.

Richard picked up the phone and punched in a series of digits.

"Okay. I want a bird to get the team to Yaviza – but subtly. Let's find a clearing north of the village and prepare an ambush so this is concluded without anyone seeing anything. Use tire flatteners, and if we can, take everyone alive. I'll forward you the tracking data real-time so you know when it's them." He paused. "Worst case, if this turns ugly, take all the targets out, but let's confirm we have the item before we fold up shop."

He listened to the reply and spoke again.

"No, but you should bring some grenade launchers just in case. If this gets cute, fry the car, too. In fact, if you can't take them alive, just fry it anyway, no matter what happens. That's fewer questions to answer later on…" Richard instructed.

Sam heard Richard's side of the discussion as he made fresh coffee. He couldn't believe the man wasn't going to ambush them on the highway as soon as possible – there were a million things that could happen between their current position and Yaviza. The way this was being handled ran counter to every instinct Sam had. But hey; it was Richard's call now. He was out of the loop. Had been cut out, actually, and was now the coffee boy.

And then Sam had an idea, so original and so Machiavellian, it surprised even him. There was in fact a way for him to regain control and emerge from this disastrous episode a winner. The best part was, if something went wrong, which it wouldn't, he could claim complete deniability – whereas if things went well he'd be viewed as having taken the initiative, showing the kind of drive that those within the upper echelons of the intelligence apparatus would need to possess. It would be confirmation he was a player, and deserved to be promoted to senior level.

Let Richard cook up his little scheme, wasting precious time they didn't have. That's not how Sam rolled. He was a man of action, and it was time to separate the men from the boys.

"Sam? Can you get in here? I need to get a chopper set up to fly a team to Yaviza within an hour," Richard yelled to the outer chamber.

"Yes, sir. I'll be right there," Sam called back. "I just need to use the john."

"Use it after you've set up the helicopter," Richard demanded.

Sam seethed at the insulting tone, but smiled as he entered the office and grabbed his cell phone.

"Fortunately, with technology, I can do two things at once," he said, and before Richard could respond, turned the corner and headed to the men's room.

Sam padded down the hall and entered the bathroom. The Embassy corridor was deserted, and the floor was eerily silent. He scrolled through his cell's contacts until he found the one he was looking for. He took a deep breath, then punched send. A sleepy, gruff voice answered on the fifth ring.

"Lewis."

"Don. It's Sam. Sorry to call so late," Sam apologized.

"Sam. Hang on, let me turn on a light." Sam heard rustling. "Alright, I'm awake. What's going on?" Don asked.

Don Lewis was an occasional drinking buddy and sometimes asset Sam had used in the past for deniable operations near the border. He wasn't on any of the Agency books, but Sam had cultivated him and used him to handle some unpleasantness a year ago involving rogue members of the Judicial Technical Police who'd been shaking down some of the narcotics smugglers in the area – including those the Agency had important relationships with. Sam couldn't use his own personnel on something requiring deniability to such a degree, so he'd floated an idea past Don that had later become a black op. The offending officers had disappeared and Don had found himself in possession of five kilos of coke the cops had extorted, which he'd quickly marketed – untraceable compensation for solving Sam's problem. Don lived in Santa Fe, in southern Panama, right along the route the cook was taking.

"I have a situation," Sam said. "A car is moving toward the Darien Gap, currently about three hours north of it. Two targets; one a Colombian cook, the other an unknown. You know that road pretty well – there can't be many cars headed in that direction at this hour."

"I'd be surprised if there was anyone else on the highway that far down. What do you need done?" Don asked. He was an ex-Ranger who'd bailed on the States twenty years earlier, preferring to do odd jobs in Central America for a roster of shady operators. It paid well and the hours were usually good. And Sam's last opportunity had turned out to be quite lucrative.

"The travelers need to be stopped," Sam replied. "And a video camera they have needs to be recovered."

"Sounds simple enough. What level of resistance can I expect, and how far can I go to stop them?" Don asked. He wanted to be unambiguous so that if there were questions later on, he had Sam's go-ahead to do whatever it took.

"Use your discretion. If you can capture them, perfect. If you need to use deadly force, so be it. My main concern is the camera. I'm not particularly interested in the rest."

"I see. So if I need to use extreme measures, that's acceptable?" Don clarified.

"Whatever it takes, Don."

"Do you have any location information for me?" Don asked.

"Yes. They're about forty clicks from Santa Fe. I'm thinking they'll continue south all the way to the end of the road, but I'd like this taken care of before then," Sam said.

There was more rustling in the background. The phone went silent for a minute, and then Don was back.

"I've got a map. I don't want to do anything in my back yard, so the next real opportunity is Meteti. I know the area well. There are a number of clearings where I could take them out around fifteen miles south of the town," Don explained, "and they're far enough from civilization so I could be gone before anyone knew what had happened."

"It's up to you. I just need to recover the camera – that's the priority," Sam said, making sure he was clear on this.

"And payment?" Don asked.

"Within a week. I'll need to move some funds around on my end. I would think thirty grand would do the trick…" Sam said.

"Make it forty and we have a deal," Don fired back. "It's a rush job, so I'll need to pay more to get talent on such short notice."

He was right. And Sam knew it. "Done. I'll get you real-time updates on their location as they get closer to Meteti. I should be able to tell you within thirty seconds of when they come around a corner or over a hill."

"You got a tracker on them, or you using their phone?" Don asked.

"Phone. Accurate to within a few meters."

Don chuckled. "Gotta love it. Call me when they're ten kilometers from Santa Fe, and then update me every twenty minutes. I'll get suited up and call a couple of guys to help out."

"I'm on it. Thanks, Don. This should be an easy one. They don't know anyone's after them," Sam reassured him.

"My favorite kind. Stay in touch…"

"You bet," Sam said, closing the phone.

Don was one of the best. There was almost a hundred percent likelihood he'd be able to take out the cook and his accomplice in a matter of seconds, then grab the camera and be gone. At which point Sam would be a hero and Richard would be jetting back to Langley; another mission successfully executed by the man on the ground he'd so badly underestimated.

Sam emerged from the bathroom, humming to himself, and made a call to get Richard's team their helicopter.

# CHAPTER 18

The road quality degraded as the police cruiser traveled further south. The pavement became haphazardly uneven, from decades of spot repairs using questionable materials and techniques. Sergio had to swerve several times at the last possible moment to avoid potholes that would have blown a tire or bent a rim.

Brief rainstorms complicated the drive because the sheets of water that dumped from the sky reduced visibility to near-zero. The showers slowed their progress to a crawl, when they were happy if they could just stay on the pavement. And then the cloudbursts would clear as suddenly as they started. But the resultant puddles in the road posed a problem – there was no way of knowing whether one was a half-inch deep, or half a foot.

Still, Sergio remained upbeat and alert.

Ernesto reclined silently in the back seat, lost in his thoughts. He hadn't spoken for over an hour, preferring to rest his eyes and relax while he had the chance.

Al looked green. The damned goop he'd ingested had worked him over, and he permeated misery. He'd always known better than to eat any of the local garbage that passed for food, and sure enough, the one time he'd varied from his diet of McDonalds and hot dogs, he'd gotten dosed. Ernesto was having no problems, but that was probably because he was riddled with parasites and e-coli already, so the new pollutants didn't have a chance at survival.

Al just hoped that enough hard liquor and nicotine would kill any critters he'd picked up from the food cart. If that failed, he supposed he could always get antibiotics. He just hated taking them, as they invariably required he avoid alcohol, which further fouled his mood.

They rolled through Santa Fe, a desultory town built around the highway, and stopped for yet another roadblock just south of it. The cops at this one seemed utterly surprised to see a car so early in the morning, and after a brief discussion with Sergio, let them through. At least their strategy for tackling the security checkpoints was working. Having Sergio driving them in his cruiser had proven to be a godsend.

As they putted down the road, the first glimmers of impending dawn streaked the sky. It had been a long night, but they were closing in on their destination, and soon Ernesto would be off into the wilds of the Darien jungle, meaning Sergio and Al would be returning to relative civilization. They were about twenty-five miles from the rendezvous point, and at their current rate of progress, would be there within an hour or so, assuming the road hadn't washed out. Allowing time for the hike from the road, they should make it by 6 a.m. on the dot.

At least something was going right.

⁂

Don had chosen a clearing fifteen miles south of Meteti for the ambush. This was a completely desolate patch of nothingness, where the jungle would swallow up any evidence of a skirmish without leaving any trace. There was no traffic on the road – the only vehicle they'd seen was an ancient Ford pickup loaded with hay. Later, perhaps by eight, there might be another car or two, however, at this hour on a Sunday the road, such as it was, was theirs.

Don's cell phone chirped.

"They just passed Santa Fe, and should be in Meteti within twenty minutes," Sam advised.

"That'll put them here in forty-five or so," Don reported.

"Good news, then," Sam said. "I'll keep you posted as they pass through town so you know that whatever's headed down the road is our boys. I doubt there's anyone else going south."

"10-4."

⁂

Sergio carefully negotiated a sharp bend, and soon they were rolling through the shabby little town of Meteti. If the total population was a thousand, including goats and dogs, Al would have been surprised. He'd done several escort jobs this year involving the same rendezvous point eleven or so miles south but he was still depressed whenever he saw the broken-down buildings and extreme poverty of the dwellings. Still, it wasn't his problem. He was just a messenger, doing the Lord's work.

"Alright, Ernesto, wake up," Al announced. "We should be at the spot within a few more minutes – Sergio, there's a clearing we'll be stopping at; eleven miles south of town, on the left hand side. Set your odometer. I'll recognize it when we get close."

Ernesto shifted around in the rear seat, and Sergio cleared his throat.

"I don't suppose there's anywhere to get some coffee in this little slice of paradise?" Sergio said to no one in particular.

"There might have been a market we passed. Probably won't be open yet, but we have enough time to circle back around if you want," Al said, checking his watch.

Ernesto nodded. Al gave the thumbs up sign, so Sergio swung back around, doing a U-turn in the middle of the rural two lane highway.

"Maybe they'll have some fresh hot pancakes, or some goat brain surprise?" Sergio suggested, noting Al's pallid complexion as he said it.

"Or a quart of cheap vodka…" Al chimed in hopefully.

ॐ≪

Don's phone chirped again.

"Looks like there may be a complication," Sam whispered in a low tone.

"What is it?" Don demanded.

Any whiff of problems at this point in an operation could be disastrous. He needed to get in front of whatever this was before it could escalate.

"The target stopped just outside of Meteti and turned around. It looks like it's going back into town," Sam reported.

"I see. What's your take on this?" Don asked. He was flying blind, and Sam was his only eyes and ears.

Sam thought for a moment. "You'll know when I do. I'll call you as soon as I get a fix on them, but you might want to mount up. You may need to get back to Meteti in a hurry."

That wasn't the plan. Don had found a location where he could stop a vehicle and hit it with crossfire from three points. That was a good plan – one nobody could survive. But trying to mount an attack on the run, with unknown parameters, in an unknown environment…that's how guys wound up dead. He didn't like what he was hearing. Then again, forty grand was forty grand, and if Sam was right, the target was clueless, so he still had the element of surprise, not to mention automatic weapons.

He raised a small yellow two-way radio to his lips, and murmured instructions into it. Moments later, two men emerged from across the road where they had been hiding, completely undetectable. They loped over to the dark green Land Cruiser and waited for Don to join them.

Change of plans.

☜☞

"Well, our luck's holding. It's closed…" Al declared, staring at the little market with corroded metal bars fortifying the windows.

"Oh well. I didn't really need coffee, anyway," Sergio said wearily.

He twisted the wheel, and pointed the cruiser's nose south again.

"Hey, look at the bright side. At least it's not raining!" Ernesto said.

A crack of thunder reverberated through the trees, and sheets of water began pouring from the heavens.

"Maybe you should be thinking something like – hey, at least we don't have teenage nymphomaniacs broken down by the side of the road requiring our help…" Al suggested.

Ernesto grinned. "I'll get right on that…"

"Why do the nymphos always have to be teenage around you, Al? What's wrong with a little older? I'm starting to get the feeling you might be a pedophile or something," Sergio offered. "Not that there's anything wrong with that. I'm just saying, is all…"

They drove in silence, the only sound the heavy rain pounding on the roof of the cruiser.

After a slow half hour, Sergio checked the odometer. "Okay, just another mile."

Al studied the surrounding terrain. The rain had softened to a light mist.

"Right before the rendezvous clearing, you'll see a yellow sign warning that the road's hazardous. Our spot is about fifty yards from that," Al instructed.

"So we'll be meeting someone by the side of the road?" Ernesto asked groggily.

"No, from the clearing we have to hike due west for half a mile," Al explained. "The guide will be waiting there for us."

Ernesto frowned. "Are you sure about this? There's nothing here but jungle…"

"This isn't my first time. I've done this before," Al reminded him. "Just do as I say and you'll be golden. It'll take about half an hour to get to where the guide will meet us."

Sergio looked in the rearview mirror at Ernesto, who caught his glance.

Five minutes later they spotted the sign and Sergio slid to a stop on the opposite side of the road on a small section of shoulder just wide enough to accommodate a parked car. Sergio left the engine running and hurried to the edge of the heavy brush. He groaned a sigh of relief as he urinated.

"Well, this is the middle of nowhere, I'll give you that, Al," Sergio called over his shoulder.

"*Si, senor.* Eees god's countreee…" Al retorted, climbing from the passenger seat and bending over to stretch his aching leg muscles.

❧

"Something's wrong," Sam said. "They stopped again, about three miles north of where you are."

"How long have they been there?" Don demanded.

"It's been almost five minutes. I think you better scramble and intercept them," Sam instructed.

"Call me if they get underway again — we're about three hard minutes south of where they're stopped. Whatever they're up to, we'll be on them shortly. I'm going silent now. Talk to you in a few," Don reported, and then signed off.

He flicked the safety on his modified, fully automatic AR-15 to the 'fire' position. The driver grinned, and the man in the back seat did the same. It was a nice morning to go hunting.

❧❦

Al and Ernesto collected their belongings from the car, and prepared for the hike to the rendezvous point. The area felt deathly still following the rain, and they could hear creatures moving around in the thick foliage.

Sergio shook hands with Ernesto and wished him luck. He seemed like a decent guy. Sergio peered into the dense brush and then glanced back at Ernesto, who was sleepily clutching his backpack to his chest and looking vaguely bewildered.

"Hey, you got a weapon, since you're going into the jungle pretty much in your underwear?" Sergio asked.

"Uh, no…I didn't think I'd need one." Ernesto looked at Al. "Do I need one? Nobody said anything…"

"Come on back here," Sergio said, "and let's see if we can get you something, so you can at least kill a snake while you're sleeping on the ground…" He motioned to the rear of the cruiser. He popped the trunk, and stood with his hands on his hips, surveying the contents.

"This should do the trick," Sergio said. He extracted a wicked looking survival knife and handed it to Ernesto. He groped around in the trunk, located the missing scabbard and tossed it to him. Al circled around and joined them.

"Whoa, Papa, when did you start carrying around the heavy artillery?" Al asked, reaching in and withdrawing a scarred Kalashnikov assault rifle.

"Hey, careful. I confiscated that from a drug bust a week ago. The dealer looked like a piece of Swiss cheese by the time the shootout was over, so I figured he wouldn't miss it. And I always wanted my own AK-47," Sergio quipped, taking the weapon from Al and slapping a magazine in place. "This one's probably twenty years old, but it's still in great shape," Sergio said with pride. Al regarded the battered wooden stock dubiously.

The silence was disrupted by the roar of a vehicle approaching from around a bend in the road.

Sergio and his two companions looked up to see who was coming. This was the first vehicle they'd encountered in several hours, and there wasn't much south of them but jungle, so they were naturally curious. Al hoped it wasn't more border control officers – that would throw a wrench in their rendezvous plan. Carmen was supposed to have taken care of that, and ensured none were around for at least an hour. He hoped she'd done so.

࿊࿊

"Jesus. Keep driving. Just keep going past them. It's a National Police car," Don hissed at the driver. This was an unexpected wrinkle. Not a deal killer, but a surprise, and Don intensely disliked surprises.

They rolled by the cruiser, and Don flipped open his phone. Only one bar of service. Sam answered on the fourth ring.

"Sam, your target is a police car with three men in it. What the hell have you gotten me into?" Don demanded.

Sam was silent, processing furiously. Why were the police involved? What did it mean? Richard had made it clear that whatever was going on with the camera, they had to be stopped.

"It doesn't matter. Take them out," Sam ordered. "And don't forget the camera. I can sanitize the rest of this."

"I hope you know what you're doing," Don said, hanging up.

The driver slowed and came to a stop in the middle of the two lane strip of asphalt, then reversed. They'd lost sight of the police car due to the curvature of the road, and now had to reverse down the narrow ribbon of pavement the hundred yards they'd come, so his gunmen would still be on the correct side of the vehicle to fire at the cop car simultaneously. They needed to shoot from the truck's passenger side, so the driver would be protected and they'd have the front and rear passenger windows to fire out of.

As they backed slowly toward the cruiser, Don had a sinking feeling. This was starting out badly.

࿊࿊

Sergio watched the ancient Land Cruiser drive by, and then heard it stop and reverse. Instinct kicked in – something was very wrong.

"I thought I saw gun barrels in that truck, and now it's coming back. Get behind the car, quick," he instructed, and chambered a round in the Kalashnikov. He threw open the driver's door, grabbed the shotgun, and tossed it to Al, who held it like it was a snake.

"What the he…" Al exclaimed as the windows exploded in a hail of bullets from the Land Cruiser, which was slowly reversing around the bend, finally coming to rest thirty yards from the police car.

"Stay down…" Sergio screamed, and then let rip a burst from the AK-47. The volley tore into the side of the Land Cruiser.

Another spray of slugs hit the police car and Al fired off a couple of shotgun blasts at the truck. The first went high, but the second took out the rear windshield.

Sergio fired again, and then Al heard two of the Land Cruiser's doors open and close. More bullets sprayed the ground around them. Ernesto yelped – a ricochet had caught him in the thigh. Blood oozed through his fingers as he gripped his injured leg.

"Get him into the brush. I'll take care of these bastards," Sergio screamed, firing again.

More shots thudded into the ground around them. Al let off another shotgun potshot at the truck, aiming for the tires.

"You sure?" Al yelled.

"Get out of here. Go do your meet. I'll handle this," Sergio said through clenched teeth. He fired off another short burst, and heard a scream from behind the truck. He thought he'd seen a man's leg there. Guess he had. "I think you owe me $800, not $500, Al," he chided, then popped off a few more rounds.

"Check's in the mail. Let's call it $750…" A slug ripped a chunk of metal from the fender by Al's head. He ducked down, scanning the jungle behind them.

Sergio sprayed short bursts at the Toyota to provide cover, and Al motioned Ernesto to crawl into the dense vegetation. Al fired another shot at the attackers while Sergio supplied staccato bursts of cover fire. Al dropped the shotgun and hastened after Ernesto, military-crawling into the heavy green underbrush. He spotted Ernesto limping ahead a few dozen yards and rushed to join him. Within a minute the gunfire receded to distant popping as the pair charged headlong into the jungle, Al supporting Ernesto around the waist.

"How bad are you hit?" Al whispered to Ernesto, who was keeping up, but favoring his good leg.

"Not too bad, I don't think," Ernesto said. "It hurts, but it isn't bleeding much."

They stopped. Al unzipped his backpack and pulled out a T-shirt. He tore it in half and tied the strips together, creating a primitive bandage. Al knelt down and inspected the wound – Ernesto had been lucky – grazed, nothing more. He fastened the cloth strips together and cinched them, covering the bloody area.

"You'll live. It's just a cut," Al said, taking stock of his surroundings. They'd come maybe a hundred yards from the road so far, which meant the track to the rendezvous point should be somewhere off to the left. He pressed through the brush to where he thought he'd seen the faint impression of a trail. "This is it. Let's move."

The plants around them whistled as random slugs tore through the vegetation. The thick foliage deadened much of the noise from the road – the gunshots now sounded like muffled firecrackers in the distance. But the bullets were still deadly. Another one shredded through the leaves by Ernesto's head, passing so near he felt the air displaced by the slug.

They instinctively ducked and ran down the trail, Al in the lead.

సా

In the SUV, Don pried the driver's door open and pulled the dead man from behind the wheel. The corpse collapsed heavily onto the road. Don's wounded wingman continued to exchange fire with the cop car, and then his foot exploded, spraying blood and bone against the fender. He screamed, dropping his weapon. Don looked at the man's leg – he wouldn't ever figure skate again.

What the hell had happened? He had two men down, was taking machine-gun and shotgun fire, and was trapped in a deadly shootout with no obvious escape – with a cop or cops. The cops seemed really pissed and were giving better than they'd received.

Don glanced at his companion and made a swift decision. Fuck this. He hadn't signed up for a bloodbath. Sam could keep his money – this wasn't Don's day to die. He'd agreed to shoot fish in a barrel, not walk straight into a kill zone.

Don sprayed the cop car and surrounding trees with a barrage of lead, exhausting his magazine. He leaned over and grabbed his partner's rifle, and emptied it at the police vehicle for good measure. Maybe he'd hit one or all of them. Maybe not.

Don hauled his companion into the back seat, and slid behind the wheel of the still-running truck. He peered out the driver's door at the road, put the transmission into drive and gassed it. The heavy four wheel drive vehicle surged forward, gaining speed despite both rear tires having been flattened from gunfire.

಄ೲ

Sergio stood, and rounding the cruiser's rear fender, emptied the AK-47 at the escaping attackers. He reached into his trunk and grabbed another full clip, slamming it into place as he jogged after the Land Cruiser. Closing the distance, he emptied the fresh magazine into the vehicle. The truck swerved and then slowed, coasting to a stop. Only twenty yards away. Sergio pulled his pistol from its holster, and fired seven shots into the now stalled SUV. The eighth round did the trick – the sizzling slug hit the gas tank and the Land Cruiser exploded in a cascade of flames, the whump of the blast searing Sergio's face and knocking him back several feet.

He sat in the middle of the road, pistol still clutched tightly in his hand, watching the truck burn in the early morning light.

God he loved being a cop.

# CHAPTER 19

Al heard the explosion and increased the pace, his lungs burning with the unfamiliar exertion. He couldn't remember the last time he'd exercised harder than walking up the stairs to his apartment – but it was amazing what naked terror could do for a guy's quarter mile time. He hadn't moved this quickly since high school.

If Ernesto couldn't keep up, that wasn't Al's problem. He'd done his job, which was to get him to the rendezvous point. Al had never signed up for shooting it out with murderous gunmen on a muddy road to oblivion – that had never come up when Carmen had described the gig. He was supposed to be a glorified taxi service, not a ninja assassin. Thank God circumstances had landed them with Sergio – if he hadn't been around they'd be worm food by now.

Which got Al thinking. Even as he followed the trail deeper into the jungle his mind thrashed over the events of the last few hours. The conclusion he arrived at was anything but reassuring. Al had lived in Panama for the last eight years and the closest he'd come to real danger was slipping in the shower whilst drunk and almost splitting his head open. Now, in less than half a day he'd been in the thick of full-on gun battles – not once, but twice. Sure, perhaps the first one at the whorehouse had been total coincidence – he'd buy that, although reluctantly. But this was anything but. There weren't a lot of ways to misconstrue armed attackers at dawn trying to stitch you with lead.

Al slowed and turned to face Ernesto, who was also flushed from the effort of running. "What's going on, Ernesto," Al asked. "Why does the whole world want to kill you?"

Ernesto glanced nervously over his shoulder, gasping for breath. "I haven't done anything, Al."

"Armed goons with machine-guns just tried to slaughter us, Ernesto. And to refresh your memory, we very recently had to sneak out a back alley because of a gun battle in the lobby of the building where I met you. So why don't you tell me why you need to get out of Panama so badly, Ernesto?" Al stared at him. Ernesto stared back, saying nothing.

"Look, let's just get away from this, and once we're safe, I'll tell you everything," Ernesto offered.

"You'll either tell me right now or I won't take you to the guide, and you'll be on your own with the gunmen back at the Transamerican," Al threatened.

"I...I stole something that's obviously very valuable to some extremely dangerous men, Al. But I swear, I didn't know what I was doing, and if there was any way to reverse things..." Ernesto looked like he was about to cry.

"Why are they trying to kill you? And who is they?" Al asked.

"I...I suppose they want to know what I did with their property," Ernesto said.

That sounded like pretty routine criminal retribution stuff so far.

"And who's trying to kill you?" Al pressed.

"I...I honestly don't know for sure..."

Something crashed and clattered overhead. Could have been a large bird, or a monkey. Or it could have been something else.

"This isn't over, Ernesto. You *will* tell me what's going on," Al hissed as he started moving down the trail again.

Ernesto nodded, then put a finger to his lips.

Al recognized that was a good idea right now. They could sort out Ernesto's drama once they were reasonably sure they weren't going to be exterminated within the next few minutes. After all, why they were being hunted was secondary to whether or not they would be killed.

Al was nothing if not pragmatic.

He looked at his watch. Quarter after six. He hoped the guide hadn't been scared off by the shooting, and then realized that a half mile into the jungle it was unlikely the guide would have heard anything. That was one of the benefits of a virtually impenetrable rainforest – sound didn't travel far.

Al unzipped his satchel and pulled out a small handheld GPS. He activated it and selected a screen. They were on a north-easterly heading, and the device, which he'd used on past trips to locate the clearing, confirmed they were almost at the rendezvous point. Maybe another three hundred yards. The technology literally made finding a needle in a haystack as simple as following the arrow and moving in the direction it indicated until X marked the spot.

After one more glance at the device he powered it off, then set off toward where the clearing should be.

They were running short on time.

And in the last few minutes, Al realized he had a teensy little problem. Namely, that he couldn't return to the road, where the killers were waiting for him – or if not those killers, their replacements. Which left him in with two choices he wanted no part of – being forced by circumstance to make it through the jungle and into Colombia, or trying his luck with whatever was waiting for him back at the road.

His belly growled. Jesus, that pig-slop from last night was foul. No doubt brimming with liver flukes and God knows what other horrors.

Some days just started off lousy, and then went downhill from there.

This looked to be one of them.

Then the clouds parted, and the sun radiated its warming light upon them. Or more accurately, they arrived at the clearing, where the thick vegetation overhead thinned enough to make the sky visible.

Ernesto sat on an old log and fiddled with his makeshift bandage. Al desperately wanted a cigarette and a cocktail, but held off on the former out of concern it might lead the death squad to them, and nixed the latter because he'd left his emergency vodka ration in his car. So he was virtuous by necessity and circumstance, rather than by choice.

He heard the sharp snapping of a branch and spun around.

The guide was here.

A small, wizened figure in baggy camouflage pants and a stained brown tank top watched them from a nearby grove of trees, an ancient machete dangling from his right hand. There had been no one there a few moments ago when they'd arrived. And then, suddenly, there he was. Carlos.

Al knew the guide was a Kuna Indian, one of the original indigenous tribes of Panama, from a tiny village on the bank of the nearby river. He suspected he had an unpronounceable name, but Carmen had told Al to refer to him as Carlos, which seemed like a reasonable compromise between whatever series of pops and grunts passed for his moniker in Kuna, and even the Spanish equivalent.

Carlos looked to be in his late sixties, but Al knew looks were deceptive. The jungle was a harsh mistress, and he might be in his forties – or eighties. Carmen had assured Al the man spoke English, but in the past their interactions had been limited to Carlos virtually ignoring Al's ice-breaking overtures in mangled Spanish, so it wasn't as though they were close.

Carlos motioned Ernesto to follow him. Al stepped forward and indicated by touching his chest and pointing that he would also be going. Carlos glared at Al as though he'd proposed sodomizing him, and shook his head. "No."

Al approached Carlos, and whispered a few words of 'Spanglish' in his ear. "I need to go with you. I can't go back – it's not safe. Bad men…"

Carlos regarded him with stoic calm then spoke in accented English. "Tough shit. This isn't a free tour, cowboy…"

Al sighed, then fished around in his shirt pocket, carefully peeling off five hundred dollars from his newly acquired wad. He figured he wouldn't be seeing Sergio for a while, so he probably wouldn't mind if his cut temporarily went to Carlos.

"That's it? Is this a joke? The best you can do is beer money? Maybe that gets you across a river or two, but to Colombia? Give me a break…" Carlos muttered, but then he snatched the cash from Al's hand, and shaking his head in disgust, motioned for them both to join him.

❧

"Sam! Get in here! Now!" Richard yelled from Sam's desk.

Sam almost choked on his tenth cup of coffee. He hurried into the office, where Richard was cradling the phone headset on his shoulder while staring at the representation of the cook's cell phone chip movement on the monitor.

"I just got word there's been an emergency call from a police cruiser about ten miles south of Meteti, which is, funnily enough, where the cook's phone chip placed them. There's been a gun battle, and at least three men are dead," Richard reported, watching Sam's face for any inkling of foreknowledge.

Sam's eyes went wide. He looked genuinely shocked. "What…what do you mean, sir? A cop? Gunfight? I don't understand," Sam exclaimed.

"Our boy was being ferried south by a police officer, it seems, and there was an armed altercation. There's no mention of the cook, so I'm guessing the cop was the transportation arrangement." Richard studied Sam. "Sam, it's wildly coincidental that there's been a gunfight involving the car carrying the cook. So much so I have to believe you had a hand in this. So why not just fess up – what the hell did you do?" Richard demanded, slamming his hand heavily on the desk.

Sam's eyes widened. "I have no idea what you're talking about, sir. Really. Look, that area of southern Panama is extremely dangerous under the best of circumstances. Especially at night. Maybe this cop came across a drug deal and they panicked?"

"I don't buy that horse-crap for a second, Sam."

"I already had a team wiped out at the whorehouse due to bad luck," Sam began. "There was no hidden scheme there, just some violent thugs with guns at the wrong place at the wrong time. Is it so impossible that there's more than one group of armed predators roving around the biggest cocaine trafficking corridor in the world in the wee hours of the morning?"

Richard said nothing. But the way he stared at Sam said it all.

"I swear, I have no idea what's going on, sir," Sam promised.

Richard turned back to the monitor. "Well, according to the tracking data, the cook is now bee-lining into the middle of the jungle. He's over a mile in, and it looks like he's continuing straight toward the border. So any chance we had of intercepting him on the road is over," Richard said angrily.

"What are we going to do?" Sam asked.

"We? …We?…*We* aren't going to do anything. I don't believe you didn't have a hand in the attack, even though I can't prove it. I don't buy coincidences that involve armed attacks on deserted roads. But I'll deal with that later. Right now I don't have the luxury of peeling your skin off, layer by layer, to get to the truth. No, I now have to figure out how to take the cook out before this goes any further," Richard hissed in frustration.

"Well, there's nobody for miles, so at least you can pretty much do whatever you want," Sam reasoned.

"Yeah, but there are no roads to get a team in, and the deeper into that jungle they go, the more dangerous any operation becomes. It's literally swarming with rebels and coke traffickers, all of whom are armed to the teeth," Richard said. "And my team is sitting almost twenty miles away, waiting for an ambush that's never going to happen." He looked at Sam in disgust.

"Maybe the cook panicked and is running blind? The intel was pretty adamant that any meeting would happen in Yaviza…" Sam speculated.

"I'm going to bet that this time, the intel sucked," Richard said.

"But…"

"The cook is heading straight for the most dangerous strip of land on Earth, and seems to be making pretty good headway, given it's the densest jungle outside of the Congo. I'm going to go out on a limb here and guess he's got some help, and that help isn't accidental. We've known all along he was making for Colombia. This is how he plans to do it," Richard explained.

"Then you have to get him on the Colombian side?" Sam asked.

Richard said nothing, lost in thought.

He really wanted to take the cook alive so he could understand what, if any, additional exposure they had to the camera's contents being leaked. Unfortunately, this operation was already running off the tracks and it didn't look like he had that option – barring parachuting his team into the middle of a hot zone, with no way out, in the hopes they could intercept the cook without stepping on any land mines or being mowed down by bloodthirsty paramilitary rebels. Richard had read the reports on the Darien Gap, and even this northern edge of it was more deadly than walking down the main boulevard in Tehran singing God Bless America, wearing a stars and stripes jacket. Every murderous faction in Central America was concentrated in that strip of jungle and each was more dangerous than the next. The Panamanians wouldn't get within miles of it, and the Colombian Army would only venture in on rare occasions, and then in only a limited area with massive firepower. It made Vietnam during the height of hostilities seem like a trip to Cancun on Spring Break.

# CHAPTER 20

They hiked further north-east, Carlos moving soundlessly in front of them. Even in the early morning, now just after seven, the oppressive heat beat down on them. Swarms of mosquitoes attacked Ernesto and Al, but seemed strangely uninterested in Carlos.

Glancing back at the pair, Carlos reached into his soiled blue nylon knapsack and tossed Ernesto a small green aerosol can.

"*Backwoods Off.* Best mosquito spray money can buy," Carlos told them. "Get all your skin and also spray your shirt – they'll bite right through it. And with Malaria and Dengue everywhere around here you really don't want bites."

Great, Al thought. If he didn't contract Malaria, he could look forward to hemorrhagic fever, where his organs would liquefy and he'd turn into a giant, bleeding hemorrhoid.

This just kept getting better.

They were being stalked by parties unknown, whose only imperative seemed to be to exterminate them; they were trekking through an area more toxic than the Burmese triangle; the place was lousy with insects and critters that would kill you just for practice; and his stomach felt like he'd swallowed molten lava – possibly from the stress, but almost certainly from the toxic rot he'd eaten last night.

Finished spraying, Ernesto handed Al the aerosol of repellant. It was nearly empty.

Unbelievable.

After another hour of pressing through the undergrowth they arrived at a brown, odiferous river. Carlos moved to a nearby pile of vegetation and lifted some large fronds, revealing an old *piragua*, a long, narrow rowboat with two plastic jugs of water in it. He offered one to Ernesto and Al, and took a long pull from his own.

"This is the Chucunaque river," Carlos began. "We need to cross it, then we continue on foot. On the other shore it gets much more dangerous, so stay quiet at all times and pay attention to whatever I do or say. I know most of the groups operating in this area, but there are always new ones, and people get killed daily, so there are no guarantees. I have a camp a few more miles inland from the river. We should try and make it there by noon."

"The river stinks," Al complained.

Carlos nodded. "You don't want to get in the water, that's for sure. It has parasites that will drill through your skin and feed on your guts – same in most of the rivers here, so try not to fall in, and leave taking a bath until you're in Colombia," Carlos advised. He regarded Al skeptically. "Assuming you make it."

"You sure that thing floats?" Al asked, ignoring his innuendo.

"It did coming over, but you're the fattest passenger I ever tried to carry, so anything could happen. Try not to capsize it." Carlos grinned at him, revealing multiple gaps where teeth had once resided.

They were across the river within five minutes, thankfully, with no drama. No alligators leaped snapping at them from the sludgy banks, no water snakes attacked. Still, both Ernesto and Al were glad to be out of the boat – it really did rock precariously and was obviously rotting apart.

Carlos grabbed his water bottle and gestured at Ernesto to do the same. He put his finger to his mouth, reminding them to be silent.

The day got muggier as they moved deeper into the dense jungle. Forty-five minutes past the river it started raining, which was a blessing from a temperature standpoint, but also a curse, as the ground soon became a muddy quagmire. Carlos wore old army boots, but Ernesto and Al both wore tennis shoes, which were ill-suited for the terrain and quickly soaked through with moisture. Carlos didn't seem to notice or be troubled by the downpour, which stopped as suddenly as it began. Within a few minutes steam rose from the vegetation, making the cloying environment even more unbearable.

How did the locals live in this? Al was dying, and he'd only been in the wilds for a few hours. He couldn't imagine what August, during the full-fledged rainy season, was like.

Eventually they made it to another clearing. Two burros were tied to a tree trunk, each with a pack on its back. Al noticed that both had rifles conspicuously stuffed in the packs, their dark wooden butts sticking out for easy access. That didn't portend good things.

Carlos untied the two burros, who ambled about in search of something to nibble. He spoke to Ernesto and Al in a whisper.

"We wait here until the worst heat of day is over, and then make for the mountains. It takes at least two days to make it through to Colombia. I got food and water packed, but only enough for two, so you'll need to share. Al, I think maybe you could use a few days on a diet, so this will do you good. But you need to ration your water. Each burro has a plastic funnel in the pack – when it rains, open the bottle and put the funnel in. That stretches the water longer."

"How many times have you done this trip?" Ernesto asked.

"About twenty times. It never gets any easier, but at least it's not rainy season yet. That's a nightmare," Carlos advised.

"Well, at least there's that," Al said, and then winced as his stomach gave a sharp stab of pain. "Christ, Ernesto, that poison you fed me at the *mercado* is killing me. Aren't you feeling sick?"

"Nah. Never better. Your system is messed up in some way. Maybe it's alcohol withdrawals?" Ernesto suggested.

Al regarded Carlos. "You wouldn't happen to have any cold beer, would you, Carlos?" Al tried hopefully.

"Sure. I keep it right next to the slot machines. Just take a right at the hookers and look for the fridge," Carlos responded.

"I figured that was a long shot," Al lamented. He sighed and pulled out his pack of Marlboros.

"No smoking till you're in Colombia," Carlos ordered, shaking his head.

"What? You're kidding me! No booze *and* no cigarettes? What is this…hell? You're the devil and I died last night?"

"Keep your voice down," Carlos cautioned. "You light a cigarette and you might as well crank a stereo and put a bulls-eye on your back. Any dangerous groups in the area will come right to you…and then you'll know what hell really is."

"All right," Al grudgingly conceded, carefully replacing the cigarette into the cardboard package.

Carlos extended a hand, flipping his fingers, signaling for Al to surrender the box.

"Oh, c'mon, Carlos. For Christ's sake. I'm an adult. If I promise I won't smoke, I won't," Al protested.

"I'm not willing to bet my life on your willpower. The gangs in this region kill people for fun. They kill each other. They kill my people. If you have a moment of weakness, they kill me, too. Sorry. You want to take this trip, you give me the cigarettes. No arguments," Carlos declared. "You can have them back when it's safe," Carlos promised.

"Fuck you," Al said, but he handed Carlos the packet.

Carlos crumpled the box, then cleared a small indentation in the dirt, and threw the package in it, burying it underfoot. He stamped on the dirt for good measure.

"I thought you said I could have them back when it was safe," Al whined.

"I lied."

⌘

On the large flat panel display, Richard studied the GPS tracking data for the cook's cell phone. The target was stationary now, and had been for over an hour. Five and a half miles off the road, but it might as well have been a hundred. There was no way he could get his men close enough to do an intercept, especially since the road would now have cops moving in from every available district.

It wasn't every Sunday morning that a single Panamanian police officer took down three gunmen in a wide-open shootout, so the rubbernecking factor would be huge. Richard would bet his salary there'd be dozens of officers at the site within the hour, if not more.

In any other area of the world he would have contrived a clandestine drop, landing a chopper nearby and executing a surgical recovery operation. The problem was he didn't have many local resources to draw upon, and had to keep this particular situation under the radar. Had this been Iraq or Afghanistan he could have arranged for a gunship to fly in and vaporize everything for a quarter mile – problem solved. But this was a friendly nation during peace time, a nation which took a really dim view of aggressive behavior – they were still touchy at having been invaded by the U.S. over the Noriega thing.

So he'd have to be creative.

That was fine – he knew how to improvise. He just hated doing so, after decades of experience had drilled into him that the difference between success and failure was planning, which translated into superior execution. But he didn't have that luxury this time around. And the stakes were too high to leave this open-ended any longer.

The chopper he'd used to fly his team into Darien was operated by a reliable long term Agency asset, so there was no question he could get the man to do a little side mission. The problem was that as the cook moved further into the Darien area, it would become increasingly dangerous to fly over it – the rebels in the region packed surface-to-air missiles as well as large caliber machine-guns, and would have no way of knowing that any aircraft overhead wasn't targeting them. So the window of opportunity was rapidly closing.

He lifted the phone to his ear, having weighed all his options and made the difficult decision. It would be messy, but sometimes life was disorganized. That's the way it was happening on this one.

A pro rolled with it.

And Richard was a consummate pro.

# CHAPTER 21

The sun beat down on the overhead canopy of vegetation, making for a stifling, humid afternoon. No wonder Carlos didn't want to move until the worst of the noon blaze had faded. Just lying around immobile was difficult enough. There was no cooling breeze in the jungle, no relief from the ever-present blanket of moist heat that enveloped their resting place. Even the brief rainstorms did little to mitigate their discomfort, as within minutes of the cloudbursts ending, the moisture converted into steam from the sun's blistering rays.

Ernesto dozed, lying against a fallen tree trunk now overrun with vines. Occasionally he swatted at his face, in a losing battle with the gnats and mosquitoes. Carlos stood by the burros, checking the packs and comforting the animals, murmuring in their ears in a native dialect.

Al spent much of the time in a clearing on the periphery, crouched with his pants down, struggling to expel the prior night's impromptu feast. It felt like someone had rubbed cayenne pepper on his rectum, and was kicking him in the lower stomach every few minutes. He suffered a constant cramping pain, punctuated by brief periods of squirting out what felt like battery acid sprinkled with small chunks of internal organs. What madness had compelled him to sample the local fare? He blamed Ernesto for his predicament. Yes, Ernesto – who was napping like a baby and with no complications whatsoever. For years, Al had only eaten products made in the good old US of A. His culinary patriotism had certainly been reinforced by this episode.

Panama City played host to every imaginable American fast food franchise, so he'd been insulated from indigenous cuisine, other than the local beer and hard liquor, which he seemed to do quite well with.

As Al squatted for the fourth time in two hours, cursing his fate, he wondered how he would get out of the mess he was in. His largest problem was not really knowing what the mess was. Ernesto had turned strangely reluctant to discuss his pursuit by gunmen, other than to restate that they were after him for petty theft. That didn't sound right – they didn't send in killers with ack ack guns over pilfered household goods. But Ernesto was asleep, and Al's convulsing colon was keeping him fully occupied so they hadn't had much chance to fully explore the details of Ernesto's transgressions.

Thank God Carlos had brought a couple of rolls of toilet paper in the burro packs – although if this kept up much longer he might wind up having to use leaves and sticks.

Ernesto came suddenly awake with a hideous scream. Carlos ran over to him, and Al concluded his sojourn in the thicket and also went to investigate. Ernesto was slapping at his wounded leg, howling in agony. Carlos whipped out his can of mosquito repellent and sprayed his wound area, then grabbed one of the water jugs and splashed his leg.

A band of fire ants had been drawn to the bloody gouge, and established a trail to the wound as Ernesto slumbered. The water and spray had done the trick, but not before a series of welts swelled all the way down his leg after the frantic ants had stung him.

Carlos patted his shoulder. "Okay, I know ant stings hurt, but we must get moving now. Your screaming has told everyone nearby where we are. It's no longer safe here." Eyes narrowed, he looked around the clearing and canopy. "I hoped we'd get a few more hours of calm before we had to go, but that's not going to happen. Grab your stuff and let's go. Ernesto, you can ride on Pablo until the swelling goes down," Carlos explained, patting the larger of the two burros.

"Where are we headed now? What's the plan?" Al asked, eyeing the brooding vegetation around them with trepidation.

"We're going into the Darien Gap," Carlos told him. "Moving northeast over the mountains until we get across to Colombia. There are a few fishing villages there – Capurgana, Sapzuro, Acandi – we say goodbye at one of those. Which one we make it to depends on the condition of the trails on that side…and the weather. From here it's about thirty-five miles, but it's some of the toughest miles you'll ever see. If we can make it in two days, we're in a race car…" Carlos said.

"Have you ever had any problems going this route?" Ernesto asked.

"I'm not going to lie to you. I know many rebel groups who live in this stretch of jungle, but there are always new *narcotraficantes* moving in and killing each other for territory, so power changes hands – some hands I do not know. We should be safe, but the best bet is to avoid contact with anyone we see or hear – many will just shoot first and worry about who they shot later," Carlos warned.

"Nice," Al muttered.

"That's if we're lucky," Carlos continued. "If we're unlucky, we could get chopped into meat by any of twenty different drug factions at war in the region, or a fifteen year old with a machine-gun could get trigger happy before we get a chance to explain who we are, or one of us could step on a land-mine that the rebels are now setting where it's easy to walk – which also keeps army troops from mounting an offensive against them."

Well that was lovely, Al concluded. If the snakes and poisonous spiders and whatnot didn't get them, and they somehow dodged the headhunters and homicidal gangs of armed predators, then a claymore could take them out just as they were within sight of safety. He considered going back the way he'd come, and then dismissed it. He knew there were bad men with guns back there but the difference was he knew they were definitely looking for them, whereas up ahead there *might* be bad men, who *might* or *might not* want to slaughter them on sight – so moving forward at least offered a slim reed of hope for survival, whereas returning to the road was certain death.

☙❧

Richard located his headset in his briefcase and plugged it into the telephone. "They're moving," he reported.

"Copy that. I can see them on our screen," came the reply. In the background Richard could hear the *whump whump whump* of the helicopter blades slicing into the sky.

"What do you think?" Richard asked.

"Obviously this would be easier with a stationary target than one moving through heavy undergrowth. It's almost impossible to see the ground through the trees, so ideally we should wait until they stop again, preferably in a clearing," the voice advised.

"I concur, but I want this over with today. Do you want to set down, or stay in the air?" Richard asked.

"It would be better to return to our last position on the ground and wait until they go stationary again. We run a lot of risks hovering over the jungle, not the least of which is that one of the locals decides to blow us out of the air just for practice. Right now, they're maybe ten minutes as the crow flies from our staging area, so whenever they stop to take a break, we can be on them." He paused. "That's how I'd prefer to play it."

"All right. Land. But be ready to move at a moment's notice," Richard ordered. "I'll stay on the com channel. Hopefully they'll stop again within an hour or two, and that's when we'll make our move."

"I just wish we had a more elegant solution. A couple of rockets with no back-blast would solve this pretty quickly," the voice observed.

"I know, but the AT-4s we can get around here are too dangerous. The back-blast would fry the inside of the chopper, taking you with it," Richard reminded.

"So we move to plan B. Less elegant, but just as effective. Hopefully."

⸙

The scene back at the highway epitomized pandemonium – police vehicles from every outpost within forty miles had raced to the site of the shootout. Groups of officers stood idly talking with one another while a flatbed tow truck struggled to drag the scorched SUV chassis off the road.

Sergio was the closest thing to a celebrity the police force would have for some time to come. 'Lone cop takes down an armed load of killers' would make for a compelling legend – even if there were some holes in his accounting of the incident.

All anyone had to do was look at his police cruiser, riddled with bullets, to get an idea of what he'd survived. According to Sergio's story he'd pulled over to take a leak and the vehicle had sped by headed north, and then backed down the road toward him and started shooting. The tire marks corroborated his version of events, so there were no questions – other than where he'd gotten the AK – which he truthfully admitted having not yet signed into custody following a drug bust the prior week. Against protocol, of course, but given his heroic actions the brass would likely overlook it.

The official report suggested that a car full of armed drug smugglers fearing exposure, and seeing the lone officer, decided to eliminate the only witness to their being on the road by gunning him down. Not so far from the truth as far as Sergio could tell. Sure, he imagined there was more to that story than anyone knew, but he also understood that, whether the gunmen had been after Al and his buddy, or had truly been paranoid traffickers bent on murder, the outcome remained the same.

Gunmen zero.

Sergio three.

With a decoration down the road for heroism, and a probable promotion as word of his actions spread.

One of the nearby vehicles contained a stringer reporter for the largest Panama City newspaper so it was just a matter of hours until his face was plastered throughout the country as a symbol of how seriously Panama took the ongoing war on drugs. As well as a figure for a new unofficial slogan for a police force in need of pride, which would go something like: 'Don't Fuck With Me Or I'll Take You Down'.

Sergio was a genuine hero, and looked every bit the part.

Why ruin a good story with inconvenient facts?

∂∾⧂

After an hour of steadily moving deeper into the Darien, Carlos signaled it was time for a break. All three men were soaked through with sweat, and they gulped greedily from their water bottles. Carlos passed out some pretzels from a small package, advising that they needed to keep their salt intake high so that the water would absorb into their cells and not just flush out as sweat.

Al took his portable GPS unit from his satchel and powered it on. By his reckoning, they'd come seven miles from the road, maybe a little more. That left thirty-three to go. If they were averaging a couple miles per hour, tops, it would take two more full days to get to the other side of the border. He considered the reality of spending another forty-eight hours in the jungle, and his heart sank. Al would have already sold his right arm for a Long Island Ice Tea and a carton of Marlboros – and it had only been eight hours. How bad would this suck by Tuesday?

Ernesto and Al sat a few yards apart, panting, resting their already tired muscles. Carlos looked like he'd just woken up after a nice twelve hour nap – soaked maybe, but not even winded, whereas his companions were tottering on their last legs.

Al supposed that if all you did was roam around the wilds in hundred degree heat, you got used to it pretty quickly. He preferred not to think about how much older Carlos appeared – Al fully understood he was in shit shape and didn't need any reminders from his well-intentioned internal voice.

Al's abdomen emitted an alarming growl, accompanied by a shooting pain in his lower intestines. Good God. Not again. This was becoming a too-regular feature of his afternoon communion with nature – a moment or two of frantic warning and then he became blow-out boy. He'd taken to carrying one of their two rolls of toilet paper in the pocket of his cargo pants, to save rooting around in the burro packs whenever he was overcome with the urge. He glanced around and saw a promising clump of indeterminate plants maybe forty yards from where Ernesto and Carlos sat.

Al half ran, half trotted to his chosen spot and soon realized he was standing in a pool of muddy water filled with flying bugs. Not good. He really didn't need his business end getting bitten while he struggled with number two, so he moved another few yards until he found firmer footing. He dropped his trousers and crouched in the now all too familiar field latrine position, eyes squeezed shut and teeth gritted from the heady combination of pain and effort. Alarmed by a nearby crackling of underbrush, he looked up to see a burro's face two feet from his. Even in the middle of nowhere he couldn't have a moment to himself and preserve just a little dignity.

Al shooed him. The inquisitive burro stared at him, standing its ground.

Suddenly the air above filled with a dense, thumping roar – the distinctive sound of a helicopter, deafening in its proximity. Al instinctively bunny-hopped for cover, pants-around-ankles style, and in the process he dropped the toilet paper roll in the swampy muck in front of him. It immediately soaked through with brown groundwater. The burro crashed past him and away from the thundering clamor, almost knocking him over.

And then the jungle clearing where Ernesto and Carlos sat exploded, detonation after detonation blasting the area into a growling fireball. Five, six, seven explosions, an area thirty yards in diameter blasted to smithereens. Al could just make out the chopper, which had risen higher overhead to avoid any shrapnel from the explosions. He listened to it hovering above as the smoke from the blasts gradually cleared. Its rotors thumped rhythmically as it remained fixed over the kill zone.

Al couldn't see the airship, but his instinct strongly recommended not sticking around to find out what happened next. He could see the smoldering fragments of Carlos and Ernesto alongside the other hapless burro, so there wasn't anything left to salvage. Self-preservation yelled at Al to get the hell out of there, and quick.

He pulled up his pants and scurried further into the jungle, trying to be as soundless as possible. The panicked burro bolted ahead of him, frantic to put as much distance as it could between itself and the helicopter. That wasn't good. If anyone descended from the chopper it would be a lot easier for them to spot a crazy, freaked out burro than Al hiding eighty yards from the detonation area. Al waited breathlessly for something to happen. He winced along with each bump and crash of the burro as it lumbered through the brush, now another forty yards past his hiding place. The helicopter maintained its position overhead.

A minute went by. As did another. And then a pair of combat boots slowly descended through the treetops, followed by a camouflage-clad torso belted into a complex harness, with arms holding a very ugly looking assault rifle.

Al willed his body to become part of the jungle floor, his face pressed flat in the ooze. He prayed he was undetectable this far away from the destruction, and hoped the attackers would be satisfied with the complete devastation the explosives had inflicted.

The man remained suspended twenty feet above the still-smoldering corpses – no longer recognizable as humans. The less inquisitive, but unlucky, burro had been blown half apart, its cargo destroyed and its torso mainly obliterated. Time halted to standstill as the dangling observer spent an eternity systematically surveying the carnage.

Then Al heard the words that chilled his blood and froze his breath in his chest.

Audible over the muffled chopping of the helicopter, now far above, a male voice said, "Target neutralized. Everything's vaporized. Pull me up and let's get out of here."

The man rose back through the trees, hoisted by the black rope attached to his harness and soon the sound of the airship receded, then faded to silence. But Al stayed glued to the muddy ground, eyes clamped shut, digesting the words he'd just heard, again and again. It wasn't so much the phrases, nor the tone.

No, the problem was they were in English.

❧❦

Richard leaned back in his chair and wiped his face with both hands. He'd removed his wireless headset but still studied the monitor, where up until a few moments before, a yellow blinking square had dominated the upper left quadrant of the aerial view of the jungle. Now there was nothing. The little yellow icon was gone.

So it was over.

He'd gotten a brief description from the helicopter and seen the video feed of the devastated blast area. It was clear nothing could have survived the attack. They'd decided on grenades, figuring that, although low tech, they would be highly effective, especially if they dropped a half dozen right on their target's head. Fired from several grenade launchers, their weight and momentum easily carried them through the thick canopy, ensuring oblivion for anything below.

He would have preferred to have gotten his hands on the camera but given the images from the video he agreed it wasn't necessary. It wasn't worth risking a half hour scrounging through body parts and debris to find fragments of it – all that could possibly be left, if that, considering the amount of destruction levied upon the small target area.

"Sam? Come in here," Richard called.

"Yes? What happened? How did it go, sir?" Sam asked, almost afraid to hear the answer. He'd been monitoring the police channels, listening to the description from the roadside shoot-out area, hoping against hope that the bodies of his accomplices were too badly burned to be identified, or at least not until well after Richard had gone back to Langley.

"Crisis averted. I think we can safely say this little episode is behind us," Richard announced. He seemed to have grown an inch.

"That's great, sir! So you were able to find them?" Sam fawned.

"All I can say is there's no longer any threat," Richard said, clearly fatigued-but-happy now that the long vigil was over.

"I don't suppose I'll ever know what was so important about the camera…" Sam muttered.

"Sam. Listen. Closely. You're lucky you aren't being packed up to Langley, to spend the rest of your dismal career cleaning latrines. After the fuck up at the whorehouse and then this suspicious shoot-out, it's really a kind of miracle you're still in charge here. If I was you, I'd focus on denying everything to the locals when they come asking – make sure and sanitize the situation so nothing can ever lead back here. So no, you don't want to know why the camera was an imperative. What you want to know is that I'm leaving now, and you'll want to pray you never hear my name or voice ever again." Richard regarded Sam with his reptilian stare. Sam fidgeted, feeling like a schoolboy.

"I'm sorry things got off to a rough start, sir, but it seems like everything–" Sam began.

Richard held out his hand, signaling 'Stop'.

"You can have your office back in fifteen minutes. I can honestly say I hope I never see this place again. I know the way out. Just clean up after me so it's as though I was never here, and we'll consider ourselves even," Richard declared, making a dismissive gesture with his still raised hand.

Sam wasn't sure whether to feel relieved or furious. He silently wished a curse on Richard's plane; it would burst into flames and crash into the sea; his scorched and bleeding body would become a twitching feast for the sharks – while jellyfish stung him for good measure. He couldn't help but smirk, just a little, at the satisfying visual.

# CHAPTER 22

Twenty minutes after the helicopter disappeared, Al cautiously raised his head and looked around. He was alone. A bird fluttered overhead in the trees. The patter of light rain played upon the canopy, the drizzle barely penetrating the tightly woven layer of vegetation.

A sudden crash from behind made his heart jump in his chest. He spun around, prepared to attack or defend himself from whatever new horror the universe had visited upon him.

The prodigal burro had returned.

Al was pleased to see the nosy beast; somehow relieved he wasn't completely alone. He reached out and scratched the scruffy latrine-stalker behind an ear, then gently stroked his long, fly-bitten nose. The burro showed its teeth – Al pulled his arm away in horror – then it gave Al a little nudge, looking for further reassurance; most likely scared out of its wits by the attack.

As was Al.

Why was a highly-trained Gringo hit squad hunting down a cook in the middle of the Panamanian jungle? And how had the cook been tracked and located? And why, if they could track him, not simply wait until he emerged out of the jungle in Colombia and grab him then? Why blow everything to kingdom come and slaughter Ernesto and Carlos in the process? Given what he'd just witnessed, was the gun battle on the road not obviously part of the same operation? If that were the case, who'd lay odds that the firefight at the brothel wasn't also connected? It was an awful lot of shooting in a short period of time. And the cook had been in all three locations when the killing started.

Al wondered what the poor bastard could have done to bring the wrath of hell down on them. Stealing someone's crap didn't really compute as a plausible explanation, but Al was unlikely to ever discover what had actually happened.

As he scratched the burro's nose it slowly dawned he had a major new problem. He had no way of knowing whether they, whoever they were, would have men stationed at the road in case anyone got away; or whether a hit squad was even now prowling down the same trail Carlos had forged through the underbrush, following it to verify no stragglers had survived the aerial attack. He really didn't want to believe that was the case, but he also had no idea what he was involved in or what kind of shit was waiting for him back the way he'd come. If they'd wanted the cook so badly, maybe they'd also be after Ernesto's travel companions. And if they'd wounded Sergio and taken him alive it was quite possible they'd gotten info out of him, in which case if he went back he would be walking into a death trap.

Al's suddenly fertile mind conjured up a dozen different scary scenarios that placed him in imminent danger, and all seemed plausible in the wake of the last few hours.

Luckily, the burro had some useful knowledge – it knew its way to their destination. As if intuiting Al's thoughts, it ambled off into the trees, untroubled by Al's internal turmoil. The sedulous donkey had the water bottles, Sergio's old machete and rifle, and the rest of the contents of the bulging pack slung on its back, so survival meant sticking with the burro.

Al almost called after it – then stopped himself. He remembered Carlos' caveat about voices in the jungle. It was possible the helicopter attack had drawn enough attention to attract armed gangs of predators, who were even now making their way through the foliage to his location…

*Pull yourself together, Al.*

He homed in on the swaying bottom of his newly appointed guide; about twenty yards in front of him and moving steadily farther away. Al picked up his pace. As unappealing as it was, his only real option was to follow the bouncing burro and hope the local cutthroats were too occupied murdering someone they knew to be interested in chopping a complete stranger to pieces. He broke into a trot – which spurred his new-found rationalizing ability; if he was going to survive he needed to get his hands on the water. And the gun. Though Al truly hoped he wouldn't need the rifle, he couldn't rely on hope to save him in the Darien Gap. Carlos had been their safe passage guarantee – but Carlos was now evenly distributed over about a hundred square feet of rainforest floor, so Al didn't really expect anyone he encountered to greet him with open arms.

He didn't need a slide-rule to work out he'd have to be extremely lucky to stay alive for the next couple of days.

But so far, luck didn't really cut it as a likely bedfellow, considering his experiences over the last 24 hours.

# CHAPTER 23

Four black gunships skimmed a few feet above the brutal terrain's treetops as they pressed toward their destination. The grimly determined faces of the SEAL Team Six commandos glowed in the red lighting of the helicopter interiors. No one had spoken since they'd lifted off from the base staging area.

The helicopters moved with an almost eerie silence, their heavily modified forms sound-deadened with special synthetic materials that also made them near radar-neutral. It was impossible to completely silence the massive turbines that powered them, but these choppers were nigh on ninety percent quieter than a stock Sikorsky Blackhawk. The tail rotors bristled with six tempered blades – not the standard four – allowing the rotor speed to be slowed while delivering the same thrust at lower RPMs. That dampened the sound from the rotors slicing through the air, as did the specially designed casings for the tail section, which rounded all sharp edges. The technology, originally developed for the Comanche 'stealth' chopper program, virtually eliminated radar signatures.

The choppers were on radio silence, so the only communications were via the headsets on a local area broadcast network, which was scrambled to prevent interception. The encryption technology was undefeatable – any detected communication would have appeared to be randomly oscillating static.

The SEAL team sat silently watching the ground fly by, mentally preparing for the mission they'd be carrying out. All their gear had been triple checked, and nothing left to chance. The many weeks of preparation would soon culminate in the real thing, and as always, it was impossible to determine how many of the team would make it out alive. There were risks to everything and it was a point of pride for these men to put themselves in harm's way. If some lost their lives, that reflected the price of being one of the elite. It was a cost each man had committed to paying, if necessary.

The group of eight older men who comprised the lead team traveled with each other in their own helicopter. The rest of the squad was fine with that – separation from the others had been the dynamic since day one, and was by now accepted as a perennial aspect of the mission. Once the ships touched down, they'd play out every step that had been choreographed and rehearsed for months. Nothing left to chance – except the fickle unexpected – and every eventuality carefully permutated. Barring their intel having gotten everything wrong, the confidence level, success-wise, was high.

As they came over the crest of the final hill before their target came into focus the pilot of the lead helicopter broke radio silence. "Thirty Seconds to Drop," he announced, almost casually. The wind buffeted the chopper, knocking it around – they'd been warned to expect thirty to forty knot gusts; the forecaster had sure gotten that part right.

A villa nestled inside a high-walled courtyard, virtually impenetrable, as though designed to repel attackers. Razor wire circled the tops of the twelve foot walls, further fortifying the forbidding barrier.

Two of the ships touched down outside the compound and the nine men inside immediately hit the ground and quickly assumed their practiced positions along the perimeter. All wore night-vision goggles and had helmet cameras.

Nothing in the courtyard moved.

The third chopper dropped the eight lead team men inside the compound walls, along with several trunks of equipment. Temporarily out of sight of the soldiers outside the walls, they moved the gear into the nearest doorway and set charges on the main entry door.

The villa was quiet – not surprising given the extremely early hour of the raid. Little activity was anticipated at four a.m. on a Monday. Only this Monday morning was different.

A muffled explosion sent shockwaves from the villa's front entrance before the eight men moved into the house in unison. After several minutes, shooting erupted from a lower floor, followed by silence. Four of the men returned to the front of the house, and carried a trunk back inside with them, quickly returning to gather up the other two.

Minutes went by.

Eventually one of the men sprinted from the main house to the front gate and opened it for the commandos waiting outside. In a practiced move, four took up positions at the front gate, two inside and two out.

The older team emerged from the house with their equipment trunks, as well as a body bag. The leader spoke into his com line – twenty seconds later a helicopter appeared over the courtyard. The men waited until it descended and touched down, and then loaded their gear – and the body – and all but two climbed aboard before it took off, disappearing into the night.

A second chopper was signaled and approached. As it hovered over the courtyard a random gust of wind swung the tail, ever so slightly, into one of the perimeter walls. The gunship immediately tumbled the remaining ten feet, crashing to the ground. The two lead men exchanged glances before climbing aboard to assess the situation.

After a brief discussion the pilot and co-pilot clambered out from behind the controls and jumped to the ground, running for the helicopters still waiting outside the perimeter walls. The two lead men murmured into their headsets and a few moments later three commandos approached carrying heavy backpacks.

Five minutes later the leader gave the clear signal and all personnel returned to the remaining two helicopters. As they lifted off the ground he depressed the button on a radio controller and the grounded helicopter exploded, fragmenting into thousands of burning pieces. Satisfied, he gave a thumbs up sign to the pilot and the two airships flew off into the dark Pakistani sky.

❧❧

Sam was just preparing to leave the office and go home for some well-deserved sleep when his desk phone chirped. He stabbed the line into active status and barked at it on speakerphone.

"Wakefield. What is it?"

"Sir, it's Gomez downstairs."

"Yes. What do you need?" Sam demanded.

"I have a woman here who says she has a drawing for you."

Sam racked his brain. A drawing? Oh. The sketch artist. Well, it really didn't matter anymore now, did it?

"Just get the drawing and hold it for me until I make it down. I was just leaving. Give me about five minutes," Sam instructed.

"Yes, sir," Gomez said. Sam could hear a conversation in the background, and then he came back on the line. "Sir, apparently there's an issue of payment. She says her services are three hundred dollars, and she was told she would be paid when she delivered the drawing."

"Tell her I don't have that kind of money lying around here on a Sunday," Sam said caustically. "She can come back tomorrow for it during business hours."

More muffled discussion.

"She says she will come back tomorrow with the drawing at ten in the morning – she's been up since very early this morning working on it, but if it isn't an emergency anymore she'll come by when you have the money."

"Whatever. Tomorrow's fine. I'll be in by ten, and I'll have her lousy three hundred bucks for her then," Sam declared dismissively.

Now that this mission had drawn to a close, Sam was again the top dog in Panama and wasn't going to dance to anyone else's schedule. He was exhausted, and with Richard gone or on his way to the airport there was no sense of urgency to tie up the last loose threads of a closed operation.

There was nothing more pressing at this moment than getting the stink of Richard's aftershave off his chair back and going home for fourteen hours of shut-eye.

And because she was being such a bitch about it, he'd make sure that the sketch artist got a check tomorrow instead of cash. That way she'd have to go stand in the queue at the bank; an inconvenience any day of the week in Panama, where the lines tended to be serpentine and slow moving. He was so sick of everyone giving him ultimatums, it felt good to be able to dish out a little misery. He'd had an assfull of being told what to do for the last day by that Richard prick, and he'd be damned if he was going to have terms dictated to him by some local sketch artist.

Sam realized it was petty, but so what?

As he was so fond of saying, they all knew where the door was…

# CHAPTER 24

Al mushed on through the dense and wet jungle, following the burro, which presumably wasn't just wandering to its favorite horsey hang-out spot, but rather was walking the path to Colombia as it had done so many times before. He occasionally checked his portable GPS and noted with at least slim confidence that they seemed to be making their way toward the banks of a river that descended from the mountains they'd need to cross to get over the border. Mountains was somewhat of a misnomer – more like tall hills; only a couple of thousand feet at their peaks. But scaling them was far more daunting a task than the elevations initially led one to believe.

The ever looming clouds burst open every two or three hours, which was good in the sense it enabled him to refill his water bottle and cooled him a bit, though bad in every other way. The moisture made the ground treacherous and ensured Al's shoes were half submerged in muck most of the time, creating additional effort on an already brutal journey.

The burro, on the other hand, seemed completely happy to be moving away from the scene of the attack point, and showed no signs of tiring or slowing. The dumpy little beast was relentlessly plodding forward with an unshakeable confidence Al found comforting.

At least one of them knew where they were going.

Al had retrieved the gun and had it strapped over one arm – another AK-47, which apparently was the VW of Central American assault rifles. Whatever – he was glad to have it, even though he recognized he was hardly a match for an armed group of seasoned jungle fighters.

So the plan, such as it was, centered on avoiding the jungle killers.

Step one: Dodge the homicidal gangs. Check.

Step two: Huh. What was step two again? Oh…right…follow the burro's bottom.

Step three: Develop religion, and pray the burro knew its way to Colombia.

Al understood he hadn't hatched a particularly richly evolved plan, nor one that was going to win any prizes for originality, however, at this point if he could make it to civilization alive he'd be glad he adopted it.

They didn't stop except once in the next three hours, and that was for another of Al's potty breaks. The burro seemed to share an affinity with Al's toilet rituals and dutifully watched over him as he struggled to evacuate the malicious toxins that had poisoned his system.

At least I've got my new pal, Al thought grimly to himself as he cinched the belt on his cargo pants back and mentally steeled himself for more walking.

Al's watch made it five o'clock in the evening, which meant this time of year he had maybe three more hours of light remaining. His goal was to reach the banks of the river and get to the lower foothills, thereby having covered almost twenty miles in one day. That would put him at the halfway point but with the hills to contend with *manana*. He was willing to push pretty hard to get the hell out of this mosquito-infested shit-swamp and figured he could make it to the Colombia side by sundown tomorrow if he really moved, and started by six in the morning – or whenever dawn broke.

He plodded along, fading in and out of a pseudo fugue state, wherein he played the day's events through his head over and over. Al recognized he hadn't done a whole lot with his life – not that he was ready to check out quite yet. Even if it was just more cheap rum and a few more by-the-hour romances, it beat the unthinkable alternative…

Al bounced, startled, off the burro's solid rear-end – it had stopped abruptly and stood rooted in the mud.

Crossing the trail thirty yards ahead were two Kuna Indian men and a woman, wearing nothing but shorts and in the female's case a *mola*: a traditional blouse/dress combination fashioned from a patchwork of colorful squares – at one time – now since faded to dull hues by the sun's rays and the jungle's acid embrace. Only one of the two men was armed, carrying an ancient bolt-lock rifle that looked like it belonged to another century. They acknowledged the burro and nodded at Al, who returned the gesture. They disappeared back into the brush surrounding the trail, their destination unknown.

After having seen nothing but spiders the size of bowling balls and occasional monkeys and birds, the silent passing at the intersection to nowhere was disturbingly surreal. Al knew there were small Kuna villages in remote areas of the Darien, but most had relocated to the coast over the last decades, after the fighting in the area had intensified.

The burro resumed its slow gait, and after swigging some more water, Al rejoined its steady pilgrimage to wherever.

Ten minutes later they heard the unmistakable popping of rifle fire in the distance – rapid machine-gun fire, lasting on and off for more than a minute. It came from the south-west, in the general direction the Kuna would have been moving through.

Al froze as the jungle went silent again.

The Indians must have walked into an ambush. Carlos had warned them about the tradition of shooting first and questioning later that formed the law of the land, and Al had just gotten a first-hand lesson of the reality of the threat. The Kuna had been virtually unarmed and only carrying small backpacks, so there was no way they had anything of value with them or posed any sort of a threat. If the shooting signaled what Al figured it did then it was cold-blooded murder of innocents for recreation or practice.

He listened for any hints of pursuit but didn't hear anything. After a few moments he thumbed off the safety on the old Russian assault rifle and nudged the burro into motion again. Every few minutes he stopped to listen attentively, no longer trudging mechanically behind his equestrian buddy. The donkey actually seemed to have better hearing than Al did, given the size of his ears, but Al wasn't willing to bet the farm on its vigilance.

They eventually came to the banks of a wide brown river, which Al knew flowed from the cloud-blanketed hills. By his estimation they could make it to the five hundred foot elevation point before they would need to stop for the night.

They followed the river upstream, sensing the gradual increase in pitch of the surrounding terrain. As the sun set, Al took one last reading on his GPS and confirmed their location. Once satisfied, he ferreted around in the burro's massive saddlebags for something to eat, only to discover that the menu was beef jerky and pretzels.

The burro munched contentedly on grass along the bank of the river before returning to Al's position in the undergrowth fifty yards from the river. Al didn't want to accidentally be stumbled upon by anyone using the stream as their nocturnal smuggling guide, so a night with the ants, snakes and spiders was preferable to being sawed in half by a stream of super-heated lead.

At least they wouldn't need to worry about temperature. Freezing wasn't an option in the tropics. A fire was obviously out of the question, for any hint of light would be an open invitation for a hundred rounds of incoming as a bedtime story. Al preferred to take his chances in the dark, huddled next to the burro, waiting for the cool light of dawn.

❦

The black helicopter transporting the commando lead team touched down on the deck of the aircraft carrier in the Arabian Sea a hundred miles off the coast of Pakistan. The men quickly disembarked and their cargo was transferred into a secure area below.

The body bag was transported to a locked area of the hospital section, where a group waited. All were CIA staffers. They quickly removed the corpse from the bag, and began preparations. After thirty minutes, they were done.

Nobody was allowed in or out of the area. Even in the middle of the ocean on the most secure vessel in the United States Navy, this was a highly classified area.

Back in Langley, a press release had been crafted days before, and it was time to start leaking both the official version of the story, as well as control the unofficial spin that was sure to circulate over the next hours. The official release indicated that Osama Bin Laden had been killed by U.S. commandos in Pakistan early that morning in a daring raid behind Pakistani lines. It claimed that photographs had been taken proving it was Bin Laden who had been shot and whose body was seized, and it further claimed that DNA evidence had conclusively proved that the corpse was, in fact, Bin Laden.

Then, after only a few hours and with no independent corroboration of any of the claims being true, the body was buried at sea because the government assumed nobody would want to claim it (that they never actually asked anyone was a detail they would gloss over) and because they didn't want his grave to become a Mecca for martyrs and prospective terrorists.

The blogosphere was filled with a combination of hate messages celebrating his death or threatening reprisals for his execution or just generally spewing venom to increase dissent and turmoil. The CIA had staffers working round the clock to craft and control the dialog, ensuring that anyone who doubted the official version of events was shouted down or branded a crazy.

In America, it had long been considered heretical and treasonous for the population to question the veracity of the government, in spite of numerous, repeated incidences where the government provably lied. This social adjustment had largely been accomplished by collaborating with a compliant media to parrot whatever the official talking points were, and demonize anyone who dared question the official version.

In this environment the clandestine machine had the power to hatch virtually any implausible fabrication and tout it to a compliant public as reality, and the supposed watchdogs in the press went along with it.

Several foreign press outlets, mainly in the Middle East, covered the amazing attack with considerable skepticism, however, in the U.S. the government's version of events was treated as gospel.

A menace had been brought to justice, and the nation could once again hold its head high. The president's meager approval rating skyrocketed, and re-election looked like a lock.

# CHAPTER 25

Lilliana approached the embassy gates on Monday morning at ten a.m. as requested. She'd managed to get some badly needed sleep and felt optimistic about the day ahead. She presented her card to the marine guard on duty and waited patiently as calls were made and her entrance was cleared.

She walked through the front doors, to be greeted by a secretary, who ushered her to a sitting area. Sam Wakefield hadn't made it in yet, but they expected him shortly. Nobody knew anything about any special project she'd been working on or any payment, so she settled into the comfortable leather seat and enjoyed the chill of the air conditioning.

Forty-five minutes later, the intercom on the secretary's desk buzzed and Lilliana was informed it would be just a few more minutes until her payment would be ready. She looked at her watch – this was turning into a half a day's wait, if one counted sacrificing her morning's work with one of the advertising agencies in the city. Employment for sketch artists in Panama was scarce, so like many moonlighters Lilliana had a day job. But dropping off a sketch that was commissioned on an emergency basis over a weekend and then having to wait forever for payment wasn't what she'd agreed to. She made a mental note to be unavailable next time anyone from the embassy required her services.

Eventually, a staffer came down the stairs and gave her a check as payment.

She wasn't at all happy. Rush jobs were usually paid in cash, not checks, and now she'd have to spend yet more time at the bank, thereby losing more working time at her job. She thanked the staffer and left an oversized manila envelope with the secretary on the way out the doors.

Lilliana was annoyed. This had been far and above the call of duty from her end, and now she was being treated like the cleaning lady.

No, she wouldn't be doing any more work for the embassy. That was for sure.

⁂

Al had gotten virtually no sleep for the second night in a row, and the deprivation was eroding his usually sunny disposition. That, and he hadn't taken a drink in thirty-six hours.

He'd started up the hill at 5:30 and had advanced only four miles through his day's slog by ten a.m.. He could have hiked up the riverbank but the constant and very real threat of crocodiles coupled with high visibility exposure to any human predators made that idea seem like a poor one. Instead, he and his trusty burro friend had forged through until they'd located a game trail that ran roughly parallel to the river, but a hundred yards in the brush. It was virtually impassable in sections, requiring strenuous work with the machete, and by ten Al reeled with exhaustion, soaked with sweat and rain. It drizzled constantly as they increased in elevation, making for a slippery morning constitutional in the Panamanian highlands.

As the day progressed, the two companions made it over the summit and Al could see the Caribbean glimmering in the distance. It didn't look that far to the coast, but Al's GPS told him he still had nine miles to go, which meant arriving anywhere near a safe area by nightfall wasn't a given. But at least he didn't have bullets shredding the leaves around him and it wasn't raining bombs, so the glimmer of the ocean gave him meager cause for optimism.

Now the question was which fishing village to try to get to. He could shoot for Capurgana, which was at the northern tip of Colombia and which had a few hotels and not much else, or veer south to Acandi, which was a larger town in that it actually had streets and some commercial boats.

He was leaning toward Acandi but the terrain looked like it naturally rolled toward Capurgana. In the end, he supposed the burro would be the key because Al really didn't know how to get to either beyond following the now fading screen of his handheld GPS.

Al's stomach affliction had eased over the course of the night so at least that part of his misery was over. As he took a break by a rock outcropping overlooking the Atlantic coast, he stripped off his soaked and bloody socks to inspect his wrinkled feet – a new source of constant pain and suffering. The skin had worn off both of his heels and several toes, and his tennis shoes were a wet, pulpy mess. Al knew this was bad news and that the infection risk was extremely high, but there wasn't much he could do about it other than hope for the best and seek out a doctor as soon as possible.

He considered stuffing some leaves into his shoes for additional padding; but with his luck he figured he'd probably select something poisonous and wind up walking the last few miles into Colombia on stumps. So he wrung out his socks, peeled off the strips of skin adhering to them and pulled them back on, wincing from the burning agony of the raw epidermis grating against the sopping cotton.

Resigned to at least another eight hours of hell on earth, he got to his feet and patted the burro; which he'd decided to call 'Ed' in a moment of weakness the night before. He'd named the burro after Mister Ed, the talking horse who starred in the black and white fifties television comedy.

"*Vamanos*, Eduardo," he whispered to the donkey, who stared at him balefully. "Come on, giddyup!"

The burro resumed its slow passage down the trail into Colombia, and Al actually felt a momentary pang of kinship with the tired beast. They were both making their way through difficult circumstances to the best of their abilities in a harsh environment.

At least the burro was holding up pretty well. Al considered whether he could ride the animal, but dismissed the idea – Ed was the smaller of the two burros the guide had brought, and slight as burros go. He also had a lot of gear stuffed into the packs strapped to his back, so there was no way he could handle Al's couple of hundred pounds of Caucasian fat reserves.

Al made a mental note to take a full inventory of the pack contents before he hit civilization – aside from scrounging around inside for food he hadn't paid much attention to the contents. And once in populated areas he'd probably do better without an AK-47 or an old machete, but if old

Carlos had any cash stashed in one of the packs or if Ernesto's battered backpack contained anything of value, then at least Al could benefit from their bounty. They certainly weren't going to be needing their worldly goods at this point.

He gingerly followed Ed down the hill, into the brush.

Next stop, with any luck, Capurgana...

# CHAPTER 26

The mood at the embassy was buzzing with celebratory undertones. It was hard not to feel a palpable sense of relief that finally, one of the most dangerous terrorists in the world had been taken down.

Obviously, the news about the pre-dawn attack soon became the only topic anyone was interested in talking about. In most offices, CNN was streaming the tidings from the monitors and televisions. It seemed that every hour some new tidbit of information was broken, adding to the sense of momentous events unfolding.

Sam spent most of his day cleaning up the mess from the weekend – thanking his contacts at the police for their help with Carmen, who was still being held pending seeing her attorney today, and denying any connection to the Caucasian men in the brothel attack. A whole lot of lying, but then again that's what Sam did best: a convincing prevaricator, even when exhausted.

So far, there had been no blowback from the botched attack on the cop cruiser, although he noted that the papers were heralding the officer as a modern-day Panamanian gladiator – sort of a tropical version of *The Terminator*. The stock photo did portray a man you wouldn't want to fuck with, Sam conceded. Looks like Don finally met his match. Too bad – it was hard to develop assets who could be relied upon to not only gun down whoever was targeted but also keep their mouths shut afterwards.

Don wasn't going to be talking to anyone now, that was for sure.

The photos of the Land Cruiser on the local news depicted a molten, smoldering steel cage with lumps of unidentifiable goop inside. The vehicle had blazed white hot for some time.

Sam was happy his little drama was over. He could return to business as usual. Of course, there was little chance of that on the day Bin Laden was killed, but then again, he didn't have Richard breathing down his neck so he could cut everyone a little slack. And truth was he still felt beat – even after taking a sleeping pill last night he'd had so much residual adrenaline and caffeine in his system it had only made him groggy. He'd finally dozed off around midnight – but it was a disturbed sleep, filled with amorphous dreams and anxious premonitions.

Given the number of hours he'd clocked the day before, he decided to take the afternoon off and visit his other *familia* – as he referred to the twenty and twenty-one year old Peruvian sisters who did double-duty as his mistresses. The older one was his main squeeze but sometimes when he wanted something really loco she'd invite sis over and they'd pull out all the stops. And if today wasn't a special occasion, he didn't know what would qualify.

Come lunchtime, Sam told his secretary to hold all his calls because he was going to be offsite for meetings during the rest of the day.

He hummed as he bounced down the stairs, thinking about his afternoon's prospects. Sam didn't even notice the envelope in his secretary's inbox, nor did she remember it, glued as she was to the unfolding Bin Laden saga on satellite TV.

There was nothing so urgent that it couldn't wait until tomorrow. Today, of all days, that was especially true.

❧◦❦

Al stood on the outskirts of Capurgana just before dusk, going through Mister Ed's packs before sending him on his way. Freedom was just around the corner for the little fellow – he hoped Ed would find some nice native girl donkey and settle down, raise little ones, or whatever burros in these parts did.

He'd ditched the weapons at the edge of the jungle and unstrapped the two packs, freeing Ed from their sapping weight. In the first he found a collection of threadbare clothes, an extra pair of ancient boots almost worn through at the soles, binoculars, a bible in Spanish, and a water bottle and funnel. There were also random odds and ends of no value – a pair of dilapidated scissors, a pocket knife, a small sewing kit. So no goldmine there.

The other saddle pack contained Ernesto's backpack, as well as a map of Panama, laminated photos of who he presumed must be the world's ugliest grandchildren, and a toothbrush. Oh, but wait – there was a neoprene dive wallet. He opened it and counted $1600 dollars, $1500 of which was obviously Al's $500 and a grand from Carmen's end, as well as another hundred bucks in tens and fives. Al pocketed it and tossed the wallet aside.

His feet were killing him, and it was going to be dark at any moment. He quickly rummaged through the cook's bag and found only clothes, a hygiene kit, a camera and a micro cell-phone. Ernesto had obviously carried his cash with him. Bad luck for Al.

Actually, worse luck for the cook, all things being relative.

Al scratched Ed behind the ears, and pointed to the jungle. "Go on, Ed. Get out of here. You're free now!" he said.

Ed, as always, just stared at him.

Al pulled the burro's big head around and gave him a shove toward the dark vegetation. "*Vamanos*," he exclaimed, slapping Ed on the butt. Ed almost decapitated him with a narrowly-missed kick – no doubt reflexive – and then trotted back to the trail.

Al watched him go, and then set out for one of the largest buildings in the little hamlet – a white Moroccan-styled monument on the beach; no doubt a hotel, considering the epic scale and the lights blazing throughout the property.

He approached the entrance and mounted the stairs. The man behind the reception desk regarded him with distrust – not surprising given that Al looked as though he'd been dragged through broken glass behind a motorcycle gang.

"I need a room for the night," Al said in passable Spanish.

"Hmmmmm. I seeeeeee. Perhaps you would like to see the rates first?" the receptionist responded politically.

"No, it's fine. I just need a room. Something simple, and I'll pay cash," Al said, figuring that was a universal language in every country.

"Dollars or…?"

"Dollars. For one night. And if there's a doctor in town, I'll need to see if you can get him to come over. I have a problem with my feet – I've been hiking for days and wasn't completely prepared…" Al explained.

"Ah. Hiking. Yessss. I seeeeee." The man made a show of studying the register. "We have a good room for you, 301, and only $80 for tonight," the man said, smiling.

Robbery, but Al had no capacity to argue. He was exhausted and in pain.

"Fine. I'll take it." He thumbed through his cash below the counter, out of view of the receptionist, and handed him the money. "And like I said, I really need a doctor for my feet. Can you get someone?" he asked.

"*Si*, of course. I'll make the call right away. Just please sign the register, yes?" the man requested, sliding a key to him.

Al signed unintelligibly. The clerk seemed utterly uninterested in seeing ID or anything besides greenbacks. Which suited Al fine.

A tired looking teenage boy approached from the back office and offered to take his satchel and Ernesto's bag. Al declined. The boy rolled his eyes, and pointed to the stairs, indicating the direction to take to find his room.

"See if you can find me a bottle of something strong and bring it up to the room along with a package of cigarettes, Marlboro reds if you can. And get the doctor over here as soon as possible," he instructed, handing the boy a ten dollar bill. The boy stood blinking at him but didn't move. Al put another ten in his hand, and he nodded and disappeared around a corner.

Al limped up the creaking stairs and found his room. He swung open the door and surveyed the aged interior with a combination of dismay and relief. After tossing his bags on a cane chair he turned on the air conditioner, which worked, to his surprise. Maybe his luck was turning. He debated a shower, but figured he'd wait for the doctor before he did anything else.

After twenty minutes of luxuriating with the AC blowing full blast the doctor knocked at the door. When Al opened it he saw the bellboy standing behind the doctor holding a paper bag.

The doctor came into the room and the boy handed him his bottle and cigarettes. Al told him to keep the change, and he rolled his eyes again. *Big spender.*

The doctor did a cursory examination of his shredded and blistered feet and handed him a tube of antibiotic ointment after writing a quick prescription, explaining that the cream should be enough, but to get the oral antibiotics if there was any additional redness or signs of infection. The house call cost $20, which was the first time Al felt anything he'd encountered in Capurgana was even close to reasonably priced.

According to the small menu on the table, the hotel restaurant provided room service, so Al ordered two portions of grilled fish for dinner, along with two cold beers. The fish appeared half an hour later, which he hastily devoured, spitting out the odd stray bone. He'd already started on his bottle of local rum, and that, coupled with a quarter pack of cigarettes, made the pain from his trip recede to a dull ache. By the time he was done with the fish and the beer he was over halfway through the bottle.

Al looked at his watch. If half a bottle of rum had made him feel almost human, then the other half would have him feeling good as Ghandi. He took a few more deep pulls on the bottle before struggling with the ointment, managing to get a glob onto both feet before he fell back onto the bed. He closed his eyes, just for a few moments, to clear his head. The AC felt like heaven, even as the room spun.

He wondered how Ed was faring since the parting of their fellowship. Damned if he didn't kind of miss the scruffy beast.

He started snoring.

❧

Sam whistled as he entered his office on Tuesday morning. He felt refreshed, had caught up on his sleep and enjoyed a few hours of adult relaxation with his mistress and her sis.

The distinctively strong smell of his private label coffee permeated his office suite; waiting to be poured. Things were back to normal. Thank God. He plopped down in his swivel chair and began sorting through the accumulated pile of paperwork stuffed in his inbox. Reports, advisements, routine forms, and a large manila envelope with his name scrawled on it.

Sam searched his memory and recalled the sketch artist from the other night. He supposed it to be a dead issue but opened the envelope anyway and glanced at the drawing before tossing it into the trash.

He swiveled toward his computer and typed in his password. His screen popped up. He began sorting through his e-mails, when his eyes strayed back to the trash can. There was something odd about the man the sketch artist had drawn. He couldn't place it, but the guy looked familiar. Sam reached into the can, extracted the wad of crumpled paper and smoothed it out on his desk. He stared at it. The face nagged at his subconscious. Sam supposed that these types of drawings probably looked like a lot of people due to their lack of specificity, but there was something about this one…

Then it hit him.

No way. Had to be coincidence.

Sam picked up his telephone handset and dialed Al's cell. It rang, and went to voice mail.

"Hey buddy. Call me when you get this. Just checking in to see how the weekend went," Sam said, and hung up.

He next called Al's little satellite office in Colon. The secretary picked up.

"Is Al there? It's Sam Wakefield," he announced.

"Uh, no, I'm afraid Mr. Ross isn't in at the moment. Can I take a message?" the secretary asked in heavily accented but fluent English.

Sam ignored her question. "Do you expect him in soon?"

"He…I haven't heard from him yet this morning, Mister Wakefield, so I don't know," she admitted.

"Was he in yesterday?" Sam asked, already dreading the answer.

"No, I didn't see him. Is there a message I can leave for him?" she asked.

"Tell him to call me as soon as he gets in, or gets my message, please."

"Yes, Mister Wakefield. Will do. Have a nice day," she said.

So Al had gone AWOL. That wasn't earth-shatteringly unusual – Al had a habit of being 'under the weather' on Mondays, and it was hit-or-miss as to whether he would show up. But today was Tuesday.

Sam was getting a bad feeling.

He dialed Al's home number, which rang four times before going to his answering machine. Sam called the cell again. Voice mail.

"Yo, buddy, it's me again," Sam began. "I was just checking in to see if you're okay. The office says you haven't been in, and I was hoping to get a hold of you. Could you please call as soon as you can?" Sam left his cell and office numbers.

He stared at the drawing a few more minutes, then shook his head. What the hell had Al gotten involved in this time? The more he looked at it, the more obvious it became to him that it had to be Al.

Sam had long been searching for ways to make Al's life miserable, and now he finally had something tangible. A delicious wave of elation swept over him. Al was no doubt into all sorts of sketchy dealings, and it looked like it had finally caught up with him. Sam could crank up the heat under the pretense he was only doing his job – this might even be a career-ender for Al. He reconsidered the unpleasant days he'd just spent with that asshole, Richard. Perhaps it had all been worth it after all. Fate had suddenly graced him with the ability to become Al's nemesis – he could inflict maximum damage on the sad fuck, and Sam wasn't the sort to pass up on that kind of opportunity.

He considered his next step, and with mischief in mind, turned to his monitor and rapidly tapped at his keyboard. Sam would get an all points bulletin out to the police, so whenever and wherever Al surfaced the cops would quickly grab him. He didn't know why the Agency had wanted to terminate the cook, so he wasn't exactly sure why Al was relevant, but it wouldn't hurt to get the word out so Al would get picked up. He was probably drunk somewhere, out on a three day bender, which would make it even better when he got nabbed – even if he denied the drawing was him, being absent and drunk for days would be a body-blow with the State Department. And if the drawing was him, Al would never be able to deny it convincingly – he was barely able to keep a grip from day to day, and had no poker face at all. Sam conjured up a mental image of a bewildered and scared-looking Al sitting handcuffed in a police cruiser. He smiled. Either way, Sam could ensure that Tuesday was a bad day for Al Ross.

He put the finishing touches on the inter-agency advisory that would culminate in a bulletin to the locals, and smiled yet again.

Sam pushed send, and walked out to Melody's desk. He instructed her to scan and attach the drawing to the memo he'd just created and sent to her. She looked at the crumpled sketch dubiously and nodded. It would be done in a matter of a few minutes.

Sam returned to his office and closed his door. This was turning into a good week already. First they off Bin Laden, then Al steps into poop up to his knees. Sometimes the wind filled your sails and everything flowed effortlessly – after years of tormenting the feckless war hero, Sam finally had a good shot at landing a knockout punch. A killer-punch, even. Take that, mister purple heart.

His phone rang, and he took a call from one of the other department heads; who wanted a meeting to go over some mind-numbingly tedious procedural issues. As the man babbled on and on, Sam felt his will to live being sucked through the phone. He eventually disengaged, and returned to considering the destruction of Al.

There was a downside to all this he hadn't immediately considered. It was possible Al had been killed when Richard's team had terminated the cook. Sam doubted Al would have been trekking through the Darien Gap, but you couldn't second-guess what a drunken idiot would do. That's what made idiots dangerous. With smart people, you could calculate their next steps by discarding behavior that would be obviously harmful to them. Smart people avoided self-destruction whenever possible. But idiots were too stupid to compute how their actions might be dangerous to themselves, so they were far harder to predict.

Sam thought it through. If the drawing was Al, which he now believed it was, and if Al had lost his mind and decided to play Tarzan with the cook, then he was as dead as Bin Laden by now. If he hadn't been with the cook, then he was probably holed up in some gin joint or whorehouse on a bender, in which case he would turn up shortly and Sam would have someone question him.

There was always the possibility that he was into something sinister and had gone to ground, but Sam couldn't believe Al would be any part of a scheme that involved him as anything other than a mere pawn – the man was a zero, a zombie. He couldn't be trusted to tie his own shoes.

No, either the resemblance to the drawing was an eerie fluke, in which case Al would still catch hell for dereliction of duty over the last two days, or it *was* him, in which case he was intoxicated somewhere after collecting money for whatever he was involved in – or at the most remote end of the spectrum, he was blown to pieces in the Darien.

But now Sam had another problem, and this one gave him pause. If Al was involved in whatever the cook had been involved in, then Richard would need to be informed, which would re-introduce a massive irritant back into Sam's life. That was to be avoided if at all possible. Sam weighed his possible responses.

What he'd do is wait and see what the police dragged in. If, as he suspected, Al was drunk out of his mind then Sam could get him into a cell at the embassy, and *then* he would call Richard, who could do his worst. That actually had some appeal for Sam. But if Al was dead, then there was no point in inviting Richard back into his life. Dead men stayed dead, and their secrets with them. In which case, Al would never be heard from again,

Richard would never have any reason to look Sam's way, and the world would continue to turn for Sam in peaceful rotation.

As with most decisions, self-interest ruled the day for Sam.

He'd wait and see before kicking the hornet's nest.

No matter what, though, Al was going to find himself in the middle of a shit-storm, unless he was already playing pat-a-cake with Satan in the seventh circle of hell.

# CHAPTER 27

A loud banging at the hotel door woke Al. He bolted upright, startled by the clamor, unsure of his surroundings. Then it all came back to him. Colombia. Gun battles. Grenade attacks. Burros.

He padded gingerly over to the door and cautiously opened it. A maid, all of five feet tall, stood defiantly at the door, mop in hand. She pointed at her watch and looked around Al and into the room, disapproval evident on her face.

Al told her he would be staying one more day, and to go away, please. His Spanish was adequate for the job – she apparently understood. She glanced one last time into Al's lodgings and then moved down the hall to the next room. He closed the door and surveyed his surroundings.

He'd obviously slept in his clothes. Again. That was evident from the smell, as well as the fact he was wearing them. The rum bottle rested on the small hotel table with a few fingers remaining in the bottom. That explained why his head felt like he'd gone ten rounds with a prize fighter.

Al stumbled into the bathroom and turned on the shower, emptying his pockets onto the small glass shelf above the sink. He entered the hissing stream of water fully clothed. He soaped his shirt, then his pants, and after removing them, did the same for his underwear. The process took ten minutes. His feet felt like he'd been dancing on razor blades.

He dried off and set about washing his socks in the sink; noting that they were good for maybe one more wearing before it was time for new ones. Al ruefully studied his reflection – not only did he have the trademark bloodshot hangover eyes, but he was almost beet red from sunburn and sported three days of stubbly growth on his face. He'd seen homeless men who looked better, but there wasn't anything to be done about it right now. Al considered shaving, then dismissed it, choosing to instead splash water on his cheeks and call it a day.

Morning cleanup over, he donned his wet underwear, wrung out his clothes, and set them out on the little porch facing the beach, spread on his chair. They'd dry in a matter of minutes in the harsh tropical sun.

His watch said it was noon. Tuesday.

So here he was, in bumfuck Colombia with no idea how he was going to get back to Panama, nor who was chasing him, nor why – assuming anyone was still doing so and the entire affair hadn't ended with the aerial strike in the middle of the jungle. Al thought that most likely – after all, 'they' had been after the cook and they'd gotten him in a resoundingly final way. Game over.

His head pounded in time with his heart. He lit his first cigarette of the day and reached over to pick up the hotel phone. The reception desk answered.

"*Bueno*," a female voice said.

"*Sí*, hello. This is *senor* Alberto in room 301," Al explained. "I've decided to stay another night. I hope you can accommodate me a little longer…"

"Fine, sir. I'll make a note of it," the receptionist said.

That out of the way, he needed to figure out how he was going to proceed from here. The obvious place to start was with the person who'd gotten him involved in all this to begin with.

He picked up the phone again and spoke with the receptionist, giving her a Panama number and asking to be connected. The girl told him it would be just a few moments.

Ernesto's backpack started vibrating and emanated a lively salsa tune. Al walked over and rooted around in it, retrieving a little pink cell phone. Great. He hung up the hotel phone, and sat on the bed, staring at the cell in disbelief.

Apparently Ernesto had very sticky fingers indeed. This was Carmen's cell phone, presumably lifted from her office when the commotion had kicked off. Which meant Al had no way of getting in touch with her – he only had her mobile number.

Nice work, Ernesto.

He considered who else he could call, but noticed the cell phone wouldn't be a whole lot of good to him as the low battery icon was blinking. Too bad Ernesto hadn't considered stealing a charger while he was at it. Al figured he might as well give it a try, though, and entered his own cell phone number from memory. A Spanish recording came on advising him the number he'd dialed wasn't in service – a result of his not dialing the area code and country code. He tried again with the country code, and went into voice mail.

Three messages, the first two from Sam. Second one sounded strident. Al wondered what Sam was in such a rush to discuss with him. The third message was from his secretary, asking him to contact the office ASAP, and that Sam Wakefield had called, requesting he call immediately.

Al jotted down the number and checked the battery indicator. It showed dead. He hoped it would last just a little longer. He dialed Sam's cell number, and he picked up on the third ring.

"Wakefield."

"Sam, it's Al. You called?" Al figured he'd start out soft and then ask him for help once he found out what Sam wanted.

"Al! Jesus. You're…" Sam almost blurted 'alive' but caught himself. "…you're not in your office. Are you okay?"

Sam sounded weird. What else was new? Sam *was* weird.

"Yeah, well, some shit happened so I haven't been able to make it in yet," Al said.

"Shit? Like what? Where are you?" Sam quickly asked.

"Dude, you're never going to believe it," Al said. "It's been a really terrible couple of days. I need to ask you a favor," he continued.

"Absolutely, Al. Just name it. You need me to come get you out of a jam or something? Where are you?" Sam offered, asking again.

"It may be harder than you think, Sam. I'm in Colombia and I need you to get me back into Panama and let me stay somewhere safe until I can figure out what the hell is going on. I've been shot at, bombed, chased…" Al blurted.

"Colombia! How did you get there?"

"Don't ask." The phone beeped, and then went dead.

Damn. Didn't that just figure.

Al tossed the phone into his satchel with a curse. That had gone about as well as everything else had lately. He went out onto the terrace and checked on his clothes. They were dry, or at least dry enough. Al dutifully smeared ointment on his feet and got dressed.

He picked up the hotel phone and ordered room service again – more fish and more cold beer. He hadn't gotten sick last night so the fish was probably safe to eat while he planned his next step.

First thing, Al wanted to slip away from the hotel after lunch, preferably unseen, so he could avoid having to pay for his room service meals or any late checkout charges. Why blow a bunch of money when he was a man of limited means? He contemplated how to most easily execute this and realized it wouldn't be simple – he had to walk past the reception desk to leave the hotel. So the best way to handle it would be through stealth and misdirection. Al was good at that.

He stuffed Ernesto's video camera and hygiene kit into the satchel and left the rest of the cook's belongings in the man's battered backpack. Having removed everything of value, he could abandon the bag there, lulling the hotel into a feeling of security. He tossed a few of Ernesto's clothing items around the room to suggest it was still occupied and put the backpack in a prominent position on the bed. It looked like Al wasn't going anywhere today. Perfect.

A knock at the door announced that room service had arrived. He opened for the waiting bellman, and in came the food. Al signed for it, generously adding a large tip to be covered later. The bellman thanked him and glanced around, asking Al's permission to take the prior night's dinner tray.

Once the man departed Al wolfed down the salty fish and finished the rum, along with the beers. Now we were talking. He felt like a new man, or at least a slightly less used one.

His watch beeped one o'clock – time to move on. He hoped there was a pay phone somewhere in the tiny village. The first order of business would be to find it and call Sam back – his clandestine contacts were Al's best shot at getting back into Panama and staying safe. He gathered his things and put the pack of cigarettes in his shirt pocket. His nerves had settled now that he'd had enough alcohol to chase away the morning scaries, and he liked his odds of bluffing his way past the receptionist.

Show time.

Al walked down the stairs, still limping a bit, and spontaneously decided to tackle the front desk head on. He approached the clerk and asked where the nearest market was. The clerk hesitantly gave him directions before Al cut him off; instructing the clerk to have his room made up and cleaned while he was out, and to please give him two bars of soap this time instead of just one; it was inconvenient to share the same bar between the basin and shower. Al told him that he'd be back within an hour, and there'd be a tip if it was done by the time he returned.

The man apologized for the soap confusion and told him that of course he would see to it that the room was cleaned and appropriately outfitted.

Al made his way out of the hotel and down the dirt road in the direction of the market. People were so incredibly gullible. It was practically a lock that the clerk would scramble to make things right. Thanks for the free fish and brews, suckers, he thought, then some unfamiliar part of him immediately regretted his insult – maybe he was going soft or afraid that karma would bite him on the ass…

He limped around a bend, picking up the pace as he spotted the market, if you could call it that. More like the local outhouse with a cash register. A group of the more listless natives loitered casually in front of it, watching the world go by as they passed a bottle around. Oh well, he rationalized. Beggars couldn't be choosers.

He hoped they sold cold beer.

☙◦❧

Sam's heart pounded and his thoughts raced in all directions after the phone in his hand went dead.

Al was alive. But in Colombia.

That was a disaster.

Then again, it sounded like he didn't suspect anything, at least not on Sam's end – potentially a huge advantage; one that he hoped he could use to lure him somewhere they could grab him.

He hated to, but he knew it was time to call Richard. The thought of the man's voice, even over the phone, sent chills up Sam's spine. But he had no choice.

Or did he?

Was there some way he could pull a rabbit out of a hat, and bring Al in on his own? As long as he had his trust, it was plausible.

Sam considered his last attempt at doing something on the sly.

That hadn't ended well.

No, in the end this was Richard's operation so Al was his problem, not Sam's. Much as he disliked dealing with him, it was better to hand it off to Richard than wait around and jeopardize things further.

He called the secure Langley number and was told Richard was unavailable. That figured. It was just like the dismissive A-hole to blow him off. Sam left his number, told the disembodied voice on the other end of the line it was urgent, and hung up.

He'd tried his best.

There was little else he could do except arrange for a bulletin to go out via the Colombian police so Al would have a hard time moving around.

Sam drafted another memo and sent it off. It would take a while, but once his counterpart in Colombia got the word out, at least they had a shot that Al would get picked up by the local cops. It was the only thing he could do until he heard back from Richard – or until Al called again.

# CHAPTER 28

Al relished his bottle of Bavarian beer as he trudged slowly down the beachfront dirt road. The beer wasn't icy cold, though cool enough to afford him relief in the muggy heat.

The downside to his foray so far, besides lightning bolts of pain in his feet with each step, was that the only pay phone in the tiny fishing village was broken. Probably had been for a year, by the looks of it.

Clearly, Capurgana had been abandoned by the tourist crowds. It was dirt poor, with not a whole lot to it other than a few lackluster hotels, a passable beach and the persistent odor of fish; Al quickly realized he would need to get to a more developed area to have any serious options. Rural was a wildly charitable descriptor for the small hamlet, and Al almost pitied Ed if he'd hung around to try his luck with the local burro talent, or whatever sexy lady donkeys were called in these parts.

Trudging farther down the road from the market, he came upon a group of dilapidated fishing boats landed halfway up the beach. Little more than elongated rowboats with ancient outboard motors. Al meandered over to the first vessel, which was tied to a palm tree. In Spanish, he asked the man who was leaning against the tree about renting it to take him to the nearest real town. The old fisherman laughed and asked which metropolis Al had in mind.

Al withdrew his handheld GPS from his satchel, powered it up, and zoomed-out the map. Acandi was only about ten miles down the coast, but there were no roads from Acandi to anywhere else, so while larger than Capurgana it didn't really do anything in terms of improving Al's transportation choices. Across the gulf was Necocli, and further south, Turbo.

Al asked the man about the three possible destinations. The old man cackled again. He sized Al up, and told him that in one of these boats there was little chance of anyone wanting to go to Necocli because the seas kicked up and got snotty in the afternoon. Forty miles across open sea to Necocli might have seemed benign on a map, but it was a possible death sentence in a small fishing boat if the weather turned ugly.

After some back and forth, the man offered to take him to Acandi for twenty dollars, and if the seas stayed mild on the way there, to continue to Turbo for fifty dollars. Al asked him why so much to go to Turbo, and he explained it was almost sixty miles by sea, taking three hours in his boat, which he insisted was the finest in the area. Al regarded it skeptically – it was maybe thirty-five feet long and five feet wide, with a single large outboard motor and a deteriorating strip of canvas mounted overhead to shield the occupants from the worst of the sun.

Al hesitated, and the man pointed out that he would have to spend the night in Turbo, sleeping anchored in the harbor, so Al was really paying for a round trip for the boat plus a hard night on the hook, even though Al would only be going one way.

Al didn't feel like he had a lot of negotiating room given the hotel would be looking for him soon. He'd saved twenty bucks on the meals, so he figured he might as well try his luck on a boat ride. He shook hands with the ancient mariner – who introduced himself as Adrian – and reiterated that if possible he'd rather go to Turbo. Adrian rolled his eyes skyward and motioned at the horizon. If the fates wanted it, they'd go. If not, it was a forty-five minute trip to Acandi.

Adrian untied the boat and Al helped him push it completely into the surf. Al climbed in, the salt water burning his feet as he did so. Adrian jumped from the beach onto the bow, climbing nimbly around Al to the rear. The outboard started with a single pull, which Al interpreted as an auspicious sign, and then they were off, cutting through the small waves at a rapid clip. Al sat in the middle of the boat's length, his weight acting as a natural leveling mechanism, offsetting the tendency of the bow to lift at speed. Thankfully the water was relatively flat – Al was prone to motion sickness – especially seasickness.

The trip to Acandi lasted only for an uneventful half hour so Adrian gave Al the thumbs up sign and pointed the bow farther out to sea. The coastline was breathtakingly beautiful, with myriad small islands and reefs offsetting the turquoise Caribbean water. A few random pelicans took up flying sentry duty off the boat's stern, as if to keep the men company on their voyage. It would have been idyllic if Al hadn't been slowly sobering up and mentally replaying the numerous fatal encounters of the last few days.

He quickly became bored with watching the water go by, and his mind turned to his main problem – how to figure out why Ernesto had been stalked and killed, and more importantly, how to determine whether he was in any real peril. He didn't want to go back to Panama if accomplished gunmen were waiting for him, and so far his instinct was that, having been with Ernesto, he remained in danger until proven otherwise. Maybe that was an over-reaction, but then again it had been raining grenades just a few days earlier, so perhaps a little caution was prudent.

He'd no way of knowing how Carmen had made out in the gunfight, and who, if anyone, she'd talked to about him escorting Ernesto to the rendezvous point, so he had to assume the worst. He wished he understood what this whole nightmare was about. Trying to operate in the dark wasn't helping, and being unable to contact Carmen posed a serious problem, assuming he believed whatever she told him. Al doubted it, but it was always possible that she had leaked Ernesto's whereabouts to whoever he was trying to escape from and thrown them to the wolves.

His thoughts drifted as the boat bounced over the small waves, eventually turning to the camera Ernesto had secreted in his backpack. Al couldn't imagine how a camera justified a killing spree. Then again, he hadn't watched the video, so he didn't know what Ernesto had filmed. The man hadn't really had any other possessions to speak of, unless he'd had blood diamonds stuffed in an orifice, so it looked like the camera was the cause of all the drama.

If so, it had to be something pretty inflammatory and of tremendous value to someone powerful or dangerous. Or both. Perhaps Ernesto was blackmailing someone in the Panamanian government? Maybe he had footage of someone big playing slap and tickle with a fifteen year old boy?

He made a mental note to check the camera once he wasn't pounding through the ocean at twenty knots with spray spattering sea water over him as he held on for dear life.

Sam's office phone rang. The direct line, not through his secretary. He picked up, and Richard's abrasive voice barked at him.

"What's so important, Wakefield? This better be good," Richard seethed.

Sam told him about the sketch artist, and about the aborted phone conversation with Al. Richard was silent for a full thirty seconds.

"And how long did you have the sketch before you made the connection?" Richard asked.

"Uh, well, sir, we got it on Monday, but with all the commotion it didn't get pursued until today, when he called. I thought it wouldn't be an issue if he wasn't…active anymore."

Another long silence.

"How well do you know this guy?" Richard asked.

"I've known him for over twenty years, since the service…but we aren't close," Sam added hurriedly.

"You've known him for that long, you're both living in Panama City, and you aren't close?" Richard summarized incredulously.

"He's an acquaintance. Someone I know from the military. Maybe we have a drink now and then, say every four months or so. The guy's got serious problems with booze, gambling, you name it…" Sam wanted to distance himself as much as possible.

"Married?" Richard inquired.

"No, sir. He's a loner. I'll e-mail you his file," Sam said. "He's a walking disaster. I'm completely surprised he's still got a job, much less with the State Department."

"Any idea what he was doing with the cook?" Richard asked.

"None. There's a lot here that doesn't add up. But it was a whorehouse, and Al's definitely that kind of guy, so who knows?"

Yet another pause.

"This needs to be contained, Sam. I'll be on a plane back to Panama within the hour. Tell me what, if any, steps you've taken so I understand what we're dealing with," Richard said, calmly, which alarmed Sam more than anything else he could have done.

"I put out a bulletin through the embassy in Bogota," Sam said. "Which hopefully by now has made it to the police, with the sketch and a general 'Approach with Caution, Hold' advisement. But you know how that goes in areas where we don't have much pull – it can take a while to circulate, and there's no telling how good cooperation will be."

"So you already put this out? Is there any way to retract it?" Richard asked.

"I don't understand, sir. I thought we wanted to bring him in…" Sam stuttered.

"Sam. I need this kept low key. Let me rephrase this. How long will it take for you to cancel the bulletin?" Richard asked, clearly annoyed.

"Colombia's tough, sir. It's so fragmented, so many factions and so much drug money circulating, there's no telling whether we'll ever hear anything. My guess is if I put through a cancellation it'll work through the system within 12 hours. Maybe less. For all I know, it hasn't even gone out to the police yet," Sam offered hopefully.

"Do it. Immediately. I do not, repeat not, want this Al character touched by the locals, is that clear? I'll be down there within six hours to deal with things. If you hear from him, call my cell. It'll be on even while I'm in the air." Richard gave him the number.

"Okay. I'm on it."

"And Sam, if he calls you again, find out specifically where in Colombia he is. Promise whatever you need to, but find out – and then call me. Don't take any action of your own," Richard emphasized.

"Will do, sir."

A thought occurred to Richard.

"Did you run a trace on the number he called you from? Is it a mobile phone? If so, let's track it," Richard said.

Shit. That hadn't occurred to Sam with everything else going on. He'd been so busy trying to arrange for Al's fall from grace, he'd spaced on the obvious.

"Not yet, sir. But I will as soon as I'm off the line," Sam mumbled.

"Sam. You had time to put out a bulletin to Colombia, but not to trace the phone so we can locate him?" Richard sighed, obviously exasperated. "Are you kidding me? Is this your first day on the job? How did you even get your position with the Agency?" Richard asked.

"I…I don't know what to say, sir," Sam began. "I know I should have done that. It's just been hectic here, so I missed it. It won't happen again. But you know it could take a few hours to triangulate the signal."

More silence.

"Sam, if anything even remotely questionable transpires before I get there, anything that even has a whiff of you buying your buddy some time by making slips, I'll personally cuff you and file treason charges. Do you read me?" Richard over-enunciated every syllable.

Sam swallowed audibly. "Loud and clear, sir."

# CHAPTER 29

At six o'clock, with a few more hours of daylight left, Adrian pulled his old *panga* boat into the bay that sheltered Turbo from the open Caribbean sea. He expertly glided up to one of the commercial docks, and pocketing the cash Al handed him, tied the boat to the piling so Al could disembark.

Al's ass felt like it had been pounded with a board for the last three hours. The waves had kicked up as the day had worn on, and they'd spent a good deal of the trip slamming over the sea's surface. He made a mental note never, ever, ever to get into another *panga* as long as he lived.

That pain steadily receded as he moved into town from the dock, his raw feet reminded him that hiking didn't agree with him any more than boating.

His first impression of Turbo placed it firmly in the world class poop-hole category. The heady atmosphere smelt like a combination of sewage, decaying seaweed and contaminated mud. Even after his brief sojourn exploring the wonders of Capurgana, which was as low end as anyplace he'd ever been, Turbo struck him as a real dump.

He'd made a mental list of things to do and finding a pay phone was priority number one. As he passed a dismally poor looking little market he quickly re-prioritized – he was parched from the trip and in need of hydration.

After a few minutes in the store he emerged with a *Ballena* of beer in a bag – a liter of high octane malt liquor. He walked up the block, if you could call it that, to where the store keeper had told him he could find a pay phone. He sorted through the coins he'd gotten as change, fed them all into the slot and dialed the number he'd scrawled on a scrap of soap wrapper at the hotel. Sam answered on the first ring.

"Hello? Al? Is that you?" Sam offered by way of greeting. His cell had obviously popped up with a Colombian phone number.

"*Si, senor,*" Al intoned, feeling somewhat better having chugged half the beer while approaching the phone.

"Where are you?" Sam asked.

"I told you," Al said. "I'm in Colombia. And Sam, I kind of could use your help."

"Sure, Al, whatever you need. I'm here for you, buddy."

That was odd. Al thought he'd have to spend a while talking Sam into coming to his aid. He knew Sam secretly harbored feelings of envy that made him a little petulant sometimes. Maybe Al had misjudged the man for all these years? He fished out a cigarette and lit it, blowing smoke into the heavy air surrounding the outdoor phone.

"What I need is for you to look into a shooting that happened at a whorehouse on Saturday night – a place called Esperanza in old town. I need to talk to the woman who runs the place, and I want to make sure she's okay," Al said. He didn't want to explain more to Sam if he didn't have to.

"Uh, okay, buddy. I can do that. But why don't you tell me where you are, exactly, so I can see about getting you back here?" Sam asked – immediately regretting his haste. Even to him it sounded too pushy, and overly interested in Al's specific location.

The phone clicked twice and went dead. Al had run out of time.

Al's frustration almost overwhelmed his gut, which had rumbled that Sam's eagerness to help was far too out of character. The guy was a prick, after all, and Al had been shot at enough times in the last few days to be justifiably paranoid, and his nerves were signaling that maybe Sam didn't have his best interests at heart. But why?

Then Al remembered the man dangling from the end of the rope in the jungle, and his comments in perfect English. Was it possible the guy wasn't a private gunman after all? Had Carmen gotten him into something that had put him at odds with the CIA? What the fuck was going on?

Maybe his nerves were shot and he was reading too much into Sam's good Samaritan thing…

Al needed more change to call back, so he decided to return to the market. Halfway there he froze at the sight of two uniformed Colombian police standing in front flirting with three teenage girls. He didn't know whether drinking from an open container was considered a no-no in Colombia and didn't want to risk finding out the hard way – the lady at the market might have put the beer in a bag for a reason. He slowly turned, and realized he was standing next to their police truck – he wasn't used to seeing the rural Colombian version of a cop vehicle so he hadn't even registered it as he'd passed by. He glanced inside, and caught sight of a white fax sheet laying on the seat.

It was a crude drawing, but unmistakably one of him. If there was any doubt, his embassy photo was on the fax next to the drawing – although that looked nothing like Al's appearance now, given that it was over four years and thirty pounds ago. And he'd actually possessed a decent amount of hair…

Al trundled back up the block, strolling as unhurriedly as his internal panic allowed, past the phone and further into town – just a random tourist backpacker exploring the wonders of Turbo.

This was bad. He knew that much. And the photo confirmed his instinct about Sam – there weren't a lot of ways the Colombian civil police in the boonies could have gotten his embassy photo other than with Agency cooperation.

What the hell was he going to do now? What did the Colombians even want with him? He hadn't done anything…

The camera.

It had to be.

Al caught sight of his tanned reflection in a dingy store window and realized with some relief that, disheveled and unshaved for four days, he looked little like the drawing and even less like his old photo. Still, he was a Gringo in Colombia, and as such would stick out. Even though he didn't bear a strong resemblance to the drawing it was too close for comfort.

He needed to change his appearance and find out what, if anything, was on the video. But where could he do it in peace?

Al turned another street corner, where the already-seedy area degraded further. A crudely-lettered hand painted sign advertized a 'Hostel' outside of a peeling building. That was just the sort of establishment he needed.

He entered the tiny lobby area, which was more like a dark, poorly-converted twelve by twelve living room with a desk on the far end.

A three hundred pound woman appraised him. "Eight Thousand Pesos, or five dollars for the night, and you have to share the bathroom," she announced dispassionately, by way of introduction.

Now that was more Al's speed. Completely off the radar, and cheaper than a meal. He quickly paid her, and she handed him a key on a grimy piece of twine attached to an old piece of driftwood.

"Number one." She indicated out into a dirt courtyard, around which were arranged five ramshackle cottages. One dwelling was labeled '*Bano*' and the others were numbered one through four.

He crossed the yard and unlocked the door of his new billet, taking in the *feng shui* of the dusty interior, which was furnished with a narrow, rock-hard mattress covered with a suspiciously colored sheet and blanket. A creaky table with a single chair complemented this centerpiece, and a delaminating mirror hung lopsidedly on the far wall. All in all a charming little boudoir, Al decided. He locked the door behind him and peered out the single window. Nice. He had a view of a dirt alley that ran behind the building – and it looked like tonight or tomorrow was trash collection day.

He flipped the wall switch, and the overhead fan began a creaky rotation, causing the single light bulb mounted in the hub to flicker occasionally. He threw himself onto the bed and stared at the filthy plastic blades orbiting the precariously mounted shaft. After a few minutes he realized he wasn't accomplishing anything so he reluctantly pulled himself to his feet, opened his satchel and withdrew the hygiene kit. Ernesto had acquired a cheap electric razor, which thankfully had the cord attached. So no worries about batteries. He'd go to work on his makeover in a few minutes – right after he got a look at the video camera's contents. Maybe it would reveal what kind of trouble he was in.

As he pulled out the camera, Carmen's dead phone clattered against the wooden floorboards after falling out of the bag, finally settling under the bed. Al leaned over to look for it but soon lost interest when he saw the myriad spider webs on the underside of the box spring. Oh well, it was a goner, anyway. His attention returned to the camera.

Sony HCR-Z5U. Expensive looking. Someone had spent serious coin on making movies.

He fumbled with the buttons and flipped out the small playback screen, eventually locating the power. The screen blinked but nothing happened.

He fiddled some more, and pushed an icon he interpreted to mean 'Play'. The screen came to life.

Three minutes later, Al shut the camera off.

He was a dead man walking.

Plain and simple. Unless he could conjure up a way to stop the entire might of the U.S. Government from swatting him like a fly, he was as dead as if he had been sitting on a pile of plutonium during his boat ride – it was just a matter of how many hours before he expired.

His hands trembled as he clumsily stuffed the camera into the satchel. He staggered over to the mirror clutching the razor and considered his enlightened reflection.

He nodded into the grime-smeared mirror – a dead man's face nodded back.

# CHAPTER 30

Sam called Richard's cell phone the second Al's call terminated.

"What is it?" Richard asked.

"He called again, sir," Sam announced.

"And?"

"He still thinks I'm one of the good guys," Sam quipped.

"Gee, Sam, that's swell. Did you happen to find out where he is?" Richard asked, heavy on the irony.

"The trace came back to a trunk line in the Antioquia region, sir."

Sam heard the rustling of paper in the background, accompanied by a dull roar he presumed was the airplane's engines.

"Okay, I have a map here," Richard said. "That's a large area. Can you be more specific?"

"I wish I could, sir," Sam apologized. "The technology down there is too primitive to narrow it down any further."

"That's a shame. About as helpful as telling me he was calling from New Jersey. And it features fun places like Medellin, population two million. You know, the home of the Medellin cartel?"

"I understand, sir," Sam conceded. "But it is what it is. The good news is we should have a GPS position for the phone he used on his first call within the hour, so we'll be able to nail him to within a few feet."

"Let's hope he still has it with him," Richard said. "I'll be touching down in Panama within an hour. I'll see you at the office in two."

❦

Al inspected himself in the mirror. He'd shaved his head with the sideburn trimmer part of the razor and trimmed his facial hair into a kind of three musketeers mustache and goatee. He hoped that as it grew in more, the goatee would be the feature people focused on rather than his whole face.

He tended to remember faces by distinctive attributes – maybe everyone did the same thing.

But that would only go so far. He needed a plan if he was going to survive. And personal grooming aside, what he was facing wouldn't ever go away. He was painted into a sticky corner and needed options.

Al paced the room, spinning scenarios in his head. He had, what, a few grand in cash? That might last him two or three months in rural shitholes like this one. Less if he went to a city. He had his passport, but it wasn't really usable if everyone on the planet was looking for him, now was it? That further limited him. He was basically broke and limited to Colombia, where he didn't know anyone and probably couldn't survive very long.

*Only that wasn't completely true, was it?*

He did have one option. Assuming he hadn't run it into the ground – as he had so many in his life.

Four years ago, a few months after being posted in Panama City, Al had spent what was easily the best year of his life with a woman from Colombia – a native of Cartagena, a popular beach city on the northern Colombian coast near Venezuela. Margarita Trigos, or Mari for short, had been working for a financial services firm in Panama City, and Al had met her at a charity mixer that had been thrown in conjunction with the embassy. Normally he would have avoided any such event like the plague but the embassy had purchased a slug of tickets and handed them out to staffers and above – and besides the noble cause of helping Panama's orphans and stray dogs, attendance included free drinks and food. A powerful attraction for Al, who was forever short on cash but long on having a good time.

So he'd cleaned up pretty well, donned a silk tropical shirt and slacks and made his way to the function; staged in the lobby of one of the large banks, which had been transformed for the evening into an entertainment zone – three bars, food stations, small tables scattered around for relaxing and enjoying the tapas and cocktails. And a live salsa band.

At first he'd felt out of place but after several vodka tonics he'd settled in, even chatting with a few groups of people he vaguely knew from the embassy. At one point, he'd gestured with his drink in his hand and bumped into a passing woman, spilling some of the clear liquid down the front of her evening dress, and almost giving her a black eye.

He'd been almost as horrified as she. Grabbing some cocktail napkins from a nearby table, he'd tried to blot the worst of the unexpected splatter off her face and bare bosom as he apologized profusely. Then she'd stopped him, and in English told him to just leave things be – she would find a ladies room and survey the damage.

When she'd returned from getting cleaned up, Al still felt terrible about the incident, and at the prodding by one of the embassy wives, approached Mari and offered to get her a drink. She'd paused for a considerable time, and then acquiesced, ordering a rum and coke. Al practically ran to get it for her. When he returned, he apologized yet again for his clumsiness.

"I'm so sorry. I normally don't slam beautiful women in the head with my drink to get their attention," he'd offered.

And she was beautiful. Al guessed maybe early thirties, medium dark complexion, raven hair, five foot one if she hadn't been wearing four inch cocktail heels, slim athletic physique. No wedding band.

"It's effective, I'll grant you that," she'd responded. "But not an ideal ice-breaker."

Al got the feeling that, in spite of his disastrous collision she was flirting with him, just a little.

Al then tried *his* hand at flirting: "Normally I drug the girl's drink, but I thought a straightforward concussion might do the trick, it being a Friday night, and all. I like to keep them guessing..."

At that point in his life he had been thinner and relatively presentable. Forty, a diplomat, decently groomed, coherent. He was not unaccustomed to interest from females since he'd hit Panama – he was plum target for women seeking a certain type of domestic bliss. At least on initial appearances. In short, Al had game.

"So what are you doing at this *soiree*?" Mari then asked him.

"I'm showing support on behalf of the embassy, in addition to boxing with the locals," he'd quipped. "My name's Al Ross...*Encantado.*"

He'd never forget the way she stared full into his eyes. A mild charge ran between them. She introduced herself.

"Hmm. I'm not a local, just for the record," she'd responded.

"No? Then where are you from? And are you with one of the embassies? Your English is very good."

"No, I'm Colombian, and I'm in Panama with one of the large accounting firms. They just brought me in a month ago to help start their new office here. I'm a CPA."

"A bean counter! I'd never have guessed. They generally don't put accountants into such attractive packages where I come from." Flattery never hurt, he'd found.

"Which is where, Al?" That look again…

He'd felt happy to share with her: "Originally? Cleveland, Ohio. A place that couldn't be more different than Panama."

"Yes, I suppose it must be."

"And you? Where did they drag you here from?" He remembered feeling a mild surprise that his curiosity was genuine.

"Cartagena. One of the most beautiful cities in the world…" she'd explained. "Are you a high-powered diplomat? A mover and shaker?" she teased.

"The State Department would be in chaos without my daily input," he'd volleyed.

They had royally hit it off, and a few cocktails had turned into a proposal for dinner the following night, which had developed into a few dates, which had become nights spent at her apartment – though she'd spent one evening at Al's before declaring it uninhabitable. Al had offered token resistance but he didn't really disagree. He wasn't the most domesticated man in the world, and hadn't had time to find a maid yet…

Life had gone by and they'd become an item, spending almost every night together for months on end. She hadn't been that interested in Al's past and had seemed okay with his divorce – less so with his drinking – but then again, he'd cut way back since he'd met her, so it was manageable. They both enjoyed a cocktail now and again and it hadn't been a problem, at least for the first six months.

Then, as with most of his relationships, he'd grown complacent and started missing dinners and showing up later and later. They fought several times, and while he recognized he was in the wrong, he also kind of didn't give a shit. Al supposed he loved her, at least to the extent he was capable of loving anyone but himself, and Mari certainly appeared to love him, but he just couldn't conquer his irresponsibility. They'd settled into an uneasy truce, but it was one that couldn't last.

On their one year anniversary she'd proposed they move in together and consider becoming serious – as in marriage serious. Al could have probably handled the discussion better – which soon degraded into a heated argument, and Al had knocked back a few more celebratory pops than normal, it being their big date, so the argument quickly spiraled into a breakup.

That had started the current three years' cycle of non-stop boozing that had torn Al's life apart. He'd tried to patch things up with Mari a few times over the following weeks but she'd been adamant that she wanted and deserved better than being the sex toy of a misogynist drunkard – hard to argue she wasn't right on that point.

Then one day he'd dialed her number on a Friday night, only to find it had been disconnected. He took a cab to her apartment, being already too tipsy to drive reliably, and had caused a minor scene banging on her lobby door. Eventually one of the neighbors returned from dinner and told Al brusquely that Mari had moved out several days before. Back to Colombia. The looks they gave him clearly indicated they felt she'd done the right thing, and that he rated slightly below the black ooze to be found at the local waste dump in terms of redeeming qualities.

He'd been despondent for months, which of course manifested in increased binging, which then resulted in even deeper depressions, requiring yet more booze to keep the demons at bay.

At one point Al had spent several days trying to track Mari down, assuming she'd gone back to Cartagena. He'd even gone so far as hiring a private detective there to locate her, but once the man had found her info, Al chickened out. What was he going to say? That he'd let the best thing in his life slip away because he was a self-absorbed, drunken piece of shit, but that he was still unsure he was willing or able to change, so he still didn't know what he really wanted? That didn't sound like a particularly compelling pitch, even to him. And so he'd simply put it all behind him and blundered forward, dulling the pain with booze, gambling, women of loose virtue and anything else self-destructive he could get his hands on, which was abundant in a place like Panama.

Three years was a long time. A good-looking woman like Margarita had probably found herself a man who was willing to commit, and likely wouldn't want anything to do with Al anymore. He wouldn't, if he were in her shoes.

Still, Al didn't have any other options. He recalled that a frequent topic of their discussions together had been her agonizing over her big brother, who had left Cartagena five years before she'd come to Panama to join the rebel forces in the south – a dangerous and stupid move, in her opinion. She constantly worried he'd been killed, or wounded, or arrested. Colombia had been wracked by civil war for decades and the FARC was the largest of the armed rebel groups – occupying huge tracts of land along the country's northern and southern borders. Many idealistic and disenfranchised youths had left their comfortable homes to live in the jungles and play out their own Che Guevara fantasies.

Maybe she would take pity on Al. She'd had strong feelings for him, he was sure of that. Perhaps there was enough residual glow, even after three years, that she wouldn't just leave him hanging out to die. Which was exactly what he had to look forward to if he couldn't drop off the map in a hurry.

Al repacked his satchel, taking care to ensure the camera was protected by the few T-shirts he'd pilfered from Ernesto's backpack. He briefly considered taking a shower – seemed like a decent idea given the day he'd had. He removed one of Ernesto's shirts and gave it a whiff – smelled clean and looked new, like he'd just bought it. *Extra Grande*, so adequate room for Al's girth.

He grabbed the key and the ragged towel that was folded on his table and exited the cottage, locking the door behind him. He approached the *bano* and pushed the door open. The odor was overpowering – a combination of industrial ammonia-based cleaner, mildew and general rot. He took in the square shower stall with its plastic curtain and jury-rigged shower head mounted to a short length of garden hose, and almost retched. But he smelled like an old bear who'd just come out of hibernation, so if he wanted to arouse as little attention as possible he'd need to do something about that. He removed his pants and underwear but kept his socks on, and again began his shower wearing his shirt, removing it once it had been soaped and rinsed, then going to work on his body. Fortunately the proprietor had stocked the shower with a full sized bar of soap, which had been worn down halfway by use but was still more serviceable than the small hotel bars at the Alcazar.

Ablutions concluded, he squeezed the water out of his shirt and slipped his shoes over his soaking socks. He didn't want to risk infection with whatever nameless horrors were multiplying on the floor, ammonia or no, so he'd take his chances with damp shoes. Hopefully he wouldn't have to go on any long hikes over the next few hours.

He wrung out his socks once back in his little love shack, and donned Ernesto's T-shirt. It would be saturated with sweat within a few minutes outside anyway, so Al wasn't too concerned with its aesthetic appeal. Even so, he reflected that a canary yellow T stretched across his belly wasn't a pretty sight. Still, that was the least of his current problems. He'd take time to diet if he was still breathing in another few days.

His satchel packed, he unlatched the window and gave it a good shove. The lower portion slid up, creating a two foot by two foot opening. That would be just enough.

Al leaned out and placed the satchel on the ground and then reversed his position, squeezing his legs and lower torso through the window before dropping the few feet to the ground. He looked around. His eyes met those of a small boy, maybe six years old, staring at him as though he'd just teleported from Mars. Al supposed it wasn't every day that the local kids saw tall, heavy white men climbing through tenement windows. Al waved at him, and the little boy spun and ran away as fast as his short bow legs would carry him.

He didn't really blame the kid.

⌒⌒

Sam's screen blinked to life as his computer beeped, signaling he'd received a message. He checked it and clicked on the icon. A satellite map of Colombia popped up and a yellow star icon blinked steadily. They'd found the phone.

Sam called Richard.

"We have a lock on him, sir," Sam reported. "He's in Turbo, which is a small town on the northern coast. Population fifty thousand."

Sam heard the rustling of paper in the background.

"I see it," Richard confirmed. "Looks like it has an airport, but it's not long enough for this jet. Arrange for a prop plane to be waiting when we touch down in twenty minutes, and I'll put a team on it and hit Turbo. It's probably a little over an hour by prop."

"You could put down in Medellin in the jet, and prop plane up to Turbo. Might cut off a few minutes, sir," Sam suggested.

"Sam. I don't want to be on record landing an Agency plane in the heart of Colombia and disembarking a team of armed men – might be a little tough to explain to an unfriendly regime, you know? So just do as you're told and get me a prop plane that can carry six passengers and some gear. I'll make some calls and arrange for it to be able to get into Colombian airspace and on the ground in Turbo with no hassles."

"It may take longer to get a plane at this hour. It's getting dark…" Sam said.

"Thanks for the update on the time, Sam. I can look out my window and see that. How about making the calls and getting it done, and calling me once you have everything in place?"

God Sam hated this man. "I'll handle it, sir. Are you still coming in to the office or continuing on to Colombia?" Sam asked hopefully.

"I'll still be in your office within an hour, traffic allowing," Richard said. "Better get busy on finding a plane. Clock's ticking."

Terrific. Sam could already foresee the next few days turning into a slow-mo instant replay of his miserable weekend. His wife was giving him enough shit already for his continual absences – and when she got upset she was meaner than a bag of snakes. He couldn't tell her anything more than it was embassy business; his usual excuse for staying out and banging his young mistress silly. If he was away from home the better part of the week with no sustentative explanation, his domestic comfort was going to take a pronounced turn for the worse – and even more so if he had to be on call 24/7 for the duration.

Maybe he could convince Richard that he'd be more effective working out of the embassy in Bogota, since his target was no longer anywhere near Panama?

As he dialed for his contact who handled air charters for him, he again wondered what Al could be involved in that would have Richard jetting across the continent with a Citation full of killers. Whatever it was, Sam wanted no piece of it.

Sometimes it was better to be the tiny cog than the big wheel.

# CHAPTER 31

The dark of night fell stealthily over the seaport town, giving Al a mild case of the heebie-jeebies as he faltered his way through the deepening shadows of Turbo. He stopped in at a small neighborhood bar and asked about a bus service to Cartagena; only to be told he'd be better off waiting till morning – the buses weren't safe after dark along that route.

Great. That didn't really work for him. He asked the bartender about alternative travel options; if that's what you could call the sweating man watching a small TV and doing his best to ignore the three customers in his establishment. The bored man looked blankly back at him before returning to gawp at the TV.

Undeterred, Al repeated the question, eating into the bartender's viewing time, until he finally suggested there was an airport he could try the next day. Al told him he really needed to get to Cartegena immediately. The man shrugged and turned back to the program.

Al wasn't getting anywhere.

He returned to the black of night, headed toward the waterfront and found another bar, where he asked the same set of questions. This barkeep, a woman, also advised him the buses weren't safe at night, but conceded that one did stop within the hour at some incomprehensible place in town. Al asked if she knew anyone who could show him the way. She screamed for someone in the back room. A ten year old boy emerged, and the woman issued a rapid-fire set of instructions in a Spanish patois of some sort. Al ordered a beer while this went on, and discovered that he got change back from a dollar on a bar beer in Turbo. At least there was a positive to his little odyssey.

The boy motioned to him. Al swiftly downed the beer and followed him out of the depressing and humid drinking house.

They walked in silence for about fifteen minutes before the boy stopped and told him he should wait just here and wave at the bus when it came by 'in a while'. Al offered him the change from the beer. The little boy snatched it from his hand and ran off laughing.

It was almost pitch black now, with only slim illumination from a bulb at the entry of a questionable edifice across the street. A car slowed as it pulled past him, and then sped up. Al had a distinctly unsafe feeling.

He had to wait until tomorrow during business hours to get in touch with the private detective in Cartagena, so he reasoned he might as well use the time to put distance between himself and Panama. Plus, if Sam was involved, which he believed with one hundred percent certainty now, there was a good likelihood that his call had been traced, which meant that at any point there could be a hit team scouring the town for him, along with stepped up scrutiny by the police. Al was keenly aware that the rules had changed, that he needed to treat everything and everyone as the enemy. One slip and he was dog food.

After what seemed like forever an old bus wheezed to a stop at the curb, where Al had been frantically waving at it. A cardboard sign in the front window announced 'Monteria' – Al's halfway point destination, as there were no direct buses to Cartagena. If he could at least make it to Monteria, an inland city of a quarter million people, he figured the likelihood of being safe was far higher than in Turbo, with a fifth the population and a possible direct hit on a trace to the pay phone. He'd already slipped up by telling Sam he was in Colombia, and there was no way of undoing that, so he had to focus on what he could change. Getting as far from the delights of Turbo as quickly as possible seemed like a reasonable first step.

He mounted the steps to the bus and paid 20,000 pesos to the driver – the market owner had been eager to change a hundred bucks into pesos at 1800 to the dollar, so Al was fat on Colombian currency. The other passengers were definitely on the lower end of the economic scale – the only thing missing was a chicken running up the center aisle.

Oh well. It was all part of the local color. He hoped this bus wouldn't be one of the many stopped by rebels or robbers at night in the sketchier areas of Colombia, which the road to Turbo definitely was. Then again, at this point he'd almost be safer if he was kidnapped.

Which gave him the germ of an idea, just a flicker, but enough to provide the first hope he'd had since viewing the video.

It would be extremely dangerous, and involve terrorists, drug traffickers, armed insurgents, you name it; but there just might be a way to stay alive.

He chose a seat midway down the length of the bus and closed his eyes, the vague outline of a strategy beginning to form.

The bus was stopped twice over the next four hours by armed Colombian soldiers, who went through luggage at random. Nobody seemed interested in Al's measly satchel. The soldiers focused mainly on the larger parcels, before waving them on after fifteen minutes or so.

They made it to Monteria around midnight. The night air was deep, dark and muggy enough to convince Al his traveling was done for the day. He felt like dung, and absent a bottle of rum there was no way he'd make it another four or five hours on a night bus through the danger zone. He'd catch the first one out in the morning.

He'd spotted a hotel that looked promising as the old bus had pulled into town and after disembarking he asked one of the waiting taxis to take him to the nearby Hotel Campenario. They pulled up outside the building within five minutes – the drive cost two bucks. Probably robbery, but again, at midnight, Al wasn't looking for a deal.

The hotel was open and charged him $15 for the night, which seemed fair given that it had AC and appeared at least reasonably clean. The desk clerk gave him a key and offered to accompany him to the second floor, room 204, but Al assured him he could find it on his own.

He did with no trouble, and after turning on the air conditioning, actually took the time to disrobe before collapsing face first onto the bed. He was out cold before the mattress stopped vibrating from his landing.

# CHAPTER 32

Two men waited outside the squalid little hostel in Turbo. One across the street, the other in the rear alley. Both of Latin complexion, they wore light cargo pants and loose shirts – the uniform of the hiking and backpacking community. Other than the fact they were standing on completely empty streets in a dangerous neighborhood at night they might have been tourists from Venezuela or Panama. A third man had paid for a room in the hostel and was currently sitting in hovel number two, listening for any signs of life.

They'd arrived via prop plane as darkness had descended on Turbo and made their way from the airport with the help of a local hired car. Their target hadn't moved since they'd picked up his signal so they'd come to the tentative conclusion that he was asleep in his *cabana*. After consulting with Richard, the decision was made to wait for him to wake up and leave, then shoot him with a tranquilizer dart and cart him to the airport.

The Agency didn't have nearly the sort of infrastructure in Colombia that it did in Panama. The Colombian regime, while friendly on the surface, was in a state of perennial armed conflict with the rebel forces that controlled large swatches of the country. The regime was riddled with conflicting imperatives due to the tremendous amount of drug money floating around – some of which made it to the politicians, ensuring that the objectives of the U.S. war on drugs were not pursued aggressively.

Most of the jungle areas of the country were littered with land-mines, rendering them impenetrable, and so Colombia existed with the dual menaces of sustained civil war and aggressively dangerous criminal syndicates operating freely throughout much of the country.

Panama, on the other hand, used the dollar as its currency, was very favorably disposed toward the U.S. and enjoyed stability and prosperity due to the new canal investment and the daily revenue from the existing canal. The police were cooperative with the U.S. and were sufficiently corrupt to allow the Agency to operate however it liked, provided it didn't arouse too much attention.

The operational idea was to grab Al when he poked his head out of his quarters, then ship him to Panama and debrief him there.

An initial line of thinking had been that all their problems would disappear if Al simply went skydiving without a parachute over the jungle on the trip north, however that had been dismissed, mainly because they needed to be absolutely sure of how much exposure the camera had gotten. Al could always have a diving accident or fall out of a helicopter later.

Their man in *cabana* two had signaled that he'd so far heard no movement or snoring that would be consistent with the room being occupied. Nobody had rolled over on the bed or gone to the bathroom in four hours. The man murmured into his cell and awaited instructions. After a few moments he got the go-ahead.

He unpacked his backpack and extracted a telescoping fiber optic lens with an adjustable tip. The cottages had four feet of airspace between them, and no side windows, so it would require a bit of art – but he was an expert at this sort of surveillance, among other things, so would find a way.

He crept out of his little shack and moved close to unit one; finding exactly what he was looking for – a space between the floorboards. Each cottage sat on a series of concrete blocks to prevent flooding during rainy season, so there was about eight inches of air space under the dwellings. He carefully fed the device through the crack and into the room, and rotated it, watching the transmission on a handheld screen. There wasn't any light in the room, which made it harder, but after a few minutes of looking around, it was obvious the place was unoccupied. He retracted the camera and moved back into his room, then called Richard for instructions.

Richard was livid. How the hell had this guy evaded multiple trained field squads, made it through impassable jungle, and now had apparently ditched them, luring them on some tangent while he slipped away?

The possibility remained he was out drinking and would return later. The phone was obviously still in the room, and there were few reasons Richard could think of for Al leaving it there if he didn't plan to return –

unless he was familiar enough with trade-craft to realize he'd be tracked on the device and had used it as a clever time-wasting decoy. Nothing in his file indicated any clandestine knowledge or background, so it was most likely Al was getting drunk at one of the numerous dive bars peppering the waterfront or possibly spending time with a hooker someplace nearby. The second possibility; that Al had figured out he was being monitored, pointed to a far less appealing scenario. That would indicate they had a much bigger problem than anticipated.

Richard weighed his choices and made a decision. The operative again emerged from bungalow two and moved to the entry of number one, expertly jimmying the lock. He quickly opened the door, slid into the room and extracted a penlight flashlight. A quick survey revealed it to be empty, as they'd suspected. Another scan, and he found the pink cell phone on the floor under the bed.

He exited the room and returned to his own, calling Richard even as the door closed.

"It's empty. The phone was under the bed," he reported.

"This is bad," Richard said. "It means he's on to us. Might have been for some time."

"What do you want us to do?" the man asked.

"Stay in position," Richard advised. "You're already in-country, so let me evaluate our options and get back to you. Try to get some sleep. This could be a long one."

Back in Sam's office in Panama, Richard scratched his head and contemplated the air duct on the ceiling. Well shit. Now they had a full-blown crisis. The country was hostile enough to operate in and they were pursuing an obviously skilled target – evading the best they could throw at him. True, they didn't know if the target had the camera, but Richard couldn't think of a lot of alternative reasons for the man to be on the run.

Richard called for Sam, who was preparing to leave for the night – he could see him packing his briefcase at the secretary's station.

"Yes, sir?" Sam said, entering the office.

"Tell me everything you can think of about this Al Ross. Everything," Richard demanded.

"There's nothing else to tell, sir. He's a drunk, is usually either wasted or hung over, has a bad gambling problem, and is a complete write-off as a human being," Sam summarized. "Oh, and he's always broke," Sam added.

"Sam, Sam, Sam. I get the feeling you're leaving a lot out. His file says he has a purple heart and a bronze star – he's a decorated combat vet. That's incongruent with the guy you're describing," Richard observed.

"Twenty-something years ago he got into a firefight, walked away with a nick and got honored for it. The guy worked in the mail room, sir. He's never had a decent explanation for what he was even doing off the base, much less with other armed soldiers. That was a fluke," Sam insisted.

"I sense we aren't seeing the big picture here. He may have been working for military intelligence, or an offshoot, even back then. That would explain a mail clerk being in a gun battle with enemy insurgents," Richard speculated, making a note on the desk pad by his phone.

"Not a chance, sir. The guy has been a loser as long as I've known him..."

Richard narrowed his eyes at Sam. "This loser has so far been instrumental in getting the cook out of Panama after evading your team, and escaped being incinerated in the jungle from a surprise aerial attack – assuming he was with the cook then – and has avoided detection for days. Not to mention that he crossed an impassable stretch of the most dangerous jungle in the world. He probably has the camera with him, or knows its location – we can't rule out that he's stashed it someplace safe, or that the cook did before he fried. And now he's behaving in a manner that's consistent with a trained operative. He hid the phone, knowing we would trace it, buying himself enough time to be anywhere in the country by now – if not on a plane to God knows where." Richard stopped and shook his head. "That doesn't sound like a stupid man to me."

"But he called me from a pay phone! Asking for help. Sounded scared and half in the bag..." Sam said.

"He's been playing us, Sam," Richard warned. "This guy has far more going on than meets the eye. That's obvious. We need to get ahead of him or this could blow up."

"Al's a sloppy, drunk zero, sir. Really," Sam tried one last time.

"For all we know," Richard mused, "he wanted to lead us to Turbo for some as-yet unknown reason. He could easily have paid someone to ditch the phone in the room, and we have to expect he's conversant enough with technology and infrastructure to know that calls from Colombian pay phones wouldn't be traceable to a specific location. He could have made the call from Medellin, for all we know – this could be a brilliant bit of deception to have us chasing our tails." Richard's face darkened. "I'm thinking it's possible he's working with another intelligence service – presumably hostile. Who's the most active in Panama? Chinese? Russians? Mossad?" Richard asked.

"Uh, the Chinese definitely have a large presence, sir, but not so much the Russians. Mossad is more Costa Rica, I think…" Sam answered, doubtfully.

"I want everything you have on all three," Richard ordered, "as well as any other potentially hostile groups in the area. Just assume Al has been playing you for years and is a double agent, if not a triple. Maybe I'm wrong, but there are way too many coincidences."

"Okay, but I think you're barking up the wrong tree, sir," Sam warned.

"And let's get the Madame back in and grill her," Richard instructed. "She's our only connection to Al now, and probably knows more than we first thought."

"What about the field team?" Sam asked.

Richard looked at him oddly.

"That's need to know. I want the intel on the Chinese within the hour, Sam," Richard ordered.

It looked like another long, sleepless night. All because of Al.

Sam's hatred of Richard was ballooning to monumental proportions but Al was running a close second. He'd be comfortably home in bed or rolling around with the sisters if it wasn't for these two shit-grubs.

He threw his briefcase onto his secretary's desk and settled in for more thankless hours of honest work.

# CHAPTER 33

Al woke to the sound of a loud conversation and laughing outside his room. Evidently the service staff enjoyed storytelling at an early hour, and every other comment elicited howls of laughter from the gathered maids.

Normally, Al would have been furious, but this morning he wasn't nursing a hangover, and he remembered he was on a short timetable – so he was actually glad to be awake. His watch said nine o'clock, so it wasn't that early, anyway.

He quickly showered, laundering his socks yet again while making the mental note that he had to get new ones today, and checked his appearance in the mirror. Sort of an ageing Rob Halford look, with a lot more padding though. Oh well, he wasn't getting any calls from GQ to be their cover model, so he wasn't that worried about a couple extra pounds.

Packing his satchel, he made a mental note that the first order of business would have to be getting on the internet to find the name of the PI he'd used to locate Mari. There weren't many private investigators in Cartagena and he'd located this one on the web, so it should be simple enough. He figured he'd call the man, get the address, and then…

And then…precisely what?

That was the hole in the short term logistical plan so far. But he'd figure it out. His gut leaned to calling Mari and feeling her out before he barged into her life begging for help – again. He had no idea what she'd been up to for three years; and a thousand days was a long time. Al hoped she wasn't married, but you never knew – he couldn't blame her if she was. He'd completely dropped the ball so it was Mari's prerogative to replace him however she saw fit.

Al checked out of the hotel and crossed the street to an internet cafe that served coffee and non-specific bits of fried, sugary dough. He ordered one of each and settled behind a monitor. His coffee arrived within moments and he savored the strong, rich Colombian roast as he munched on his health nuggets.

After ten minutes of searching the web he had the PI's information, and used the voice-over-IP phone in the corner to call him. After some back and forth, the man remembered Al and looked up the number and address he'd filed away for Mari. Al scribbled away frantically, repeating the information back to him to ensure he'd gotten it right before he hung up.

He had the lady at the cafe call him a taxi and soon arrived at the seedy downtown bus terminal's ticket window. Still, compared to Turbo it was Club Med. The roads were paved and there were actually relatively new cars on the streets, and stores that looked as though they stocked reasonable goods. The next bus to Cartagena left at eleven a.m. and arrived at three. Al bought a ticket and went across the street to a store that featured mannequins posed in jeans and T-shirts in the window display. He bought another shirt, a pair of underwear and a package of three pairs of white athletic socks. Satisfied with his shopping expedition, he returned to the station and sat in the waiting area, prepared to board when they announced his bus.

A group of soldiers carrying machine-guns and accompanied by a tired-looking beagle walked through the terminal, eyeing everyone suspiciously. Al was relieved that they gave him no more scrutiny than anyone else. He supposed that given the country abounded with armed homicidal factions intent upon inflicting as much chaos as possible, a nearly-bald Gringo with flamboyant facial hair didn't really rate a second glance.

The bus was three quarters full but in better shape than the one from Turbo – this one had leather seats and appeared to be only a decade old. When the driver started the engine, meager air conditioning even wafted down from the broken overhead vent – an unexpected luxury.

He busied himself with applying ointment to his feet and changing his socks, to the considerable disgust of the woman across the aisle from him, and then reclined his seat to watch the scenery go by. From what he could make out, Colombia, like Panama, mainly consisted of tropical jungle punctuated by large cleared farm tracts and the occasional city. The road wasn't terrible, and aside from several more inspection stops by armed soldiers the trip was uneventful.

As he dozed on the slow-moving bus, Al went through a mental list of actions he needed to take when he arrived in Cartagena. First he'd grab a late lunch, and then see about buying a temporary cell phone. In Panama you could get a card with a certain amount of airtime on it, then you entered in the phone number and an access code, and the system credited the phone with the airtime. He hoped it was that straightforward in Colombia. It would be a lot easier than trying to find pay phones and carrying around pounds of coins.

The issue of how best to approach Mari was tougher. He just hoped that any affection they'd shared during their year together had created at least a small amount of residual glow.

No point in agonizing over it. He'd know where he stood with her soon enough.

∂∘⟨

Carmen had been released on Monday evening, after routine questioning from the police. Her attorney had gotten her out, with the promise of charges to be pressed over the shooting – but everyone involved knew the threat was hollow, as Carmen's contact list read like a roster of past and current government luminaries. There was slim-to-no chance she would actually be prosecuted for defending her place of business from known violent drug lords engaged in a killing spree on the premises.

She'd put out feelers to see if there were any rumors on the street about her having double-crossed the Colombians, and there weren't. So as she'd suspected, the threats of the man who'd questioned her about the cook were empty. As connected as she was, she would have heard within a few hours of them being circulated – so it all had been bluster and bluff.

Carmen had an opulent apartment in a condo development along the waterfront, and had resolved to take several weeks off while she had Esperanza cleaned and repaired. She'd contacted the contractor who had done the renovation and he'd been more than happy to get the job of fixing the bullet damage and restoring the interior to its prior glory. Work was sporadic since the economic crisis and a lot of projects had been put on hold, so he had a full crew he could throw at the brothel – they'd be back in business within ten days, he had assured her.

Several of the girls had quit and moved to other establishments, but most stayed with Carmen, as they made more money with her than they could anywhere else. Carmen's clientele was the higher end of the audience that paid for love, and tended to tip a lot bigger than the poorer locals or economy tourists.

Many of Carmen's young ladies came from Colombia, Ecuador and Peru; where beautiful peasant girls with no future at home were lured by the draw of easy money to be had in the north. Carmen went to great lengths to ensure they were treated well at her place, and not subjected to the kind of danger and violence that often accompanied a life in the trade. Still, many of the girls had drug problems – a function of plentiful, cheap cocaine. But that was true of working girls in most countries – Carmen's weren't any better or worse than average in that respect.

Carmen didn't do drugs herself and denied ever having been a hooker. She was vague on her reasons for operating a brothel, however, the prosperity she enjoyed couldn't be denied. From her perspective she was merely tendering a service for which there was substantial demand. She was like a high-end restaurateur or an exclusive disco owner, only there was a guaranteed happy ending associated with time spent at her place.

The girls came to her willingly – she made it clear she wouldn't do business with the cartels that traded in human flesh. Carmen's girls were there because they liked money, enjoyed sex, and had no other options. She had a doctor on call who routinely did health inspections, and she even helped those who were interested to open up savings accounts and calculate their career earnings required to retire. That was the dream; to work a few years, and either hook up with a wealthy regular who wanted full-time companionship, or amass enough money to open a legitimate business and go straight. Many actually did wind up with older men looking for willing, youthful beauty, although it was far from an everyday occurrence. And some did retire and open clothing stores or coffee shops.

True, the majority eventually drifted to other establishments or to other towns, but the life was what it was. Carmen didn't pass judgment – she simply catered to the wants of some of the most powerful men in Panama, many of whom were involved in writing or enforcing the law. So her appreciation of morality was understandably colored. There was a complete double standard for the powerful and rich. Being a woman in Latin America was like being a second class citizen to begin with. Being a poor woman was even worse. Money was a kind of power, and there few ways for a single woman of limited means to acquire any. Carmen had chosen her road and it had made her wealthy and relatively untouchable.

As she padded around her condo soaking in the view of the ocean, she was also calculating the cost to get Esperanza back on its feet. It was a financial setback, that was for sure, but she'd get over it.

After showering and putting on a dusting of makeup, she slipped a light cotton summer dress on and prepared to meet some friends for lunch. In the tropics, even a simple one-piece cover-up was considered appropriate during the day – it was invariably hot in May, but nothing like as muggy and awful as August or the surrounding months. The rainy season was tough but she'd lived with it all her life and so was used to it. She inspected herself in the mirror with satisfaction. She was holding up well after thirty-eight years on the planet.

Carmen grabbed her purse and keys, locked her door and waited for the building elevator. In the lobby, she greeted her doorman with a cheery wave and breezed through the doors into the damp heat of the day.

Halfway down the block two men approached from the opposite direction. A black sedan pulled to the curb alongside her. One of the men flashed a badge and instructed her to get into the car. She half turned to run back to her building but the second man grabbed her arm and forced her into the car. The few pedestrians on the block avoided eye contact, preferring not to become involved. Carmen decided not to fight it – it wasn't like she wouldn't be back on the street within a short time. This was probably just the second phase of questioning by an over-zealous detective.

Then she noticed the passenger in the front, next to the driver.

Jenkins.

"Hello, Carmen," he said. "Seems like we have a lot more we need to chat about."

She felt a sting on her arm – the man who'd climbed in next to her had injected her with something. Her vision blurred and everything went dark.

The car pulled from the curb and accelerated around the corner, onto one of the large main streets.

❧

"She hasn't told us anything we don't already know," Jenkins said to Richard on his cell.

"So she's sticking to the story?" Richard asked. "This was just a chance encounter? A simple cook who was looking for a cheap way across the border without paperwork, escorted by a down on his luck embassy simpleton?"

"That about covers it," Jenkins replied. "She swears she only used Al because of his diplomatic passport – and because he worked cheap."

"Do you believe her?" Richard inquired.

"I'm not sure what to believe, Richard. The account hangs together and makes a certain sense, but on the other hand, she's clearly a skillful liar; look at the business she's in," Jenkins observed.

"We need to get everything out of her." Richard paused. "Whatever that takes."

"I understand. We'll get it," Jenkins assured him. "I can be very persuasive."

"I know. But there's a limit to how far we can go and still release her. She's connected, and we don't want to stir up any more local trouble," Richard warned.

"You need to make a decision, then. How far are you willing to go?"

"As far as you need to in order to be confident you got everything," Richard replied.

"That could get messy. Just so you know."

"The time for delicacy's over" Richard said.

"Okay then, I'll get cracking on it," Jenkins said, his tone flat.

"Call me once it's over."

# CHAPTER 34

Cartagena turned out to be a large, vibrant metropolis, much more developed than Al had expected based on his experiences with Turbo and Monteria. This was a bustling cosmopolitan ocean-side city, perhaps not modern by first-world standards but definitely not the boonies, either. Traffic clogged the streets and thousands of pedestrians milled about in the city center.

The bus arrived at the depot and Al stepped out of the climate controlled interior to be assaulted by the inevitable humidity and heat. Even though they were near the ocean, the equatorial swelter was never far off. It had rained several times a day almost the entire time he'd been in Panama, and Colombia didn't seem much different.

Al walked down what appeared to be one of the main streets and soon found an electronics shop that featured cell phones in its display. Inside the store, he quickly discovered that while the phones were more expensive than in Panama, they weren't that much more. He selected a small Erikson that cost under $50 and also bought a hundred minutes of talk time on a card. The woman behind the counter was amenable to charging the battery for him so he could use it immediately. Al killed the required battery-charging hour by grabbing some grilled fish and beer at a neighborhood restaurant next door. Upon his return to the store, he peered at the array of sundry technological marvels on display in the window. He wondered whether he could sell the video camera and just keep the storage medium, and quickly thought better of it. With his luck it would surface like a bad penny and lead his pursuers straight to Cartagena.

Once the cell phone was fully charged the woman handed it to him, complete with the box, the manual and charger. Al dutifully packed it into his satchel and walked back out onto the hot sidewalk.

It was the moment of truth. He couldn't believe it, but his stomach was tightening up from anxiety. The whole world wanted to kill him and he found that less stressful than calling an old flame...

Al suspected this was only one of the myriad ways he was really screwed up.

He carefully entered the number the PI had given him. The phone rang four times, followed by a generic machine-created voice advising him in Spanish to leave a message. He hung up, checked the number again – and got the same recording. This time, he waited for the beep and began his fumbled message...

"Ahhh...hi, Mari...at least I hope this is Mari...I know this is probably very strange, but this is a voice from your past...it's Al...hopefully you remember? I...uh...I was hoping to talk to you...I have a number you can call..." Al left his cell number and stood dazed in the hot sunshine, staring stupidly at his new phone.

Well that kind of sucked. He had no way of knowing if it was even the right number, and certainly no way of knowing whether she was in town or not. He dimly recalled that her mother and sisters lived in Cartagena too, but not much else. Those years had been effectively blurred by time and an ocean of rum.

So now what? It was two o'clock and Al had nothing to do; no plan other than hoping Mari would call him sooner rather than later. Ordinarily he might have wandered around the town but his feet were still largely out of commission. He didn't want to shred the barely healed skin any worse than he already had. And finding the nearest bar in which to get obliterated seemed like a poor idea, even to him. He needed to keep what few wits he had about him.

Then again, one more icy cold *cerveza* couldn't hurt.

Al walked down the block and spotted a cafe with plastic tables on the sidewalk in front of it. The small green awning over the picture window advertised Bavaria beer, so Al figured they'd know how to serve a frosty one.

He sat at a shaded table. Moments later a teenage girl emerged and took his order. Al watched her reenter the restaurant with interest – no matter how old he got or what country he was in, cute girls always had that special appeal.

Mari had certainly been cute. Among many other things. Her face was very reminiscent of J-Lo, with a body to match. Al had always marveled at how stunning she looked and how lucky he was to have her – *but not enough to commit, obviously*. No, surrendering himself to a sort of boozy purgatory had been a far better choice than having a serious relationship with the best woman he'd ever met.

Al was great at making those kinds of tough choices.

When his beer arrived he dropped a bill in the girl's hand and told her to keep the change. She smiled at him with polite disinterest, no doubt thinking, *Grandpa with a lobster head and effeminate facial hair, on sale here, special price today…*

Wallowing in self-pity was hardly a good substitute for a plan, so when he'd finished his beer and still gotten no call from Mari he decided to check out her neighborhood, and maybe stop in, just in case the phone number had changed.

She lived in an area by the beach called Crespo; which was on the northern side of town near the airport, according to the cab driver he'd just flagged down. It would be a twenty minute ride and cost five dollars.

The cab pulled up to a twenty story white high rise condo development across the street from the beach – which was gorgeous, even by Miami standards. Al paid the driver and stepped onto the sidewalk, savoring the crisp sea breeze as it rippled inland. Now this was more like tourist country.

Studying the address, he realized that the new building wasn't his destination – Mari had to be on the other side of it. He proceeded to explore further down the block and spotted a more traditional, two story home, also painted white. The number on the wall matched the paper in his hand.

He swung open the gate and entered the front courtyard, and taking a deep breath, mounted the three stairs and knocked on the front door. His heart skipped a beat.

Nothing.

Al knocked again and listened carefully, alert to any sound coming from the interior of the house.

Silence.

He turned and descended the steps, and halfway to the gate, froze.

Mari stood in the gateway. Holding the hand of a small child. A little girl, by the looks of her locks.

Al stammered a greeting. "I...hello, Mari...I...I know this is a surp–"

Mari approached him from her position at the gate and slapped his face as hard as she could. Al saw stars for a moment.

"What the hell do you think you're doing here? How did you find me?" she hissed at him.

"Mari. I'm sorry. I know this is probably a shock. I called earlier, but nobody answered. I left a message..." Al offered.

She slapped him again. Not quite so hard, but it still stung.

"Get out," she said, barely controlling her voice. "Get out of my life right now, and don't come back. Ever."

The toddler started to cry.

"I...Mari, please. Let me explain. I don't mean to disrupt your life. Really," Al blurted, and then addressed the child. "Shhhhhhhh. *Por favor. No problema*. Shhhh..." He returned his attention to Mari. "God, I'm so sorry, I didn't mean to cause any drama. It's just that I'm in really bad trouble and I had nowhere else to go...I...I'm sorry, Mari. For everything. You're right...this was a bad idea. I'll go now." Al's marginal fortitude had deflated with each syllable. He should have never come.

What had he been thinking?

Fearful of another of Mari's well executed blows, he sidestepped her and the infant and stumbled to the gate. "You look great, Mari. I hope you're happy and you found someone who deserves you. I'm sorry for coming..." he apologized again, then closed the gate behind him.

Mari and the toddler stood watching him limp down the sidewalk back toward the big condo development, clutching his knapsack, defeated. Mari kneeled in front of the little girl and dried her tears with the hem of her skirt as the wind off the water tugged gently at their hair.

She returned to the gate, closed and bolted it and they slowly walked back toward the house, the scary red-faced man now just a bad memory for both of them.

Mari withdrew a key, which was suspended on a necklace around her neck, and bending down, unlocked the deadbolt. The little girl ran inside and Mari slammed the heavy wooden door behind them.

⤬

That could have gone better, Al reflected. He rubbed his face, which was now adorned with two bright red handprints, and considered his next move. It was pretty safe to say that any assistance he'd hoped to get from Mari was a dead end.

This was obviously the worst day ever to quit drinking.

He decided to continue down the beachfront road, watching for the telltale bright yellow that would indicate a taxi. There was plentiful traffic, but no cabs. That figured – it was now rush hour and people were heading home in droves. This was a residential area with no hotels he could see, so there wouldn't be a plethora of cabs loitering about hoping for gimpy Gringo fares.

After several blocks of hobbling he came upon a seafood restaurant – a little neighborhood place whose business obviously came from the locals. He limped through the doorway, to the *ting ting* of a bell, sat down – and ordered a beer.

Mari was still in good shape, at least judging by the force she'd brought to bear behind her slaps. He couldn't take that away from her.

He replayed the look on her face, part horror and part something else; something difficult to define as she stood with the ocean in back of her, the breeze tussling her flowing mane. Mari was still beautiful – if anything even more so over the intervening three years. Al, on the other hand, was bald, sunburned and sporting a peculiar goatee, along with a couple of extra pounds. He swallowed the beer in three gulps and ordered another. She didn't know what she was missing. Broke, bald, fat, running from the law, no prospects and no future, a boozehound with commitment issues and a pronounced limp...

Maybe she did have a fair idea what she was turning down.

The waiter brought his second beer. He picked it up and skillfully quaffed half of it in a single gulp.

A muffled warbling sound emanated from his pants.

Al coughed his second glug of beer through his nose. Eyes streaming, he tried to arrest his choking, struggling for breath while he fumbled for his phone in his pants pocket.

He retrieved the little cell phone, but it was silent.

Maybe he'd hit a button when he'd shifted to swallow the beer.

It started warbling again.

He stabbed at the green call button with urgent anticipation. He put the cell to his ear.

"What kind of trouble?" Mari asked.

❧

Al opened the gate, being careful to close it behind him. He approached the front door and mounted the steps. He braced himself and knocked. A few moments later the brightly painted door swung open. Mari stood in the doorway, eyes red, tears streaking her face.

"You miserable bastard. It took me years to get over you, and then you show up here, where I've built a life without you, fighting to forget about you every day but also wondering how you were doing..." Mari contained herself. "It's pretty goddamned selfish of you. Then again, you've always been selfish. That for sure hasn't changed..."

"Mari..." Al started.

She threw her arms around him and hugged him close to her, sobbing. The little girl stood in the living room, watching them from down the hall.

He hugged her back. It felt so good.

After an eternity, she let him go, and smoothing her hair back in place, composed herself. She dried her face with her hands and took a deep breath.

"Well, you might as well come in and tell me what happened," she said and turned, walking toward the living room.

"Uh, okay," he replied. As long as he lived, he'd never understand women. He closed the door and turned, finding himself confronted by the toddler, holding a sippy cup in what could only be called a defensive position.

"Cute kid..." Al started, calling down the hall to Mari.

"Say hello to your daughter, Melissa," she responded.

The little girl stared up at him with frightened eyes.

His were more so.

# CHAPTER 35

"I don't understand..." Al stammered. He'd been doing a lot of that lately.

"It's simple, Al. A little friction, a little moisture, bees pollinating flowers...and poof, there's a baby."

Al had followed the child into the living room, setting his knapsack down on the floor and then falling into a heavily-padded easy chair.

Al tried again. "No...I'm clear on how that happens. I just don't understand the rest of it – does she understand English?"

"Not a word." Mari sat across from him as Melissa played on the floor between them.

"And the rest of it?" Al repeated.

"I wanted a real life with you. You didn't want one with me. I found out two weeks after we split I was pregnant, but your sentiments were abundantly clear so I left Panama and came home. Seven months later Melissa was born. And now here we are..." Mari explained.

Al frowned. "I'm her father? And you never once thought about telling me?" He couldn't quite understand these new feelings or why he felt so put out by the kid thing. But he was.

Somewhat.

"I thought about telling you," Mari explained, "about a hundred times a day for the first year, and then only twenty times a day the second year. I was down to maybe once a week, and then you showed up again." Mari stared at him. "Do you have any idea what it's like to go through a pregnancy and then raise a child by yourself? Even an inkling?"

Al shifted awkwardly in the easy chair. "Well...no, not exactly..."

"Here's a hint. In a Latin culture, it's really, really, really hard. Even with my Mom and sisters to help, it's really hard."

"I had no idea, Mari. If you'd have told me..."

"What? What would have changed? Look me in the eyes, and tell me you wouldn't have thought I was trying to trap you. Just tell me," she dared. Then she sighed. "I know you, Al. I know how you think. I don't think it's right, but I don't blame you for it, either. You can't help it."

Al hated that she was right. "How old–"

"Do the math," Mari snapped. "She's two. Actually, twenty-eight months."

Al sat speechless as he gazed at the fruit of his selfish loins. This new revelation orbited his already overwhelmed noodle. The world had changed shape beyond restoration – that much he knew. He attempted to speak, but all that came out was a choking burble.

Mari gathered up Melissa. "I need to put Mel down for her nappies, and then you can tell me about your crisis and how you want me to help you. Just stay where you are – I'll be back in a second," she said sweetly.

Al was left to his thoughts. Mari returned after five minutes.

"Keep your voice down," Mari said, "She gets really grumpy if she misses her nap." She studied Al. "At least she looks like me. Not that the egghead thing isn't attractive," she teased.

Al rubbed the stubble on his head. "Oh, this. It's a long story…" Al began.

"Yeah. I'll bet. When did you start wearing the little fun beard? Halloween?" Mari asked.

"It's a disguise," Al insisted. That sounded lame.

"Wow. Man of a thousand faces."

"Look…" Al protested.

Mari giggled. "I'm sorry. It's just that you look so…I don't know. Like one of those big sad dogs – a mastiff!" Mari clapped her hands then put her hand over her mouth, trying to subdue her howls of laughter.

He'd forgotten how funny she was. "I deserve every bit of this, and more. I've earned any mockery you want to serve out," Al conceded.

"Woof!" Mari exclaimed, exploding into more bubbly giggles.

Al couldn't help himself. He started laughing too. He gave a halfhearted bark.

"Woof…"

Tears of merriment flowed as they both laughed uncontrollably.

It was probably the tension being released from the situation. Either that, or he really did look like a hound.

Mari held up her hands. "Okay. Stop. Seriously. Tell me what happened. Why are you here?"

"Well, it all started with me driving a cook to southern Panama," Al began...

After half an hour he sat back, the saga told. He'd left out some bits to protect her, but the story was largely complete.

"So what's on the camera?" she asked.

"You really don't want to know, Mari," Al said. "Seriously. It would be dangerous for you to know anything more."

"I see." Mari considered that, and seemed to accept the logic. "So what do you want me to do?" she asked. "How can I help you? Are you asking to live in the basement for the rest of your life?"

Al slowly laid out his plan, explaining the details and why he felt it would work.

She stared at him like he'd never seen before. "You've really lost your mind, haven't you?" she asked.

"No. Listen. This is the only chance I have to stay alive. Trust me on this – they'll kill me even if the camera magically appeared in their hands, because I know too much. And they'll never stop trying to find me. I don't have any other option I can see," Al insisted.

"Al. The people you are talking about trying to make a deal with are some of the most dangerous on the planet. They'll kill you just as soon as talk to you," Mari said.

Al sighed. "I know, but I can give them something of huge value in return for very little. It's a win-win."

"It's suicide, is what it is," Mari countered.

"No, Mari. Suicide would be not doing it. I'm not saying it will be easy, just that I think I can propose a deal that would ultimately make everyone happy and keep me in one piece," Al explained.

Mari was silent for a long time, mulling it over. It was a bold, ingenious plan, but extremely high risk. "Help me set the table for dinner. You'll stay and eat with us, won't you?"

"Uh...of course I will..." Al said. He considered saying more but his new found wisdom recommended otherwise.

Mari got up from the sofa and walked into the kitchen. Al's eyes followed her.

So he had a daughter. With Mari. He was a father.

Al wasn't sure how he felt. He'd probably have been more affected if he wasn't running for his life. As things stood, being his daughter probably carried far more liabilities than rewards. And now he had to worry about anyone ever finding out about her. He'd never have come if he'd known he might be endangering his own child by being there.

Oh, come on. Who did he think he was kidding? Of course he would. That's just who he was.

It was who he'd always been. And therein lay his biggest problem.

Al had made a career of being selfish and self-absorbed; quick to seek an easy way out rather than taking responsibility for his actions. It was partially what had driven him to always do the seemingly wrong thing – he was always convinced at some level he could beat the system and find a shortcut. This now questionable ethos had defined Al as long as he could remember.

His first marriage had ended in disaster, after he'd taken to drinking breakfast and cheating on his wife. They'd been married since their mid-twenties and Al had undoubtedly benefited from the union – her father had been a high ranking member of the State Department, and Al, the Desert Storm war hero, had been the perfect son-in-law to help into a new career. Al had actually gone to law school before joining the marines, which was one of the reasons he'd been helping defend soldiers during court-marshals – in addition to running the mail service in Kuwait.

He was an educated man, who could be depended upon to innovate more efficient systems and keep the current systems honest, as well as act as low-rent counsel to ill-behaved marines in military court.

That he'd attempted to pass the Illinois bar three times, and failed each time, was left off his resume. In his rendition, he'd been seized by a patriotic desire to make a difference in the war against terrorism, or oppression, or whatever it had been that time, and so signed up to be a marine. In reality, he'd been wasted on gin for several days after growing increasingly despondent over his failure to ever become a lawyer, and during his multi-day drunk had been convinced by a friend that what he really needed to do was become a marine – mainly because they got laid a lot in some of the bars he frequented, and because a stint of military service on his CV might result in favorable treatment when applying for jobs.

So a slightly shaky Al had gone to the recruiting station and filled out the forms, and been enthusiastically accepted by the service.

And thus had begun Al's bold strides toward the greater good, along with rigging a smuggling operation so he could personally benefit from the theft of sacred icons. That had gone badly wrong, but he'd been decorated for it, which had in turn transfixed the attention of one extremely beautiful, but alas not particularly bright, Susan Brixton, who not only became the one-and-only Mrs. Al Ross, but also badgered Daddy into getting her man a gig with the State Department so they could live in fun places and attend really cool parties.

Thus Al's parabolic career trajectory was launched. But rather than catapulting to fame and fortune, Al's limited interest in doing much besides drinking and trying to figure out how to cheat the system kept his options limited. His first posting was to Uruguay, which his wife hated because she was a strict vegetarian, and everyone spoke Spanish, and it was nothing like Chicago, *at all*. That minor posting lasted six years, during which time Susan managed to accumulate seventy pounds despite her dietary restrictions, and learned to despise Spanish-speaking folk even more than she had when she'd arrived. Al had occupied his time by developing an advanced fondness for *Grappamiel* – a fifty proof local beverage – as well as for the seductive charms of the local working girls. It wasn't so much that he felt compelled to cheat on his wife, as much as it never occurred to him not to.

His next posting was to Belize, which contrary to many self-serving descriptions as a tropical paradise, was in fact a fourth world hellhole. The only thing Susan had liked about it was that English was the national language. Her father, had he lived to see it, would have been horrified by the posting, and would have by then recognized that Al was being shipped to swamps because he was a marginal talent, at best. Fortunately, the old man had succumbed to heart disease while they were still living in Uruguay, so he never saw the precipitous decline of his family's fortunes.

While in Belize, besides indulging a prodigious appreciation for flavored rum and the local *Beliken* beer, Al had taken up with the underage daughter of one of the large landowners near Belmopan; she had been as entranced with the idea of a diplomat as a lover and probable future husband as Susan had initially been. Al had thought it a splendid idea, but had neglected to tell his new paramour about his still current marriage to Susan.

Unfortunately for Al, Susan discovered the short-lived affair and promptly divorced him for justified and provable infidelity. That had cleaned Al out financially – not that he'd ever accumulated much money. In addition to every cent he'd ever earned, he'd also managed to spend most of his wife's half million dollar inheritance. It had been a difficult parting – Susan had discovered the couple *in flagrant dilecto*, drunk and horny in their matrimonial bed on what turned out to be Susan's last abridged shopping trip to the tax-free zone on the border of Mexico.

In Al's defense, the daughter had been a very adult-looking seventeen year old.

To say that the incident had left a stain on Al's resume would be an understatement.

Following this local 'disturbance' he was posted from Belize to Guatemala for a few years, and then ultimately to Panama; mainly because State didn't know what to do with a drunk misanthrope who was also the world's losing-est diplomat, but who still had his looks and a reasonable level of smarmy charm. It seemed to State that sticking him further into the jungle was as good an idea as any, because State hated firing anyone, even if they deserved it in spades.

Al had spent his whole life dedicated to selfish and self-centered activity, resulting in the destruction of every relationship he'd ever had, including the best one – his year with Mari. He'd always taken, never given, and now found himself yet again needing someone else to behave selflessly to save his worthless ass.

For the first time, as a kind of revelation sparked up in his soul, Al questioned his value on the planet and whether his way of living was worth the price he'd paid. This unusual introspection caused his head to pound and spin, which he attributed to a falling blood alcohol level, but something deep down knew it was disgust at his choices to date.

Now he had a baby daughter he'd never met until he'd shown up expecting angelic mercy and heroism from a woman he'd scorned, and it would be a miracle if he survived the week. He already recognized any possible life with Mari, the best woman he'd ever met, was over, but he'd never considered that it might also exclude him from knowing the only child he'd ever had.

So far, Cartagena sucked.

Al padded into the kitchen to see if he could do anything to help with dinner.

After they'd eaten, Mari and Al sat on the couch, Mel having been put to bed. They discussed Al's scheme, which Mari refined considerably.

"I called a friend, and by tomorrow my brother will have a message that I'm coming to Cali for a day or two. He'll figure out a way to meet me – we've done it before," Mari explained. "Then I'll introduce you to him and you can make your proposition."

"That's great, Mari," Al enthused.

"Maybe not so much, at least not initially," she warned. "He'll want to gut you like a pig when he realizes you're Mel's father."

"I wonder if we could leave that part out?" Al suggested.

"No, I think he needs to know. If he ever finds out later, your safety would be jeopardized – he'd put your head on a stake and feed your body to the crocodiles."

"I'm sensing there may be a problem in all this," Al ventured.

"No, I'll tell him that I left you, which is true. He'll still want to tie your intestines to a tree and make you walk around it until you die, but over time he'll mellow. He knows me," Mari said.

"What if he acts before he's had time to consider all the facts?" Al asked.

"Well, the worst that can happen is you die, which it sounds like will happen if you don't see him," Mari reasoned. "So what have you got to lose?"

"Put like that, how can I resist?"

"Seriously, though, it's probably best if I meet him first," Mari said. "If I think there's any danger for you, we'll just have to think of something else."

"Is he really that bad?" Al asked.

"They call him the "Borderland Butcher. He's one of the top officers in FARC. But I've known him all my life – he's really as gentle as a lamb," Mari assured him.

Al's eyes widened. "The Borderland Butcher?"

"Usually, just *El Carnicero* – 'The Butcher'," Mari said. "'The Borderland Butcher' is more his official title."

"So…" Al clarified, "only for formal situations. With family he's just The Butcher?"

"Exactly. But I think it's all exaggeration to create fear in the hearts of his enemies," Mari suggested.

"It's working on me," Al said.

"You see? That's why they call themselves these things," Mari reasoned, glad Al had finally gotten it.

"Given that he's a top dog with FARC, isn't it possible there's a side of him you haven't seen, that maybe has developed over time?"

"Al. I'm his crazy sister, and I dumped you, and never told you we have a daughter together. He may be a violent psychopath, but he's still a man. So let's hope he'll see your side in this," Mari said. "At least he wasn't around when I was crying myself to sleep every night for a year," she continued. "I hope Mom didn't tell him."

"Hmmmm. So if we go to Cali together, who's going to watch Mel?" Al asked.

"Oh, Momma and my sisters will. They absolutely love her," Mari gushed. "I'll call them tonight and see what time they can come over tomorrow."

"And getting to Cali?" Al was almost afraid to ask.

"We'll hire a plane. A small four passenger one, so you won't have to document anything."

"If you recall," Al reminded her. "I don't do well with motion."

"You'll be fine," Mari replied. "The alternative is being slaughtered by Gringo death squads."

"You have a marvelous way with words."

"After three years, one forgets the little things, no?" Mari chided.

The discussion went on for another hour, as they argued the fine details of the plan. But in the end it was Al's only shot.

The talk turned to Mel, and the childhood he'd missed sharing with her so far. She sounded like a good kid and it was obvious that she was the light of Mari's life. Al wondered what it must be like to care so profoundly about someone besides yourself, and again felt an uneasy stirring.

At ten p.m. Mari went to a closet, got a sheet and a pillow out and invited Al to make himself at home on the sofa. Her only request was that he sleep clothed so if Mel wandered in for any reason she wouldn't be permanently traumatized by the sight of his unclad body.

What else was new? Seemed like a fair deal to Al.

At least he had clean socks.

# CHAPTER 36

The following morning, Al woke early and was showered, shaved and in shape by the time Mari emerged from her room with Mel.

Mel regarded Al with seriousness, and held out her hand. "*Buenas dias,*" she recited, lisping over the soft consonants.

"*Encantado, Senorita Melissa,*" Al replied sonorously, shaking her little hand with as much gravity as he'd ever shown at a diplomatic event. "She can talk?" Al wondered aloud to Mari.

"She started young, at eighteen months, forming simple words," Mari explained. "At this point she's up to three and four word sentences." Pride bloomed in Mari's face. "She's advanced for her age."

"I don't have any experience with this…" Al explained.

"I wouldn't expect you to," Mari said as she headed into the kitchen to set about feeding Mel.

The two sisters and Momma arrived at nine a.m. and were introduced, in turn, to Al. He got the feeling Mari hadn't fully explained his relationship in the family, although he sensed that Momma wasn't particularly warm toward him. He asked Mari, who told him that no, as far as they knew he was just a friend, nothing more.

He supposed that painted an accurate picture, at this point.

Mari explained to Al they'd be taking a taxi to the nearby airport – she'd arranged a small plane to take them to Cali for a thousand dollars plus hotel expenses; the pilot would wait for two days in Cali to fly them back.

"That seems expensive," Al grumbled.

"You can always take the bus," Mari countered, "which takes several days and runs the risk of requiring your passport to be checked as you get further south."

That about covered that issue.

Al quickly calculated; with the flight and some hotels, he would burn a third of his money. Then again, he wasn't going to need much if this didn't work – his retirement would be measured in hours, not decades.

Every cloud had a silver lining.

Which might have been a poor choice of phrase, given Al's reaction when he saw the plane Mari had hired. He'd been in economy cars that were bigger. Mari seemed unconcerned. Al needed a drink. Or ten.

The captain, Jorge, patted the side of the dilapidated plane with pride, assuring them that they were in for a treat. A 1978 Cessna Turbo Skylane. Finest plane in the air. Hundred and fifty knots per hour would get them all the way to Cali with no refueling. And Jorge proudly told them that he'd wisely bought his fuel for most of the flight in Venezuela, due to the radically lower costs. He'd have to charge $1500 if he did the whole trip using Colombian fuel.

"Isn't the plane almost thirty-five years old?" Al asked Mari.

"That means it hasn't crashed for thirty-five years," Mari observed. "Relax, you're in safe hands."

She had a point. Sort of.

The plane interior smelled like ass. Maybe all small plane interiors did.

"Where's the co-pilot?" Al asked, noticing the dual controls.

"*No necesito*," Jorge replied. "Don't need one."

Al wasn't convinced. "What if you have a heart attack or something?"

"Let's hope I don't. If I do, try not to hit anything," Jorge advised.

"How about the bathroom?" Al asked.

Jorge handed him an empty *Gatorade* bottle. "Liquids only."

Al could already see this was going to be a hoot. He gazed at the clouded over sky skeptically. The thunderheads looked ominous.

So did the pilot.

They were airborne within ten minutes. Al watched the altimeter as the small plane rose to nine thousand feet and steadied. Jorge seemed suspiciously close to nodding off. Every so often they'd lurch and bump and plummet alarmingly. Al left finger grooves in the armrest. Mari looked like she was sightseeing.

He was convinced they were going to go down at least a dozen times over the Andes, when they were only three thousand feet above the mountain tops. Jorge would let out a 'whoo' every now and then following a particularly alarming loss of altitude or sideways wind shear.

They touched down in Cali just a little over three hours later. Al felt like he'd been doing sit-ups the entire time – his abdomen was cramping painfully from the stress.

"Maybe on the trip back it will be bumpy. There are supposed to be storms moving in over the next couple of days," Jorge said as they left for their hotel.

Just making idle small talk.

Al's stomach did another flop – he made a mental note to knock back a liter of Absolut before the return flight.

# CHAPTER 37

The FARC (Revolutionary Armed Forces of Colombia) have existed since 1964, when insurgents from the Colombian Communist Party armed themselves to combat regular army units bent on breaking up communist strongholds around the country. It had developed over time into an armed militia that to this day controls almost half of Colombia's territory.

FARC forces are significant players in the Colombian cocaine production and shipment trade, having escalated from 'taxing' production to becoming involved in manufacturing and trafficking. Estimates of revenue exceeding $100 million per year from these activities are probably conservative, and FARC is known to be instrumental in many aspects of the business.

Although Colombia doesn't like to advertise the fact that almost half the country is under the sway of, or completely controlled by, an armed militia which makes its living via the drug trade, kidnappings and extortion – the fact is that the nation has existed in a state of *de facto* civil war for half a century.

While some of the grievances that drove FARC in the early years have passed into obscurity, one of its central themes remains vital – the subjugation of manual laborers and murder and terrorism against union activists by agents of American multi-national corporations...

Along with strongholds in and around the Darien region, FARC controls most of the south-eastern portion of Colombia, the Andean plains region, and much of the area along the Brazilian and Ecuadorian border.

Viewed by some as armed thugs and murderers, and by others as the voice of the proletariat against foreign imperialism and oppression, the truth is complex, and likely somewhere in between. It's undeniable that armed clashes tend to be brutal and indiscriminate, and yet it's also obvious that the group is a political force to be reckoned with.

Venezuela has attempted to temper the tone of the rhetoric surrounding FARC, and has encouraged the group to disarm and to stop employing kidnapping and similar terrorist/criminal tactics – with minimal success.

The U.S. Government's official stance is that FARC is a terrorist organization, but as with many such stances, the position that its duty is to stamp out global terrorism is highly elastic, given that the total narco-profit pie is a massive number – some estimates place it at nearly a trillion dollars a year globally. Money of that magnitude has to find legitimate homes in mainstream industries; multiply this by thirty years and apply simple compounding at a nominal rate – say 3% per year – and it's easy to see that a large piece of the global economic pie has had to pass through or has been generated by narcotics trafficking.

One illuminating example of how the U.S. talks out of both sides of its mouth when it comes to terrorism and organized crime is an embarrassing photo from 1999, when Richard Grasso, the Chairman of the New York Stock Exchange, was photographed in the cocaine production territory of Colombia hugging the then second in command of FARC, Raul Reyes.

Another is a slew of lawsuits alleging that Chiquita, through its subsidiary in Colombia, funded payments to the AUC – the 'United Self Defense Forces' – a paramilitary organization that was in reality a murder-for-hire and extortion group that killed hundreds of union leaders and 'agitators' who were pushing for better wages and working conditions in the banana industry in Colombia. While the U.S. Justice Department fined Chiquita $25 million in 2005 for what it termed 'extortion' payments to the AUC, a host of internal company documents recently released under the Freedom of Information Act suggest that the payments were much more than protection money.

Whatever one's views, it's obvious from even a cursory review of the history of Central and South America over the last fifty years that what are perceived as American interests have resulted in massive numbers of violent deaths, and the populations of the affected countries have long memories.

They hold a grudge.

෧৵

Sam was back at the embassy, having grabbed a few hours of sleep at home. He now occupied a temporary office down the hall from his permanent one. Richard, as far as he could tell, had done no more than catnap in the office since his arrival.

The interrogation of Carmen had yielded no new information, other than confirmation that Al occasionally moonlighted as an escort for customers who wanted to cross a border with no questions asked. Given that Al didn't actually transport them across any borders he technically wasn't doing anything wrong, and it seemed like he was more of a feel-good chauffeur than anything else.

So far, the foreign intelligence angle hadn't provided any additional illumination on the enigma that was Al. If he *was* a foreign operative, then he was deep cover and had been spectacularly good at acting the part of a harmless, drunken oaf. That either made him a dangerous fool or an even more dangerous genius capable of years of sustained, convincing role playing.

Richard swiveled in Sam's office chair taking stock of events and their implications. Jenkins had continued the questioning until he'd been sure there was nothing more to tell, and had dumped Carmen's body in an outlying area where she was unlikely to be found for weeks. The jungle typically consumed anything that hit the ground very quickly so any complications were unlikely. Richard hadn't shared this with Sam because he didn't want the idiot to complicate his life further with any vague ethical considerations about the value of foreign nationals' lives.

The team was still located in Colombia but had nothing to do. The decision was made to get them to Bogota, as there was a U.S. Embassy there, but they were at a dead end on leads. Until Al made a wrong move or contacted them again they had nothing.

That didn't sit well with Richard, however, he'd learned to be extremely patient during his thirty-five year tenure with the CIA. He had run ops all over the world, in all manners of hellholes, including Colombia and Ecuador, so he felt comfortable with the local dynamics. Compared to places like Nigeria or Sudan or the Balkans, this was positively uncomplicated and serene. So he'd just watch and wait, and be ready to pounce once Al surfaced.

Sam had cancelled the police bulletin, as instructed, and now Richard was thinking maybe that hadn't been such a great idea. Then again, they really had no choice – they couldn't afford Al getting picked up, and a room full of cops viewing the camera's contents. That would broaden Richard's headache exponentially.

They'd questioned all of Al's associates and known contacts but the man had no close friends or confidants. No mate, no steady, no poker buddies or weekend pals. It was as if Al was some kind of ghost. He had no credit cards, though his credit rating was below terrible anyway – then again, that could have also been a skillful ruse to sustain his cover. And worst yet, his generation of passport didn't have a chip in it, so it couldn't be tracked. Unless it was entered into the system somewhere and flagged a computer, Al was essentially invisible.

That worried Richard. Under normal circumstances the first thing to do was follow the money, understanding that amateurs virtually always slipped up and eventually used an ATM or credit card. But a search of Al's apartment had yielded his ATM card on the coffee table – next to his cell phone – so no hope there of an easy tag.

That's where things got complicated – if he was a pro, he'd ditched everything and likely had an emergency stash of cash to access until his handlers could get him somewhere safe. If that was the case and Al disappeared they had an epic problem, namely the equivalent of a hydrogen bomb ticking away, to be used by America's enemies at the worst possible moment. The fallout would be devastating; the credibility of the nation ruined, and the repercussions would cut across partisan lines. It could literally start World War Three.

There was simply no way they could allow the unthinkable to happen. Richard had even run scenarios where a major land and sea attack could be launched in Colombia, annihilating a whole town if need be, to contain the damage. It could be made to look like a rebel attack of rival elements fighting. Or whatever. But in reality they had no target, and no clue as to where to begin looking. There was no guarantee Al wasn't long gone and currently jetting to Moscow, or Beijing, or God knew where.

These were the crisis situations that wore on him, as one of the top field directors and trusted confidant of the Director. He was one of a handful, the inner circle, and knew the whole story; or at least as much as anyone knew aside from the Director – and possibly the President, though there were many operations that required deniability, and so the Oval Office was kept in the dark on them; for their own good, really.

But exposure of the camera's contents would destroy everything. There was no denial that would be plausible. It was the worst of all possible situations.

# CHAPTER 38

Mari and Al checked into their hotel – a three star establishment five blocks from the primary business and tourist center. The modest focal point of the hotel was a coca plant growing in the small courtyard that housed the pool. They had a single room, but two beds; Mari hoped she had made it abundantly clear this wasn't going to be their re-kindling vacation.

Sure, they had things left unsaid – and now Al knew about Mel. For better or worse, things had forever changed. It seemed Al had changed too. Mari reminded herself this was about saving the life of Mel's father. Nothing more. At least, that's how she had articulated it, and Al had agreed – in that way of his.

Once Mari had checked in, she met Al down the street from the hotel for a late lunch and gave him a room key. She instructed him to stay in the room at all times until she came for him. She'd already slipped the desk clerk some cash to ignore whoever accompanied her – in a society where mistresses were common you often didn't want to recognize whoever a young lady was with.

Nobody knew that Mari's brother was high up in the FARC; for her protection and his. Many of the fighters went by false names or aliases, and nobody needed to know who was who when a man had proved his loyalty over a harsh number of years. Mari knew her brother, 'The Butcher' was beholden to and connected to no one, and that's the way it would stay. If there was any hint that she was his sister, she'd have been in mortal danger from the Colombian government, but Mari felt safe enough in her society – where secrets were closely guarded for generations.

They finished their lunch and returned to the hotel, where Al was studiously ignored by the suddenly-absent clerk. Once in the room, Al searched around for a mini-bar but it wasn't that level of place. Mari advised him against ordering anything from room service unless he wanted to risk his life, so it was looking to be a dry trip for Al, other than the beer he'd had at lunch.

At four o'clock Mari's cell rang. After a listening to a few words, she wrote down a number on the corner of a paper napkin, which she then screwed up and put it in her pocket.

"I need to use a pay phone and call this number within fifteen minutes. I'll arrange a meeting with my brother then. I may be gone for a few minutes, or maybe hours. Either way, don't worry, and stay put. And under no circumstances call or order anything until I get back. No joke, Al," Mari instructed, giving him a withering look. She knew him very well.

Mari grabbed her small purse, checked her reflection in the mirror and hung the 'Do Not Disturb' sign on the door as she closed it.

Al listened to Mari's footsteps echoing down the passageway, and then she was gone. He tried taking a nap but the adrenaline from the flight and the anxiety over Mari's brother overwhelmed his usual ability to sleep virtually anywhere at the slightest pretense. He tossed and turned until common sense told him he may as well try to distract his overworked brain. He switched on the TV to try out the Spanish language programs. Ugly Betty was the only program he recognized – he hadn't realized it was Colombian, not that he particularly cared. He only recognized it because his secretary was a devotee, regaling him with plot summaries on a regular basis. Usually when he was tediously hung over.

The darkening sky triggered Al's concern for Mari and he was getting seriously worried until finally he heard the key turn in the door.

Mari entered.

"So how did it go?" he asked.

"How did what go?"

"Uh, well, I don't know. Your meeting?" Al hated when she fucked with him. This was too good an opportunity for her to pass up though, obviously.

"Oh, that. Pretty well. We can discuss it at dinner. I'm starving. There's a good restaurant a few blocks away, according to the desk. Let's try it," she suggested, before waltzing in the bathroom and locking herself in. "I'll be ready in five," she called through the door.

Al played along. What choice did he have?

She finally emerged, all sweetness and perfume, grabbed his arm and walked him toward the door. He grabbed his satchel and they made their steady way to the restaurant. The streets were bustling with the dinner crowd and Al detected no aura of menace or danger on the well lit street.

Once they were seated and had ordered, Mari gave him the data dump.

"You'll meet him tomorrow. Seven a.m.. We have to go to a coffee shop a few minutes from the hotel, and we'll get a message from someone telling us where you have to go. It will be just the two of you." She folded her arms. "I'm to stay out of it."

"Does he want to cut out my heart and eat it in front of me?" Al asked.

"I think we got past that part. I guess you'll know for sure tomorrow. If he changes his mind, I'll remember you every Christmas," Mari offered.

"That's touching. But seriously – is he holding a grudge?"

"You'll be fine. Just don't make any sudden moves around him," she warned.

"Are you serious?" Al demanded. He couldn't tell.

"Mostly no – okay, maybe a little. He's on edge being near an urban area," she explained.

"The Butcher is a little testy, but hopefully I'll be fine," Al concluded.

"It's the best I could do. Have you got any better options I haven't heard yet?"

Al burst into low-volume song: "*We're off to see The Butcher…*"

The reference was lost on Mari, who'd learned her English in elementary school, before perfecting it throughout high school and college, that and watching Bruce Willis action films.

Their food arrived, and Al floated a different topic as they ate. "Mel is very cute, and very smart," he began.

"She should be. She's my daughter," Mari stated.

He tried again. "I never thought I'd have a daughter…"

"Al, you don't… I do," she explained matter-of-factly. "You had a few seconds of muscle spasm. I have a lifelong commitment."

"And what if I don't feel that way?" Al asked. "I mean, now that I've seen her? Now that I've seen *you* again?"

"Spare me the melodrama, Al," Mari snapped. "You had a chance to stay with me, and if you'd loved me you would have. You didn't. So there are no obligations."

"You never called me to tell me," Al argued.

"I had my cell number forwarded for a year. Were your fingers broken?"

Al shook his head in defeat. "I thought you knew me well enough to understand I'm an idiot sometimes…"

She stared at him. He had a fleck of food in his goatee, and was sweating down his sunburned bald head.

"Sometimes?" Mari repeated.

"Haven't you ever done something really stupid you now regret?" Al asked.

She stared at him again, incredulously. Waited a few beats. Eventually Al figured it out.

Time for a different approach.

"I appreciate what you're doing for me, Mari," Al offered.

"I'm doing it for Mel."

And there they let it settle, though Al believed, or hoped, there might just be more to it than that.

They finished their dinner and walked back to the hotel, the streets still populated, only now with young people headed to the nearby clubs. The same desk clerk abruptly found something that needed doing in the back office when he saw Mari entering the lobby. Mari and *The Invisible Al* made their way upstairs.

A tense silence permeated the room as they took turns brushing their teeth and getting ready for bed – Al taking a shower so he'd save time in the morning.

Eventually, they silently slipped under the sheets on their respective beds. Mari turned off the bedside lamp.

"I'm sorry, Mari, about everything," Al murmured. "Sleep well…my friend."

"Me too, Al…me too."

The following morning, Mari's phone alarm sounded at six. She went into the bathroom for her morning routine while Al tried to drowse. Mari emerged at six-thirty.

"God you snore loudly nowadays," she declared.

"Good morning to you, too," Al responded.

"Really. My cousin had an English bulldog, and that's the only other noise I've ever heard that sounds like you," she said. "You didn't snore four years ago."

"I have allergies." Al explained.

"You're fat," Mari offered.

"I have issues," he tried again.

"Like eating too much. And not exercising, and drinking all day long…" she listed.

"I was thinking of respiratory deficiencies," Al said.

"I hear smoking helps those," Mari observed.

"I'm trying to quit," Al lied.

"Snoring? Or eating too much? Or smoking?"

This wasn't going well. "I'm sorry I disturbed your rest, Mari."

"We need to leave in a few minutes," she said – right, as usual.

Al dabbed ointment on his ragged feet, pulled on his clothes and grabbed his knapsack. He was ready to hit the road in three minutes flat.

"Were you planning on zipping your fly?" Mari queried.

"Oops…I'm still asleep," Al said.

She didn't say anything.

They made their way to the street and walked four blocks to an intersection where a small coffee bar was serving espresso and pastries. They took a table on the sidewalk and ordered *cafe Americanos*. The coffee arrived and they sipped it in silence. Nobody approached. No one called.

After twenty minutes, the waiter brought the check, handing it to Al. He glanced at it and fished around in his pocket for change.

"Look at the back of the check, Al," Mari instructed.

A single sentence was scrawled in Spanish.

"Walk south on Calle 2 – start now," Mari read. "This is it. I'll pay. Good luck, Al."

The cafe stood on the corner of Calle 2. Al got his bearings and looked for the position of the sun to establish direction but it was hidden somewhere behind an expanse of rolling clouds. He extracted the GPS from his satchel, powered it on and immediately turned right, walking steadily down the quiet street. Two blocks later a car pulled to the curb beside him and a voice from the backseat called his name through the halfway lowered window. Al stopped and the door swung open. He got in, and a man jumped in beside him. They roared off into traffic.

Forty minutes later they were deep into the countryside, having left the city behind them. They turned off the highway and navigated a series of ever smaller roads until they were bumping along a dirt track cut into the dense growth. They arrived at a small caretaker's hut and pulled over. Two men holding machine-guns stood on either side of a Nissan van. A third man rolled the sliding door open and gestured with his head for Al to get inside.

He did, and another man already in the van slipped a black hood over his head. The van engine started and soon they were bouncing down a rural trail, after making a series of switchbacks and turns. They stopped ten minutes later and Al was guided out of the van and into the interior of a structure. The hood was removed, revealing a man in his late thirties, seated on a threadbare loveseat, black and white photos of anonymous Colombians framed on the wall.

The man gestured. "Sit."

Al sat.

"Mari tells me you are someone important to her, and that I shouldn't kill you – yet. She says you have a proposition for me that is sensitive and could make a tremendous difference to my organization, as well as to the eventual balance of power in Colombia. That's quite a promise. So I agreed not to hack your head off with a machete if you could interest me within five minutes of meeting you. You're now down to four and a half," the man said in good, if accented, English.

"Julio?" Al asked.

"You're wasting time. But yes, that is one of my names."

"My name is Al. Mari swears you're trustworthy, which is why I'm here," Al started.

"You're an American. What would you know about trustworthiness? You now have four minutes," Julio advised.

"I know you value her," Al said, "and will understand the value of what I'm about to offer you. When we're done, I'll tell you what I propose and what I want in exchange."

"What you want in exchange?" Julio's eyes widened. "How about being allowed to leave with all your organs? You now have three and a half minutes."

Al slowly raised his knapsack, and handed it to Julio.

"Open the bag. Inside, you'll find a camera. Open the screen, turn on the power and push the button with the single arrow on it," Al instructed.

Julio cautiously opened the bag and removed the camera. He watched the screen for five minutes, in silence. Then he powered the camera down and put it on the sofa next to him.

"No fucking way," Julio said, shaking his head at what he'd just seen. "No fucking way…"

"Yup. Now here's what I'm proposing…"

They spent the next hour going over the outline of Al's plan. Julio stared at the ratty ceiling, lost in thought. After a heavy, almost infinite silence he nodded, as if coming to a decision.

"What do you want, if I agree to this?" Julio asked. "And why wouldn't I just kill you now, and take this, and do whatever I feel like?"

"Because you're an honorable man. Because you gave your word. And most importantly, because your sister would never forgive you," Al answered honestly.

"And your demands?"

Al listed them. Four items.

Julio appeared to consider them thoughtfully before rising to his feet.

"We have a deal. My men will take you back to within a block of where they picked you up. Give me forty-eight hours to arrange things and I'll get in contact with Mari." He shook Al's hand. "You took a huge risk bringing this to me. I really wouldn't hesitate to knife you where you stand and watch you choke on your own blood," he warned.

"I bet on your sister."

"I'll keep the camera," Julio said. "Good luck with her," he concluded.

"Thanks. I'm going to need a lot of it. Luck, I mean," Al quickly added. "I'll be in touch."

Julio walked to the door of the house they were in and snapped his fingers. A man entered, holding the hood, and pulled it over Al's head again. Al felt something thrust into his hands – his knapsack; now empty save for the little GPS unit.

And just like that, it was over.

The drive back to Cali was anti-climactic. They changed cars twice, and after an hour Al found himself blinking in the mid-day light, standing on the sidewalk of Calle 2.

# CHAPTER 39

Julio watched the video in silence as the van's wheels crunched down the dirt track and away from the little house.

He liked Al's plan. What the man had wanted in return was laughably easy to provide. The difficult part would be dancing with the elephant – negotiating with the U.S. government so FARC got what it wanted without bringing down the wrath of the entire American military machine. But the reward was potentially massive and would make FARC extremely powerful and wealthy, positioning it to replace the existing government of Colombia at some point in the future – something the FARC had never believed possible during its entire existence.

Al had just handed Julio the means with which to manage the U.S. and get it to work toward FARC's interests. It would also reposition Julio within the organization to be the natural successor to Alfonso Cano, the current Commander in Chief. In five years, or ten maybe, he'd step down, or die, and then Julio would be the one to assume control – which was virtually guaranteed...once he'd negotiated this deal.

The risk was worth it.

Of course, it would take a bit of work to set up a secure communications channel that couldn't be traced, but he had a contact that could do it via the Internet. He thought through how best to transmit his demands, and smiled at his idea.

The CIA's Director swiveled his chair to face the telephone. The Agency was taping the call and attempting to triangulate a geographical location for its origination, however, they couldn't get past the IP masking software – the signal was being bounced to IP addresses around the world, seemingly at random, every 30 seconds. The Director realized at some level that it didn't matter – it was the substance of the discussion that was key. They'd already dispensed with identifying the key participants – now they were down to terms.

"I'm listening," the Director said, his distinctive lisp emphasizing the sibilance.

"What we require is for your government to allow our shipments to pass unmolested into U.S. ports. This should be simple enough to achieve. Twice a month, a container or two will arrive on a designated cargo vessel…and you'll ensure that the contents make it through customs unobstructed – with no tracking or other subterfuge," the Colombian stated.

"And you honestly think we can arrange for thousands of pounds of cocaine to make it onto American soil every month with no DEA or law enforcement interference?" the Director clarified.

"I believe you're more than capable of accomplishing this," Julio explained. "It's not as though there aren't tons making it through every week already. What I'm proposing is that in exchange for our discretion, you eliminate the losses we experience on occasional shipments and enable us to ramp up our supply to better accommodate demand."

"And if something goes wrong on our end? Something unforeseeable?" the Director asked.

"You will reimburse us for the lost shipment at a cost we stipulate," Julio said. "In all honesty, I don't care if you transfer hundreds of millions of dollars to our accounts every month and confiscate most of the shipments, or allow them all to go through. That's up to you. If your country really wants to stop most of the inbound cocaine traffic, you can stop the containers and pay us the value."

"You realize this is unprecedented," the Director hissed, "and flies in the face of decades of policy and stated goals of our government, when it comes to drug control and supporting terrorist organizations?"

"That's the second part of the deal. Over the next three years, your government needs to temper its rhetoric regarding FARC and slowly transition to a position where it recognizes us as a legitimate political faction within Colombia. Within another two, I would expect that policy will support FARC's agenda to becoming a mainstream contender for Colombia's government," Julio continued. "In return, FARC won't feel it necessary to engage in kidnapping or extortion as mechanisms to achieve political change."

"What guarantees do we have that you'll honor your part of the bargain?" the Director asked.

"Every month, you'll not see the recording splashed across every PC screen in the world. Each day, you won't wake up to a world where the U.S. Government is exposed as liars, cheats and frauds, and rendered incapable of governing or negotiating with other, legitimate regimes. That will be your guarantee. There are now multiple copies of the tape in secure locations around the globe – if you doubt my willingness to broadcast them, simply do not agree to my terms within the next twelve hours and we'll have nothing more to discuss," Julio warned.

"But you're asking the impossible." The Director's voice had taken on a slight wobble.

"I'm not asking. I'm proposing a solution to the biggest problem your nation has faced in two hundred years. If you don't accept my terms, or think you can propose different ones, then do nothing…and twelve hours from now you'll be facing political extinction. You know how to contact me. You have twelve hours. I suggest you stop posturing and start getting the approvals you need to ratify our arrangement," Julio advised. "Oh, and just in case you're getting any clever ideas; if we get hit with a missile attack or I choke on a chicken bone or get run down by a car, the tape will immediately be circulated globally. So you better take all precautions to ensure I live a long and prosperous life," Julio continued. "You have eleven hours and fifty-nine minutes."

The call terminated.

The Director stared at the phone for a while before turning to face the other occupant of the room – the White House Chief of Staff, Jeremy Temens.

"What the fuck are we going to do?" Jeremy demanded.

The Director wiped the sweat from his brow. "I think we need to brief the President. It's actually not a bad deal, all things considered…"

"Are you insane?" Jeremy sputtered. "The U.S. Government is going to become the silent partner of the largest cocaine exporter in the world, as blackmail payoff?"

"Jeremy, this is very simple. It's a matter of survival…the least of two evils. Sure, we can all agree that drugs are bad and wrong and cause suffering and crime and the like, but in my opinion, the fallout of the tape going public makes that moral position a non-issue. We can't allow it to surface. Ever. I would have thought that's obvious. You're just lucky he didn't demand an F-15 filled with suitcase nukes to be personally delivered by the first lady to a Medellin airstrip."

The Director couldn't believe Jeremy actually imagined there were any other options at this point. So a few more kilos of coke got into Miami or Los Angeles than usual – was that the end of the world as they knew it?

"It's just morally reprehensible," Jeremy complained. "And it'll be tough getting the President to go along with it. Remember – the consequences of a shift in our political stance toward the FARC can never be undone."

The Director shook his head. "No, it won't be hard to get him to see reason. It's his, and the country's, ass. It's an easy choice – a no-brainer. And as to Colombia, so what? So a new set of pistol wavers becomes a legitimate force of change – is that really any different than Arafat being hailed as a peacemaker? Come on. Grow up, Jeremy."

"How did we ever get to this point?" Jeremy asked, visibly mortified.

"We got just a little too clever and pushed our luck. And we lost. So let's just accept this as a cost of doing business, do what we have to do, and move on," the Director advised. "Call the President, and let's go visit the White House and get this over with."

The Director had no remorse and was pragmatic about his counsel. The administration had decided to craft a stunt that would boost the sitting President's approval ratings the year before an election – and justify its aggressive policies in the Middle East. Sure, the prior administration had set it all in motion by its actions, but nobody had forced the current President to up the ante and go along with this now-disastrous public relations scheme.

It had all seemed so simple, up until the tape had surfaced.

All they'd had to do was create a media event, and the public bought it big time; and if the rest of the world had doubts, it stayed silent. Nobody wanted to rock the boat and incur the wrath of the U.S. Government. It wasn't worth it, and anyway, no good was served by airing skepticism about a *fait accompli*.

So there had been a dramatic assault, a triumph of good over evil, and an heroic mission that could make the country feel good about itself in the midst of a financial crisis in which the largest financial institutions and banks robbed the nation blind. It had been a perfect plan, with no downside.

Amazingly, none of the mainstream media even questioned that the number one most wanted man in the world's body needed to be confirmed as being the genuine article by someone besides the U.S. government, and that by dumping the *corpus delicti* all proof that any of the claims were true was gone. It seemed almost orchestrated.

*How did anyone really know that it was Bin Laden?*

"Because we say so."

*How do we know he died in the raid, or that he even ever existed except as a CIA straw man?*

"You'll just have to trust us on that."

*How do we know he was even alive at all, and didn't die ten years ago, as many web resources claim – not to mention his obituary in a prominent Egyptian newspaper in 2001?*

"Trust us."

As to the corroboration, the Government grudgingly allowed groups of U.S. elected officials to see photos that purported to be of 'Geronimo' – Bin Laden's corpse. Were any of these photos subjected to any kind of real analysis by impartial experts to ensure they weren't clever dupes? No, of course not. What the public got treated to was the spectacle of red-faced talking heads saying things like, "Yup. Y'all gotta know that's one dead Osama," after viewing the snaps. Was any of the DNA independently verified as being genuine, or not having come from other collection opportunities fifteen or more years earlier? Unnecessary. After all, the government would never lie about something like that.

No, instead, the administration simply insisted what it was saying was true and offered no proof other than the strident volume of its insistence. Just as it insisted that the Gulf of Tonkin had taken place in order to escalate the war in Vietnam – before it became common knowledge that no such thing occurred. And just as it insisted that it had no foreknowledge of Pearl Harbor – even though telegrams documented the top brass had full and credible warnings from Australia two full days before the strike. No, the stupid rubes bought it, lock, stock and barrel. They never learned.

The government knew that its population wouldn't question its spin, and it cared little about international skepticism. Just as it didn't care about international skepticism about prior false claims; like the supposedly irrefutable one concerning nuclear missiles in Iraq that could hit Israel within minutes. And just as it responded with mockery to several authenticated videos by Bin Laden claiming Al Quaeda had no part in the attacks of 9-11. Those were 'distortions' and 'lies', whereas the one video where he purportedly took credit for the attacks featured a man 40 pounds heavier than Bin Laden with a nose a full centimeter wider than the genuine Osama, wearing rings in contradiction of Muslim practice – even hard-liners considered this parody a fake. But to the U.S. government that video was twenty-four karat gold, and shame on anyone for questioning it.

No, the CIA and the administration understood that if they made a claim, and had the media repeat the claim over and over, they could make even an obvious lie into a new kind of truth – at least for the U.S. population – and if it was later exposed as false, the new proof could just be ignored away or dismissed as an irrelevant mistake. After all, nobody was infallible.

Several generations of political correctness had bred a population that confused patriotism with credulousness and felt it was unpatriotic to question anything the power structure claimed was true. The government now relied on that combination of ignorance and apathy for tacit approval of its deeds. It realized that reality didn't matter any more – there was no right or wrong, there was no 'what actually happened' versus invention; there was simply what the government said happened. All other speculation was squashed as wacky conspiracy nonsense…or treason.

That a nation founded upon the principal of a small government that should be distrusted and held accountable by its constituents could morph into a state-run machine where the apparatus determined what was fact and what was fiction, and the masses swallowed it up without question, had been unthinkable a few decades ago. The former U.S.S.R. was castigated for its ludicrous internal public relations messages of happy tractor workers and a benevolent ruling group of equal privilege. Back then, those were examples of totalitarianism or fascism.

Apparently not when the U.S. did it.

No, the CIA understood that; he who controlled the message, controlled history.

So history would record that the U.S. had gone in and killed Bin Laden, and he'd gotten what he had coming.

The crowds celebrated across the nation, and the President became a kind of hero overnight.

And they all lived happily ever after.

It had been perfect.

Except for Albert Ross and the fucking camera.

☙❧

Al and Mari checked out of the hotel at eleven, and after grabbing breakfast in the lobby restaurant they caught a taxi to the airport.

Jorge was waiting for them by the battered old plane. Al cursed that he hadn't belted down a few fortifiers at the hotel, but given Mari's mood, it hadn't seemed like a good idea. So he was going to have to do the return trip sober as well – a state of affairs that hadn't done much for his mood, either.

Mari's cell rang as they were buckling into their seats. She looked at the caller ID but there was no number listed. Odd.

A digitally distorted voice spoke a single sentence: "Your friend will get everything he requested." And then the line went dead.

Mari turned to Al, who was struggling with the seatbelt, and deftly fastened it for him.

"So what did you ask for?" she said. "What was your end of the deal?"

"I told him I wanted a new name and passport with a guarantee of his organization's protection...and a bar on a beach somewhere warm where there aren't any Gringos, and where the U.S. has no reach – like Venezuela...or Cuba. And a little pocket money to cover operating expenses until it hits its stride," Al explained.

"A bar, huh? How fitting. How much did you ask for...this pocket money?" Mari inquired.

"Half a million dollars. I figured that would last a while, even if the bar didn't do so well."

Mari raised an eyebrow. "You know that's a fortune someplace like Venezuela."

"Yeah, but in the business your bro' is in, it's about twenty minutes' worth of profits. I'm not greedy," Al reasoned. What he didn't tell her was that he didn't plan to touch more than a hundred grand of it – ever – the other four hundred was Mel's college fund.

"No, you're a lot of things," Mari observed, "but greedy isn't one of them."

She buckled herself in and patted Jorge's shoulder to signal they were secure.

As the old plane taxied up the bumpy runway Al felt something rolling under his feet and leaned forward, retrieving the object.

The empty *Gatorade* bottle.

He hoped Jorge wouldn't need to use it; or at least had one of his own.

It was a long trip.

# CHAPTER 40

Al said goodbye to Mari and Mel and walked out the iron gate to the waiting taxi. The arrangement was to go into the downtown area and wait at a restaurant called El Mirador, where someone would contact him. Two weeks had passed since they'd arrived back in Cartagena after a turbulent flight on the little plane. Al had gotten his new Venezuelan passport and driver's license three days ago, delivered to his hotel in a plain envelope, along with a deposit slip in his new name for five hundred grand at Banesco in Caracas, Venezuela.

Al was now Alfredo Guerrero, presumably of Italian heritage – or perhaps Swiss or French descent via Mexico. All he really had to do was practice spelling his last name because he'd chosen the first after his favorite pasta dish and so was unlikely to forget it. He'd selected the last because it meant 'Warrior' in Spanish. He figured if Julio could be 'The Butcher', he could at least be a soldier of some sort. Conveniently, Alfredo shortened to Al, so he was safe on keeping the first name straight, even after a couple of cocktails.

He'd gotten his photographs for the new identification taken on his first day back in Cartagena, after which he did a surreptitious drop at a dive hotel in one of the seediest neighborhoods in town. Al looked like virtually any somewhat seedy middle-aged white man in the shot, although he felt he was considerably better looking than most. Admittedly, the shaved head look wasn't his best, but then again he was still breathing and no commandos had shown up to cut him down with a hail of lead so he was staying with it for now. He figured if he waited long enough all his hair would fall out anyway, making it a far lower-maintenance style in the long run.

Al made it a point of meeting up with Mari, and if possible, Mel, every day. He and Mari were still distant in places, but he felt like she was thawing a little. That he'd blown it badly was obvious to him – but he couldn't turn back the clock so he was reconciled to pushing on to whatever the future held as bravely as he could. He'd made it clear that he was interested in trying to patch things up but Mari was apparently still resentful – her feelings were still hurt, even three years after the fact. He couldn't say he blamed her. She'd spent a lot of time working on getting over any connection to him; it was foolish to expect her to be interested in re-kindling.

The cab arrived at the restaurant. It was a typical seafood-themed Caribbean place with dancing shrimp painted gaudily on the walls and salsa thumping out from the ceiling-mounted speakers. He sat at the table by the window, as instructed, and ordered the grilled fish and a Bavaria beer. A glance at his watch told him he still had twenty minutes till the rendezvous time and he could see no reason to starve.

The plan was to drive from Cartagena to Maicao near the Venezuelan border, then take a bus across the border to Maracaibo, which was a large city of over two million. From there he could transfer to another bus, taking him to Caracas, where he would be met and escorted to his new home in Carenero, roughly fifty miles east of Caracas.

The condo that had been leased for him was actually down the road from Carenero, in the larger town of Higuerote – a four mile drive – but the bar was by the yacht club in Carenero, so he'd be commuting every day. That was fine by Al – it was about as far as he could imagine from prying eyes, not that he had any fear he was still as valid a target – but you never knew.

Better safe than sorry.

The passport was genuine so he had no concerns that traveling would be any sort of problem. Whoever had arranged it had been thoughtful enough to get an entry stamp for Colombia dated a few days earlier so he would appear to the Venezuelan system to be returning home. Al knew nothing whatsoever about Venezuela except that it was on the Caribbean, had nice beaches and good weather, and enjoyed extremely poor relations with America, which was the most important thing.

His fish arrived and he tucked into it with enthusiasm. That had been one of the notable transformations his forced exile had brought about.

Everywhere he went now, he ordered the grilled fish, and, not only had he yet to be poisoned, he actually found it an enjoyable meal.

The waiter brought the bill. Al checked both sides of it, just in case.

Nothing.

After a few more minutes a mid-forties woman in fashionable jeans and a colorful blouse entered the restaurant and approached Al's table.

"Alfredo, *Corazon*, how have you been? I thought that was you," she cried, extending her arms to him.

Al, who had never seen her in his life, played along and stood embracing her fondly in return. To all the world it looked like good friends re-uniting after a lengthy period apart. The woman surveyed the restaurant over his shoulder as she hugged him, then whispered in Al's ear.

"Let's go to my car. The restaurant's clear. Hurry."

Al gathered his knapsack, now considerably fatter with the new shirts and shorts he'd bought, as well as six pairs of socks. He followed her through the doorway and down the shambling block to a parking garage. They walked silently to her car, and soon were hurtling down the road at the peculiarly Colombian clip that struck Al as borderline suicidal. She passed trucks on blind curves, never touched her turn indicators and redlined the motor as often as possible. Al was only half sure they'd make it in one piece but he figured she knew what she was doing.

He tried small talk with the woman, whose name he didn't know, but she wasn't chatty. Obviously this was business, and her job was to get him to the border without a tail, nothing more.

Al settled in for the ride and closed his eyes. At least that way, if they crashed and burned he'd never know what hit him.

And so began his new life.

# CHAPTER 41

Julio sat on a folding canvas chair in his field headquarters deep in the southern jungle, watching the small playback screen on the camera. It never ceased to fascinate him, even weeks after the arrangement with the U.S. Government had been finalized.

The date and time flickered in the lower left hand quadrant of the video, as a wizened, olive-skinned man in grey cotton pajamas sat at a metal table, sipping a glass of water, stroking his beard and responding to questions from an off-screen voice in a foreign language. He looked unwell, with a gaunt, jaundiced complexion and palsied hands, and appeared bewildered at times; at others, extremely fatigued. The date was April 18, 2011, at 3:22 p.m. and Osama Bin Laden didn't seem well at all. Julio had seen enough death to recognize it hanging in the air…and this was a man who was poised at its threshold.

Al had filled Julio in on the part the cook played during their hour long discussion – Ernesto had been making special meals for eight years at the villa. It wasn't difficult to do the math and figure out that the world's number one most wanted man had been in U.S. custody for at least that long. They'd likely grabbed him during the offensive in the mountains and caves of Tora Bora, assuming they hadn't had him even before then.

Julio always paused the tape in the same spot – one where Bin Laden stared straight at the camera with a look of despair and resignation in his eyes. He'd been beaten long ago, that much was clear. This was a man with no hope.

Julio had never tried to have the dialog transcribed – it was far too sensitive for any eyes but his. He'd secreted one other copy with his mother, who was unaware of what the flash drive he'd messengered to her contained – he'd instructed her to lock it in her old floor safe and forget about it. He knew she'd do as he asked without question. That's how mothers were. If anything happened to him, he'd left sealed instructions with a trusted associate in Bogota to go see her – then share the contents of the drive with the world. The friend was a schoolteacher he'd grown up with who had nothing to do with FARC or any political movement so Julio was confident that the instructions would remain sealed in the envelope, undisturbed unless he died an untimely death.

So far, twenty-eight shipments had made their way through U.S. ports with no problems whatsoever. He had no reason to believe that the new smooth passage wouldn't continue in perpetuity. Political realities were the same the world over – if you wanted power you had to resort to risky plays, and if you had power you'd do anything to maintain it. The U.S. was no different. The bargain would be honored in the same way that mutually-assured destruction had served as an effective deterrent to nuclear holocaust – if both parties understood their existence would be extinguished the moment they violated their pact, then neither would breach it.

The world hadn't changed during his lifetime and he doubted it would any time soon.

Humanity was a selfish organism.

⤙⤚

Using a rolled-up situation report, Sam swatted at a particularly persistent fly in seething frustration. The fly proved more dexterous than Sam.

Freshly separated from his wife, and with a challenging new posting, he viewed his current station as a temporary setback on his life track. Sometimes you got thrown curves. You dealt with them as best you could and put one foot in front of the other.

He never understood what had gone so wrong at the end of Richard's final visit to Panama. Richard had folded up his tent a few days after the final call from Al and departed without saying a word. He'd never offered any explanation, nor any guidance. Just left as abruptly as he'd arrived.

Sam's relocation orders hit several months later and came as a surprise, to say the least. Not to mention that they resulted in the sudden termination of his marriage. His wife had made it quite clear she'd stuck with him under the expectation that their life would change for the better, not the worse. When he'd told her they had to move within ten days, she'd packed her bags and returned to her family's home in the States.

He could see her point.

This posting was about as far from the power center of the Beltway as he could imagine. But it wasn't as though he had fifty job opportunities, and he was a company man so he'd toe the company line whether he liked it or not.

Part of Sam felt he'd been sentenced to purgatory and another argued that if he was able to persevere in his new assignment there'd be a shot at redemption with the Agency for sins he must have committed – even though nothing jumped out at him as obvious. Things had just gone sideways on him for reasons he didn't comprehend. He suspected that Richard had tanked his career out of spite. But Sam was resilient – he'd outlast the prick.

An explosion boomed outside on the street, beyond the heavy walls of the fortress-like embassy, and he ducked, more out of habit than anything else. One learned these things quickly. He peered out the heavily fortified window – it was nothing, just a backfire.

Still, better safe than sorry. The next time it could be real gunfire.

He tossed his Styrofoam cup of vile instant coffee into the trash, cursing his fate, then took a deep breath, committed to making the best of a miserable start to yet another miserable week.

The lights flickered, then the wall-mounted air conditioning unit quit with a sorry groan. Sam stabbed at the button of his intercom. Nobody answered.

As was usually the case when he most needed immediate assistance.

If there was a worse assignment than assistant station chief in Ndjamena, Chad, Sam had yet to hear of it.

# CHAPTER 42

Al fiddled with the top of the grill he'd installed, adjusting the angle so the fat ran down the grooved top pieces and into a channel collector, which in turn angled down into a reservoir. He'd developed the contrivance after dealing with flare-ups from burger grease.

At first he'd just kept the small palapa-topped open-air bar a beverages only establishment, but then he'd come up with the idea of building a cooking station off to the side of the large central bar. He'd run electricity to the grill area for a small refrigerator and now offered a menu consisting of cheeseburgers or grilled fish. The local fishermen came by every morning after their catch and provided him with fresh filets, and Al had enlisted the baker in town to make something that at least partially resembled a hamburger bun. He was introducing progress to the region, bit by bit.

Paradise Cove opened from 11 a.m. to 10 p.m. and was situated mere footsteps from the marina. It featured gorgeous water views and a congenial, relaxed atmosphere with a tropical twist. Al had a decent clientele now and there were usually at least a couple of customers hanging around at any given hour, drinking, laughing and telling stories. He wasn't going to get rich operating the place but now that the food thing had kicked in he calculated he'd be able to cover all his overhead, including his living expenses, with a little left over every few months. It was all he needed. There was something to be said for having a simple life, where your only concern was ordering more cases of beer or making sure your bartender wasn't stealing too much.

He'd lost eighteen pounds since he'd relocated three months earlier, mainly because his diet now consisted almost entirely of fish and rice, and he'd cut back on his boozing to only a few sociable beers. That, and he bicycled from town to the bar, which made for twenty minutes of exercise mornings and nights – a total of forty minutes more per day than he was getting in Panama.

Al had also quit smoking – mostly. He'd still have a cigarette now and then, but it wasn't habitual anymore – he'd given up buying them. The bar stocked a few brands but he had a rule for himself that he wouldn't touch his own supply, just as he had a new rule that he would only sip a few beers each evening with his customers.

For the first time in his life, Al felt a sense of balance. He supposed that after being almost killed several times in the jungle and having narrowly escaped extermination by the most powerful government in the world, it put the important things into perspective. Just breathing every day was a nice treat – not a right. Viewed in that light, he had a good life.

The grill-top pinched his index finger. Al muttered a silent oath, then raised his hand to his mouth and sucked on his injured pinky, which failed to do anything to ease the pain. Maybe a little ice?

At ten-forty in the morning the bar wasn't open yet, so Al was alone other than his day-shift cleaner, who was scrubbing the wooden table tops and trying to appear busy. Al moved behind the large circular bar and dug a few ice cubes from the holding area below the colorful tile countertop, holding them against his wounded digit.

A boat in the marina started its engines, and the dull roar startled a group of birds on the periphery of the seating area, spurring them to take flight. It sounded like a big yacht. Al grabbed a pair of old binoculars from below the cash register and looked to see what was making the racket. His gaze landed on a large custom sports fisher, at least a 90 foot Carolina with sleek lines and a twenty foot beam. They saw a lot of big money boats there – the fishing was considered to be some of the best in the world, and perhaps more importantly, fuel was cents per gallon instead of dollars.

Al returned the glasses to their position beneath the bar, and sipped his lime and mineral water.

His cleaning woman called his name, trying to get his attention. "*Senor* Al," she exclaimed. He could barely hear her over the boat's engines, and then suddenly the roar diminished into silence, other than Jimmy Buffet playing quietly from the bar speakers.

"*Senor* Al," the woman repeated.

Al turned to her, curious as to what the latest emergency was.

Two shimmering figures stood at the edge of the bar's patio. He couldn't make out who it was because the sun cast a mirage around them. Squinting at the colorful shapes, recognition hit, and the world tilted, just for a moment; his heart skipped a few beats, then the sensation of being on the deck of a pitching ship receded and he slowly regained full awareness of his surroundings.

He rounded the bar, marveling at a sight he'd never dared hoped for.

Mari and Mel waved at him.

"Hello, Al," Mari said.

# ABOUT THE AUTHOR

Russell Blake lives full time on the Pacific coast of Mexico. He is the acclaimed author of the thrillers *Fatal Exchange*, *The Geronimo Breach*, *Zero Sum*, The Delphi Chronicle trilogy (*The Manuscript*, *The Tortoise and the Hare*, and *Phoenix Rising*), *King of Swords*, *Night of the Assassin*, *Return of the Assassin*, *Revenge of the Assassin*, *Blood of the Assassin*, *The Voynich Cypher*, *Silver Justice*, *JET*, *JET II – Betrayal*, *JET III – Vengeance*, *JET IV – Reckoning*, *Jet V – Legacy* and *Upon a Pale Horse*.

Non-fiction novels include the international bestseller *An Angel With Fur* (animal biography) and *How To Sell A Gazillion eBooks (while drunk, high or incarcerated)* – a joyfully vicious parody of all things writing and self-publishing related.

"Capt." Russell enjoys writing, fishing, playing with his dogs, collecting and sampling tequila, and waging an ongoing battle against world domination by clowns.

Sign up for e-mail updates about new Russell Blake releases

http://russellblake.com/contact/mailing-list

8431427R10139

Made in the USA
San Bernardino, CA
08 February 2014